To Pat ...
Enjoy ...

MURDER IN NEGATIVE SPACE

Neal Sanders

The Hardington Press

Murder in Negative Space is a work of fiction. While certain locales, historical events, and organizations are rooted in fact, the characters and events described are entirely the product of the author's imagination.

Also by Neal Sanders

Murder Imperfect
The Garden Club Gang
The Accidental Spy
A Murder in the Garden Club
Murder for a Worthy Cause
Deal Killer
Deadly Deeds
A Murder at the Flower Show

In memory of Cheryl Collins
who, among her many achievements,
used her photographic skill to forever preserve
the beauty of thousands of floral designs and gardens

MURDER IN NEGATIVE SPACE

Prologue

"Worthless garbage."

Valentina Alexandrovna Zhukova pulled apart the delicate head of a seemingly perfect iridescent blue iris. Picking up another iris, she briefly inspected it and destroyed it in the same manner.

The six women and one man around her in the Grand Ballroom of Boston's Convention Center Plaza Hotel paid little attention to this latest outburst. Zhukova was not speaking to them and the acts of floral mutilation had been going on in one fashion or another for more than two hours.

"I can find better material than this on any street corner in St. Petersburg," Zhukova sneered. "World class city. World class flower market. *Govno.*" She smashed the heads of another half dozen irises.

A thin, pale woman climbed down from atop a ten-foot ladder. "Valentina Alexandrovna, maybe we take short break." The woman spoke the words softly and soothingly in English. They were intended to be heard by the other people in the room, as well as by Zhukova.

Zhukova glared at the pale woman. "Always the conciliator, Ludmila Karachova. Always the one to make do with second best."

The two women now stood just inches from one another. Zhukova was twelve inches taller than Karachova. She was blonde with high cheekbones and an athletic build to Karachova's mousy brown hair, round face and shapeless body. Zhukova, who appeared to be about forty, was attired in expensive black slacks and a brightly colored designer tunic over a crisp white blouse. Karachova, at least ten years older, was in shades of brown.

The pale woman took Zhukova's hand and whispered something in Russian. Whatever she said had a calming effect. She spoke for perhaps thirty seconds, smiled, and released Zhukova's hand.

Ten seconds elapsed. Zhukova turned and addressed the other people in the room, few of whom had paused in their work to regard the dynamic between the two Russians. "Jet lag," she said. "I am not usually this kind of person. Jet lag is my reason. Please forgive my outburst."

Everyone nodded and murmured appreciation and understanding. Two by two, they returned to the task at hand, creating and assembling four massive hanging floral designs suspended above the center of the massive Grand Ballroom floor. Each design incorporated a three-foot-diameter spherical aluminum truss; a series of thin metal straps that all but disappeared beneath the flowers embedded in water-retaining foam.

Arranged in a square and twenty-five feet apart, each of the spheres hung by a heavy chain from the ballroom's twelve-foot ceiling such that the bottom of the apparatus was seven to eight feet above the floor. When completed, viewers would be able to see the designs from anywhere in the room, including from directly underneath each sphere.

One member of the team directed from the floor and passed up floral material. The other went up and down a ladder, positioning material and placing it only when the designer on the floor nodded his or her assent.

Outside, it was nine o'clock on a damp, chilly early April evening. Inside the cavernous ballroom, there was no time and no clock. There was only a competitive pressure. Four teams each comprised of a designer and an assistant.

Oddly, the competition was heightened because these designs would never be formally judged by any panel. But over the next five days these four airborne spheres would be seen every morning, afternoon and evening by eight hundred of the world's best floral designers. Each attendee would spend more time looking at these designs than at any of the others in the adjacent Boston Convention and Exhibition Center. These designs would be overhead at every meal, every keynote address and at the final awards ceremony five days hence. A month after the attendees returned home, the 250,000 square feet of floral creativity in the Convention Center would be a blur of color and form. These four designs would be embedded in memory for years to come, and every attendee would have his or her favorite.

Nine o'clock became midnight and midnight became two in the morning. Zhukova's outbursts continued, though with less frequency. At three o'clock, as if by common consent, the group declared their designs complete. Wordlessly, they dragged buckets of leftover flowers to a side room, packed carts with the tools of their art, and left the room.

* * * * *

Two hours later, the first crew opened the doors to the Grand Ballroom from the adjoining kitchen and service area. Four men pulled two large wagons filled with tablecloths and linen to dress one hundred tables for breakfast. Just ahead of them, three men pushed vacuum cleaners and wagons containing cleaning supplies. They chattered in Spanish or Portuguese about family, work and news from home. The first man to enter the ballroom pulled a cleaning supplies cart, grunting under its weight. The second man pushed the same cart and glanced up only when he was fully in the room. When he did, his hands let go of the cart and went to his face. He stood at the room's entrance, his mouth open. He crossed himself.

"*Dios mio,*" he said.

Forty feet in front of him, suspended from the base of one of the flower-filled spherical aluminum frames, a blonde woman in black pants and a white blouse hung grotesquely by her neck. Her feet were eighteen inches off the floor, her white blouse was streaked and spattered with red, her eyes open but empty. Pools of dark blood coagulated on the carpet below her.

One by one, the other six men stopped and followed the one man's gaze. Some crossed themselves and murmured religious incantations. Others merely stared before offering less ecclesiastical comments.

Chapter 1
Wednesday, April 8

At 5:27 a.m., Lieutenant Victoria Lee parked her Honda Civic in an open space in the cramped lot behind District C-6's headquarters on West Broadway in South Boston. Her official starting time did not commence until 7 a.m. but, as she was quickly learning after seven weeks on the job, the demands of the position could not be shoehorned into an eight, ten, or even twelve-hour day. By the time her detectives reported for duty at 7:30, she was expected to have reviewed all active case files and be ready to pepper those detectives with intelligent questions. Her Captain could arrive at 8 a.m. or he could already be at his desk, and his questions could begin flying even before she was in her office.

Vicky – the 'Victoria' was foisted on her by Anglophile parents and was truncated to 'Vicky' at seventeen on her first day of college – Lee was well aware of the eyes that were on her every day. She was thirty. She was a woman. She was Asian. And, a few weeks earlier she had been promoted to Lieutenant after four years as a patrolman and five years as a detective. Those who did not know her assumed the rapid advancement was because of gender and ethnicity; a matter of pandering to noisy political constituencies. It did not help that she appeared even younger than thirty. Conversely, those who had worked with her cheered her on.

As she did every day, Lee wore a skirted suit and white blouse. She owned perhaps eight or nine such outfits, more or less identical except for color and all purchased online. Today's outfit, pulled in rotation from the right-hand side of her clothes closet, was red. Her lone concession to jewelry was a pair of half-carat diamond studs, a birthday gift from her parents two years earlier. An unadorned black leather shoulder bag completed her ensemble.

Her first stop, even before refreshing her cup of coffee, was Dispatch. There she could get the first, raw information about overnight events. From a law enforcement point of view, South Boston came alive at about 10:30 p.m., when people began leaving the bars and restaurants along Seaport Boulevard and Northern Avenue. From then until 1:30 a.m. there was a steady string of '911' calls or cruisers reporting suspicious behavior. Most of it – ninety percent of it – was fueled by alcohol.

The balance was what those on West Broadway called 'real' police work. Sexual assaults, drug arrests and muggings were growing problems with the increasing number of hotels and tourists along the waterfront. Shootings, at least, were still rare. Domestic violence – DV in police shorthand – generated at least half a dozen calls each evening.

The Dispatch desk was the communications nerve center of the District, a low semicircle of electronics at the center of which sat Jasmine Jones, the overnight communications officer. Her job was to monitor every radio conversation, responding instantly to requests and to apportion the District's resources in support of every call.

"What do you hear, Jasmine?" Lee posed the question to a tall black woman wearing four-inch gold hoop earrings complementing a vividly patterned black and gold sweater. The earrings swayed in an exaggerated arc with every movement of the woman's head.

"Got a good one going right now," Jasmine said. "Seven minutes ago we got a call from Security at the Convention Center Plaza Hotel. They found a woman hanging from some kind of flower arrangement in the ballroom…"

"Play me the call," Lee said quickly.

Jasmine pressed two buttons with the tips of her long, gold fingernails.

"9-1-1."

"Yeah, this is Security at the Convention Center Plaza Hotel on D Street. We've got a body here. A woman. Looks like she was stabbed or shot, and she's hanging from some big metal ball with flowers sticking out of it…"

"Where exactly are you?"

"The Convention Center Plaza, on D Street…"

"Where in the hotel, exactly?"

"Oh, the Grand Ballroom. Mezzanine level. She's…."

"Units 217 and 93, please respond to a report of a body of a woman at the Convention Center Plaza Hotel, 400 D Street. Proceed to the Grand Ballroom on the mezzanine level and notify upon arrival."

The call went on for several minutes as Jasmine pulled information out of a night security guard named Theo who quickly proved to be out of his depth in responding to questions. It was not helped by the background noise of people around him offering opinions on what to tell the police. EMTs were also summoned although the security guard made clear he believed the woman was dead.

"What about detectives?" Lee asked.

Jasmine shook her head. "I had two DV calls within fifteen minutes of one another about an hour ago. Protocol is to wait for the initial report from the uniforms…"

She was interrupted by the excited voice of a policeman coming over the speaker. "Jesus Christ," the policeman said. "There are these four big balls of flowers hanging from the ceiling. There is a woman – Caucasian, late thirties or early forties – blood all over the front and back of her shirt and she's been hanged by the neck with some kind of purple wire…"

Lee motioned for Jasmine's earpiece. "Officer, this is Lieutenant Lee. Get a cordon around the area. No one except authorized personnel gets within fifty feet of that crime scene. I'll be there in ten minutes."

Lee returned the earpiece to the dispatcher. "Get Lois Otting out of bed and get someone from public affairs up to speed. Get the full homicide technical team over there. Where is Jason Alvarez?"

"He's on one of the domestic violence calls."

"Call him and tell him I need him at the Convention Center Plaza. Tell the shift commander I'm going over to the crime scene."

"Respectable white woman, probably a tourist, hanging from a flower pot," Jasmine said without a hint of sarcasm. "Someone needs to be there who knows what they're doing." Then the dispatcher cocked her head. "Flowers. That's how you got famous in a hurry. That thing at the flower show. The guy in the pool…"

Lee gave a hint of a smile. "My legacy. I'm glad the flower show comes but once a year."

Chapter 2

The Convention Center Plaza was one of half a dozen new hotels that had sprung up in recent years on the perimeter of the Boston Convention and Exposition Center a few blocks from the South Boston waterfront. At eleven stories and clad in glass and red brick, it was identical in height to the surrounding hotels, distinguished only by the subdued, backlighted 'Plaza' sign on its top floor.

These hotels' fortunes rose and fell with whatever event was booked into the 'BCEC' as it was known colloquially. A medical convention a week earlier had resulted in a flood of calls as thieves preyed on well-heeled conventioneers and their families out walking too far from the sanitized and heavily patrolled waterfront. Before that, a computer game developer's conference drew nearly 100,000 youthful attendees; a measurable fraction of whom consumed too many street drugs or alcohol.

The LED sign at the entrance to the convention center read, "WELCOME IFDA APRIL 8 – 13". A stylized hand held out a bouquet of what were probably supposed to be roses.

A florists' convention? Lee wondered.

Three police cars and an EMT van pointed Lee to the right hotel entrance, and an escalator indicated the Grand Ballroom was one flight up.

The enormous ballroom itself was ablaze with lights. A hundred bare round tables, each with eight chairs, filled the room except for an area in the center of the space. There, the four flower-filled spheres were suspended from the ceiling, with four ten-foot ladders nearby. The tables that would have been closest to the spheres has been pushed back, creating a solid perimeter with a single access lane for police and EMTs.

And, hanging from one of the spheres was what until a few hours ago had been an attractive woman with short blonde hair in a white, blood-stained blouse and black slacks. Around her neck was a purplish-colored wire of a type Lee had never seen. The woman's feet cleared the ground by roughly eighteen inches.

Slavic features was the first thought that went through Lee's mind.

An argument was well underway at the front of the room and Lee gravitated to it.

"…there *is* no place else. In two hours, eight hundred people expect to… they've *paid* for this breakfast… surely you can just curtain off…"

Lee took her leather badge holder out of her purse and flipped it open.

"I'm Lieutenant Lee of the Boston Police Department. May I ask the problem?"

A white-haired woman in her late sixties, overweight and bereft of makeup but nonetheless attired in an expensive silver-colored suit to which a heavy brooch was anchored, heaved an audible sigh of relief. "Thank God someone is finally in charge."

"And you are….?" Lee left the question open.

"Mitsy Fairchild," the woman said in a tone that managed, in just two words, to express amazement that anyone in the room didn't already know her on sight.

"And what is the problem?"

Fairchild turned her attention to Lee, made some assumptions, and began speaking. "At 8 a.m., I have *eight hundred* people coming for the opening breakfast – a *major* event. Some of them may be here even *earlier* because they've been at the *Flower Market* since 4:30. This *policeman*…." With her ample chin she indicated a uniformed officer half her age standing next to her, "….says this is a *crime scene* and the room will be *closed* until further notice. I assume you can see the need for an accommodation to our *needs*." Her case stated, the woman crossed her chubby arms and waited for Lee's inevitable acquiescence.

Lee glanced at the policeman's name badge. "Officer Torres is exactly right," Lee said. "Here's what you're going to do, Ms. Fairchild: there's a convention services manager on duty right now. Find that person and have him or her check the Westin, the Marriott, Hyatt, Renaissance, and the Seaport and see if their ballroom is available. My guess is that the convention people – who are very good at this – can move the food and the staff, and everyone will assume it's just a misprint in the program."

"You can't be serious…" Fairchild's face showed a willing non-comprehension of Lee's instructions.

Lee indicated the woman hanging from the sphere. "Do you know that woman?"

"*Everybody* knows that woman," Fairchild said, without actually looking at the body. "She's Tina Zhukova and she's one of the most *gifted* floral designers in the world."

"And so your suggestion is that we ought to just cut her down, pack up and clear out of the place, and let you get on with your breakfast?"

The question took the woman aback. "Well, no, but can't you just curtain off the immediate area?"

"Take a good look, Ms. Fairchild." Lee pointed at the body, fairly forcing Fairchild to follow Lee's arm and finger. "She didn't do that to herself. Someone killed her," Lee said. "My job is to catch that person. Are you in charge of this convention?"

"Just the meals," Fairchild said, her voice faltering. "Winnie Garrison is the IFDA chair."

"Why isn't she here?" Lee asked.

"She's at the Flower Market with several important guests."

"I assume she has a cell phone. Call her and tell her she needs to come to the ballroom right now; not in an hour. Then go talk to convention services. Then, we're going to talk about IFDA and why everyone knows Tina Zhukova."

* * * * *

Medical Examiner Lois Otting watched as Mitsy Fairchild walked over to talk to a group of women that had gathered near the entrance to the ballroom. She had observed and heard the exchange.

"God, you sure turned on the charm for that old battle-axe," Otting said. "I'm going to make you up one of those 'Miss Congeniality' sashes."

"She's upset that she has to move her breakfast," Lee said incredulously. "Someone she knows is dead, there's blood all over the floor, and all she can think about is putting bacon and eggs in front of eight hundred people."

"Oh, I think some of them will opt for the yogurt and granola, but it does seem a bit too callous," Otting said. The comment earned Otting a smile from Lee. *Cool down. Take it easy.*

Lois Otting was an inch either side of five feet and, weighing in at two hundred pounds, could be charitably described as plump. But she was also, in Lee's experience, the best medical examiner in New England and one of the best in the country.

Otting was also an unconventional dresser, especially being awakened from a sound sleep at 5:40 a.m. She had shown up at the hotel in a pair of pink Lululemon yoga pants, a New England Patriots sweatshirt and a bright orange overcoat that appeared to have been rescued from a dumpster. The effect ensured that no one would inadvertently back into her.

"Do you know anything yet?" Otting asked.

Lee shook her head. "Her name is Tina Zhukova and she's quote-unquote one of the most gifted floral designers in the world, according to Ms. Fairchild. And we have apparently wandered into the IFDA convention, which I know nothing about except that everyone is at the Flower Market, wherever that is."

"The Flower Market is just down the street from my office,"

Otting said. "Albany Street. You've passed it a hundred times. Huge, long one-story building. Kind of hard to miss."

Lee shrugged. Her cell phone chirped a unique musical snippet.

Otting whispered, "I'm going to get started with Miss Zhukova."

Lee looked at the caller ID though she knew from the ring tone who was on the other end of the line. She muttered an obscenity. It was her Captain.

"Yes, Sir," she said.

"What's going on there?"

Lee began walking toward the body. "I've been on the scene less than ten minutes, Sir. It's definitely a homicide. Tina Zhukova, white, late thirties or early forties. Three wounds to the torso; two to the back, one to the chest. And then suspended by the neck with some kind of wire. She's part of a convention group called IFDA, something to do with flowers. The sphere she's hanging from is a giant flower arrangement. One of four in the room. The ME just got here, I have four uniforms keeping people away, three EMTs here now and a full technical team due any minute, and I've asked for a detective who would otherwise be going off duty in an hour. I've also asked for someone from Public Affairs."

"Russian, you think?" the Captain asked.

"Or eastern European," Lee replied. "She's Slavic by appearance and the name is Russian. I'll know more in an hour unless you need me to come back."

"Come back?" the Captain said. "I was calling to tell you that you're the primary on this. It's a hotel at the BCEC. If she's a tourist, the media is going to be all over this, and I don't mean just the local people. We don't need any unsolved murders of tourists in Boston. Get back to me in an hour." The phone screen indicated 'call ended'.

She looked up. "Jason!" and beckoned him to hurry. Detective

Jason Alvarez, age thirty, had proven indispensable six weeks earlier in solving the murder of the New England Botanical Society's executive director, a crime that had taken place a mile away at the Harborfront Exposition Center.

Except for the perpetual serious look on his face, Alvarez was almost boyish looking, with black wavy hair and dark eyes. He wore a brown wool sports jacket, a white button-down shirt and a narrow, muted striped tie that looked as though it might have been handed down from his grandfather.

"You have your computer, right?"

Alvarez nodded. "Nice to see you, too, Lieutenant."

"Sorry," Lee said, shaking her head. "You're the second person this morning to tell me I need to slow down. You're both right." She paused to catch her breath. "In ten minutes, I want you to tell me everything you can find out about a flower group called IFDA and a world famous floral designer named Tina Zhukova, and don't ask me how to spell that." Indicating the body, Lee added, "Miss Zhukova is our guest of honor. And if you have time, get me something on Winnie Garrison, who is the head of IFDA."

Lee left Alvarez pulling an iPad out of his briefcase, and walked over to the policeman who had been being badgered by Mitsy Fairchild when she first arrived. He was watching Otting's examination of the body.

"Officer Torres," she said, "This is a hotel and I'll bet there's a kitchen behind those double doors." She indicated two doors with portholes in their fabric covering. "And I'll also bet that kitchen has been brewing coffee since five o'clock this morning. I want you to use your charm and, if that doesn't work, your authority to requisition a gallon of that coffee and a dozen mugs." She smiled, as did Torres.

"Right away, Lieutenant."

Chapter 3

"IFDA is the International Floral Designers Alliance," Alvarez said. "As far as I can tell, it exists solely to put on a flower show every two years in a different country. This year it's Boston, two years ago it was Italy. The next one will be in Malaysia."

"A flower show," Lee said. "And to think less than an hour ago, I told someone I was grateful that the flower show was only held once a year."

"It's a different kind of flower show, Lieutenant," Alvarez said. "This one is just flower arranging or, as they call it, floral design. None of those big landscape exhibits or anything like it. Just eight hundred floral designs in fifty categories. IFDA's press release said there are people from sixty countries participating. It opens to the public on Friday. Twenty-five bucks a head to see the designs. Actually, I heard something about it on the radio."

He tapped his computer's screen. "Edwina 'Winnie' Garrison is Chairman of IFDA. She's from California and she and a small committee put on this whole thing. This organization runs on big donations, and Ms. Garrison is part of the 'Platinum Circle'. Assuming her husband is Frederick Garrison, it explains why Los Angeles' biggest independent law firm is also a Platinum Circle member."

"Which brings me to Valentina Alexandrovna Zhukova," Alvarez continued. "She has two stories to tell. The first is that she is in fact a world-class floral designer. She is described in several articles as 'The Queen of Negative Space' which is some kind of floral design term. She lives – lived, excuse me – in St. Petersburg, but she lectures, judges, and writes books."

"And?" Lee asked. "You've got something else on that computer screen."

"Does the name 'Marshal Zhukov' mean anything to you?"

"Should it?"

"If you grew up in Russia, he's a saint. Georgy Zhukov, Marshal of the Soviet Army during World War II or, as they call it in Mother Russia, The Great Patriotic War. He was the guy who lifted the sieges of both Moscow and Leningrad and chased the *Wehrmacht* back to Berlin, where he accepted the Nazi's surrender. He is also Ms. Zhukova's grandfather. Zhukov fathered four daughters by three women, only two of whom he was married to. Valentina is the daughter of one of the legitimate ones, and her father was career military. I have a full page of Google images showing Valentina with Vladimir Putin. She's extremely well connected."

"Just what I need," Lee mused. "Vladimir Putin to take a personal interest in this case."

There were raised voices from the far side of the ballroom. A tall, slender woman was trying to push past two policemen who were forcibly blocking her way.

"Let's go see if this is Winnie," Lee said.

It was. Edwina Garrison stared at the still-hanging body of Valentina Zhukova, a look of shock and non-comprehension on her face. "Who would have done this to her?" Garrison asked. "And why?"

"Those are the questions we need to answer as quickly as possible, Ms. Garrison," Lee said. "May we go somewhere and talk?"

* * * * *

Edwina Garrison was not the kind of person Lee had expected. She was easily seventy but was attired in blue jeans – very expensive ones, but still jeans – and a down vest over a 'UCSB' sweatshirt. Her silver hair was pulled back into a pony tail and she wore minimal makeup that was visible as makeup only on close inspection. On the whole, she gave the impression of someone who was both comfortable with her actuarial age yet possessed of an uncommon vigor.

She also had every fact about the convention on the tip of her tongue. She was eager to help and readily accepted that a police investigation trumped the concerns of a flower show, even one that had been meticulously organized for two years. Finally, Lee quickly concluded Garrison possessed an earnestness that showed in her responses to questions: this exhibition was her child.

"You have to understand that floral design is a passion for many people," Garrison said, "but that outside of the United States, Western Europe and Japan, finding an outlet for that passion can be very difficult. There are more than 350 garden clubs in California, for example. If I want to learn about design I can go to Flower Show School. If I want to exhibit, there are club shows and regional shows and shows associated with fairs. But what if I live in Ecuador or Kenya or Turkey? That infrastructure doesn't exist. There are two international groups – we overlap in some ways and are complementary in others – that fill the universal need to be around other designers."

"You must have to be fairly well off to travel from Kenya to Boston just to exhibit in a flower show," Lee observed.

Garrison nodded her concurrence. "That is a factor. But this is an event that people look forward to for two or even four years. In two years we'll be in Kuala Lampur. Our designers won't come just for these five days; they'll be in the country for weeks. This is just the 'tent pole'. Also, certain of our designers come from restrictive societies. Those restrictions don't follow them to Boston."

"Everyone knows one another?" Alvarez asked.

"There's a core group that has exhibited at every IFDA event since Sweden in 1993," Garrison replied. "We encourage that bond of friendship and we pick up additional 'regulars' at every show. But perhaps a quarter of our entries this time are from American exhibitors for whom this is their first show. My goal in bringing IFDA to the United States was to make 'regulars' out of these first-timers. We also expect to draw upwards of fifty thousand visitors on Friday, Saturday and Sunday to see the designs. We'll try to impress on them that they could be exhibiting in Malaysia in two years."

"When do you start organizing that Malaysian show?" Alvarez asked.

Garrison laughed, but then held up a hand to excuse her action. "I'm sorry for that involuntary response, Detective," she said. "As of Sunday evening, I'm officially retired and I go back to my sheep farm in Santa Barbara. The next President of IFDA is a lovely Malaysian woman named Zara Jretnam. She understudied me for two years just as I understudied my predecessor, who was an absolute fireball from Milan. These five days are both my glory and my swan song. I am just so very sorry that there had to be tragedy associated with the show."

"Let's talk about Valentina Zhukova," Lee said. "Did she have enemies that you know of? Professional rivals?"

Garrison shook her head, a rueful look on her face. "This is a very civilized group. I know many of these people – hundreds, in fact. I know all of the Committee members and many of the regular attendees. Some people don't get along with other people but nobody 'hates' anyone else. And, as for 'rivalries', we are all amateurs when all is said and done. Some have outsized reputations within the floral design world, and those reputations translate into speaking fees or book contracts, but very few have a livelihood riding on whether they get a Gold or a Silver. It isn't that kind of a competition. It's collegial and it is supposed to be educational and fun."

Lee pressed. "Then how did she come to be putting together that design last night? I thought everyone was buying flowers this morning? Did she enter that group specifically?"

Garrison paused before answering; collecting her thoughts. "The vast majority of the exhibitors have paid their own way here, paid an entry fee to compete, paid for their hotel and meals, and are paying for their own flowers as we speak. We also have what we call 'invitational' and 'honorary' exhibits. For those, we – and I mean the Committee – extend an invitation a year or more ahead of time because we want the best of the best. We provide those designers a highly visible showcase for their talents."

Garrison continued. "I can still vividly remember the meeting where we discussed the ballroom exhibit. There were a few names common to everybody's list. Tina's was one of them. We contacted Tina that day and offered her both the place in the ballroom exhibit and a lecture spot. She readily agreed and with very few conditions."

"What were the conditions?" Alvarez asked.

"The one we expected was that we would pay both her airfare and that of her assistant. Most designers use a knowledgeable local volunteer to do the grunt work – and those chosen consider it an honor to be selected – but for as long as anyone can remember, Tina has worked exclusively with a woman named Ludmila Karachova. But she didn't ask for her own airfare or to be comped for her hotel and meals; only for those of her assistant. That was quite generous on her part. She did, however, request a speaking slot on Friday afternoon – prime time – but that was fine because we all felt she would be a big draw. On the whole, her requests were extremely reasonable."

"Did she ask about the other people with whom she would be doing flower arrangements?" Lee asked.

Garrison smiled. "You mean, the other 'exhibitors' and their 'designs'. Those are the terms of art in our world, just as the police have their own terminology. Valentina was the first person we asked and we didn't know if the others we were inviting would agree. But as it turns out, she didn't ask though, in the case of an invitational, she could have made that a condition."

"We'll need to speak to the other participants – both the designers and their assistants, including Ms. Karachova," Lee said. "From there, we'll widen our circle."

"I have someone who can arrange that," Garrison said. "But I also have a thousand duties that are about to come raining down on my head, and some of my Committee members are, quite frankly, valued more for their financial connections than for their management expertise. I realize I can give you an overview of what we're doing here, but you need to catch the person who committed this horrible crime."

She continued, "You need a guide – a translator. You need someone who knows the language and has some sense of the politics. That person also has to have no loyalties in this. As we've been speaking, I've been racking my brain to think of the right person. If you give me until, say, ten o'clock, I can give you a list of names."

"A guide," Lee repeated. "I think I may already have someone in mind."

Chapter 4

Liz Phillips laughed. "Yes, I know what IFDA is and no, you're not waking me up. In fact, right now I'm at the Flower Market playing nursemaid to a group of seven Pakistani women, where my principal role is to patiently explain to them that they can't haggle over the price of flowers or take just one orchid out of a box of ten."

Lee felt a surge of hope. "Could you lend me your expertise for a few hours today? I'm told I need a flower show Sherpa, and I suspect your qualifications are excellent."

"Can you tell me what it's about?" Phillips asked.

"I have a murder to investigate. Someone connected with IFDA, but we're keeping the name under wraps pending notification of next of kin," Lee said. "I need someone whom I know has no dog in the fight and who won't be intimidated. Can you help me?" Lee tried to keep any pleading note out of her voice, but she was convinced Liz Phillips could be the key to a quick solution.

"Yes, as long as you know what you're getting," Phillips said. "I've been to Flower Show School. I'm a member in good standing of Judges Council. I exhibit or I judge a few times a year. But IFDA is 'way over my head. These people are big league. I was at the Convention Center yesterday putting staging in a straight line, and I'm here this morning at the Flower Market because IFDA needs every warm body it can find."

"I know exactly what I'm getting," Lee said. "I'm getting someone who knows the language and how these things work. I'm getting someone I can trust. That's perfect. I'll see you as soon as you're done there. And thank you."

* * * * *

Phillips touched the button that ended the call on her cell phone. *Incredible*, she thought to herself.

Six weeks earlier, she had been shocked to learn, along with the other staff and volunteers at the Northeast Garden and Flower Show, of the murder of St. John Grainger-Elliott, the Executive Director of the New England Botanical Society, sometime after the Opening Night Gala. Only because she was walking near the area of the investigation, Phillips had been singled out by Lieutenant Lee to help explain how the show worked. Time and again, Lee had come to her with questions about timetables and responsibilities and show practices.

The more she explained, the more Lieutenant Lee and her team were able to zero in on the actions that had led to Grainger-Elliott's death and ultimately to find his killer.

And now, Lieutenant Lee was asking for her help again. But why? Yes, she was an amateur floral designer like everyone else at the IFDA meeting, but she certainly was not part of the IFDA hierarchy. She barely even knew the names of the committee members.

She wasn't even entered to do a design. The entry fee was a stiff six hundred dollars and, while she could easily afford the expense, it annoyed her Yankee sensibilities that an organization would put a price on entering a competition where the arranger would also incur several hundred dollars of costs for flowers and other materials. Phillips had never entered a competition where an entry fee was charged, and she didn't intend to start with IFDA.

But three weeks earlier a plea had gone out to Boston-area garden clubs seeking volunteers to help in dozens of areas. As President of the garden club in Hardington, a suburban town eighteen miles southwest of Boston, Phillips felt duty-bound to answer the call.

And it wasn't that she was needed elsewhere. Her husband, David, was in Pittsburgh all week, 'rescuing' a failing company. He had accepted the assignment in January and, based on previous experience, she would see him infrequently until the company was either sold or liquidated two or three months hence. David's chosen line of work provided a very good living for the two of them; they were more than just 'comfortable'. But she was fifty-five and had been married for nearly thirty years to a man who showed no inclination to retire. Each morning he was away, Liz Phillips realized she was learning how to live her life on her own.

* * * * *

At 7:30 a.m., Lee ushered Phillips through a cordon of police who blocked the entry to the ballroom and began filling her in on the investigation. The body of Valentina Zhukova had been taken down but four techs continued to take measurements and photos of the site.

"In fifteen minutes, we're going to meet with six of the seven men and women who worked last night with Zhukova," Lee said. "I don't want you to ask questions, though you can feel free to tap me on the shoulder and quietly suggest something if you don't like what you're hearing."

"Before we meet with them, I want to show you something." Lee pulled a clear plastic evidence bag from a box. It contained a short length of heavy gage but flexible purple wire. "Have you ever seen anything like this before?"

Phillips nodded. "Of course. It is aluminum florist's wire or, I guess, crafts wire. Floral designers use it all the time. It adds height to a display or it adds color or interest. It comes in half a dozen colors – gold, green, blue…"

"Would a floral designer have a ten-foot length of it for any reason?"

"It's sold in forty-foot-long rolls," Phillips said. "Chances are, a designer has several rolls in different colors in her cart."

"Cart?"

"The first thing you do when you get serious about floral design is to buy a rolling cart," Phillips explained. "You fill the cart with every tool you need to do a design: knives, scissors, a camera, a couple of kenzan…"

Lee held up a hand. "Kenzan?"

Phillips struggled for words. "A little, round, heavy piece of metal with spikes on it. You use it to anchor flowers."

"Got it, Lee said. "Go on."

Phillips ticked off items with her fingertips. "Glue dots, wire and wire cutters, surgical gloves…"

Lee again held up a hand. "Why surgical gloves?"

Phillips nodded. "You may be working with material that has thorns or you may have an allergy. I buy them fifty pair to a box."

"So, if my techs don't lift any fingerprints, surgical gloves may be the answer. What else is likely to be in that cart?"

Phillips thought for a second. "Three kinds of glue and four kinds of tape, plus extra Oasis. All that is missing are the flowers and an assortment of containers."

"So it's likely that, if I ask these women if they have a roll of this wire in their carts, they would say 'yes'."

"Sure, may I ask why it's important?" Phillips asked.

"Because this is what someone used to hang Valentina Zhukova." Lee replied.

Phillips gulped and stared at the wire. After a moment she said, "You understand that everyone who came to Boston for this show brought a cart, and that most of those carts have a spool of that wire."

It was Lee's turn to blink. "Eight hundred carts? It would cost a fortune to ship through a cart…"

"A hundred dollars for excess baggage is nothing," Phillips explained. "I just helped seven women from Pakistan buy more than two thousand dollars of flowers and, afterwards we went next door to Jacobsen's, and they spent several thousand more dollars on accessories. What they don't use themselves they'll sell or give to their friends back home. You don't come to IFDA if you're worried about what it will cost to ship through your cart. These women were wearing Armani. They flew eight thousand miles to participate in a flower show. I couldn't help but overhear them talking among themselves. When they run out of places to shop on Newbury Street, they're headed for New York for a few days. The cost of shipping a cart gets lost in the round off."

"There went my easy theory," Lee said, looking at the bag with the segment of wire. "I've never seen this stuff before, and you're telling me everyone in the hotel has a spool."

Phillips nodded. "I'd check their carts, but I'm not sure that having half a spool proves anything. I save my end pieces. I probably have ten feet of it in my cart at home."

Lee drummed her fingers, a look of disappointment on her face. She flipped open her note pad. "Let me run some names by you. Eva Kirk. She's from Germany. Tomás Suarez, he's from New York. May Wattanapanit. She's from Thailand."

"I certainly know who Tomás Suarez is," Phillips said. "I have two of his books. He's originally from Argentina, and he does incredible tropical designs – lots of orchids and things like that."

Phillips continued. "Eva Kirk spoke here in Boston last year. There's a big floral design lecture held out in Waltham, and it's usually by someone well-known internationally. I went and so did about five hundred other people. Her lecture was informative, her English was excellent – not always true of those speakers – and her designs were really innovative."

Phillips continued. "The funny thing was what I heard afterward – scuttlebutt, not something I know first-hand – about what happened when she was finished. According to two friends who are on the committee that puts on the lecture, Kirk was handed a check. Kirk opened it and said it wasn't what she agreed to: she wanted to be paid in cash – and in Euros. It took about an hour to convince her that it wasn't going to happen; that it was a check payable in dollars or she did it for free."

"Tax evasion?" Lee asked. "If you pay in cash, it never gets reported?"

"That's as good a guess as any," Lee replied. "Her fee was probably two thousand dollars but she was also reimbursed for travel and meals. Not megadollars but not inconsequential. I've never heard of May Watta… the Thai woman, but that doesn't mean anything."

Lee wrote down something in her notebook. "The helpers are Kathy Thomas, Helen Weiser and Yvonne Capella. I'm going to interview Zhukova's assistant, who traveled here with her from Russia, separately. She also took the news very badly and had to be sedated."

"I know all three," Phillips said. "They're all great designers in their own right and members of Massachusetts Judges Council – that's the organization of people who have gotten through Flower Show School, passed all their exams, and exhibit and judge regularly."

"Is there anything I ought to know about any of them?" Lee asked.

"Just that they're the right people to have been asked to do this. They get to spend several hours working with a top designer and being the assistant means you truly understand the choices that were made. You can look at a final design and draw conclusions about the designer's thought process, but unless you were there through the editing and changes, you don't have the complete story. Think of it as being able to look over an artist's shoulder, except that the painting is completed in about three hours."

"The information I have is that they started at 6 p.m. and didn't finish until around 3 a.m.," Lee said.

"Nine hours?" Phillips looked at the four designs suspended above the ballroom floor. "I've heard about designers at the Chelsea Flower Show in London taking twelve hours to perfect a design, but not here. All four designers probably knew about the design in the round months ago. They probably did a practice design – or two, or two dozen – at home over the past few months. They bought their flowers yesterday morning. They probably ordered special flowers, but it doesn't mean the vendor will get in everything they ask for, so they may have had to adjust the design on the fly and choose different flowers. They conditioned their flowers for about fourteen hours, but some things they purchased may not have opened like they wanted, so they adjusted again."

Phillips continued to study the designs. "But nine hours to assemble the design? That's a lot. Usually, in competitions, you have three hours, max. This is more like one-upsmanship."

"What do you mean?" Lee asked.

"It's like what I heard happens at the Chelsea Flower Show," Phillips replied. "You look at what everyone else is doing and you think, 'I need to do better'. So you take out everything in your bag of tricks and try to outdo everyone in the room. You stop looking at the clock and you find the energy to do what has to be done."

"You know these aren't being judged," Lee said.

Phillips nodded. "It doesn't matter. I'll bet this ballroom is going to be used for all the meals and important lectures. Impress the people in this room and you'll get invitations to lecture in thirty countries next year. Be the lame entry of the four and your phone won't ring at all. I think that's what was driving them: visions of glory and fear of being outdone on a highly visible stage."

At that moment, Alvarez cleared his throat from the ballroom entry door. "I have everyone," he said. "May I bring them in?" In a lower voice, he said, "I also have some more research. We can talk afterward." Glancing at Liz Phillips, Alvarez said, "I remember you. Welcome back to the world of crime."

* * * * *

The five women and one man filed in, looks of apprehension mixed with weariness on their faces. They had gone to bed sometime after 3 a.m. and expected to sleep six or seven hours. Instead, they had been roused at 6 a.m. and been told to make themselves available for questioning. Now, they stood in the same ballroom. Fifty feet away and behind a barrier of tables were the four designs and the cleared area underneath them, including a missing five-foot diameter of carpet under one of the designs removed for analysis of the puddle of blood on it. The four ladders still stood where they had last been used. One ladder now rested on bare concrete.

Lee motioned the six to sit at a round table by the ballroom entrance. She and Alvarez took the two remaining chairs at the table, Phillips sat just behind Lee.

"I need to understand what happened here last night and this morning," Lee said. "I need to understand the dynamic among you and, more important, I need to learn about Valentina Zhukova's state of mind. Tell me what Ms. Zhukova said and how she acted. Also, if you know anything about Ms. Zhukova outside of her standard biography, this is the time to talk about it. Someone killed her. Please help me catch that person."

Lee indicated Phillips. "Some of you may recognize Liz Phillips. She has been asked to coach me on the world of floral design, and I've asked her to observe this proceeding. Let me stress that you are not suspects. You are, however, the last people to have seen her alive other than her killer. So tell me what happened last evening. I'll start with Kathy Thomas who, I believe, was assisting May Wattanapanit."

Thomas appeared to be in her fifties, though with a mane of curly gray hair and a deep tan that indicated she had not spent the winter in New England.

"Do you want the truth?" Thomas asked. "The real truth and not something sanitized because the person is dead?"

"Pulling punches won't get us the answers we need," Lee replied.

"Then, Tina Zhukova was a prima donna who spent nine hours complaining about everything. I've worked with great designers and none of them ever felt compelled to shout insults at the people around them, throw flowers, yell at her assistant, and kick everything in sight. She may be the Queen of Negative Space but she's also the queen of negativity. I had to listen to her complaints from the time she walked in right through until three in the morning. She complained about the food, the room, the flowers, the weather, her fellow designers, her flight over and the IFDA people. What I wanted to do was walk over and slap her. What I did was keep quiet and vow that woman would never be hired by any organization in which I had a voice."

"I think it was an act." Those words, spoken quietly, came from May Wattanapanit, a slightly built woman of about sixty with gray hair pulled tightly to the back of her head from a severe part down the center of her scalp. "Her goal was to distract us. Keep us from thinking about our work. If we allowed ourselves to become angered by her rudeness – and it was certainly rudeness – then we would stop doing the task we were there to do. I saw Kathy's anger and how it affected the way she placed material. She jabbed flowers in too deeply and without sufficient care. Yes, it was an act."

Eva Kirk shook her head. She was a stout woman, somewhere in her fifties, though with dark blonde hair cut short and well-layered. Her black trifocal glasses gave her an academic look. "Before last night I never had the pleasure of working with Miss Zhukova. Yes, I believe May is correct that it was an act at some level. But I also sensed that something was greatly disturbing her last night. Her tirades came from something deep inside her; an anger or inability to cope with something. Her assistant had to repeatedly calm her. I felt helpless. But, like May, I put it out of my mind while it was happening. Only now, with her death, do I wonder if her actions are linked to her death."

Yvonne Capella, an attractive woman in her early fifties, showed a keen interest in what the others were saying. Lee saw her biding her time, waiting for the right opportunity.

"Ms. Capella, you appear to have something to say," Lee said.

"We were supposed to be here at six," Capella said. "Valentina was late, and Ludmila had to make excuses for her. When she wasn't in the ballroom at 6:25, Ludmila acted like something was very wrong. There was fear on her face. Then, when Valentina finally showed up, they spoke in Russian for nearly twenty minutes. That's when the tantrums started."

Tomás Suarez, younger than the other designers by a decade, was silent through the recollections shared by the others. Lee looked for changes in body language but saw what appeared to be boredom. This interview was of no interest to him.

"Mr. Suarez, do you have anything to add?" Lee asked.

Suarez gave a slight shrug of his shoulders. "I do not know why everyone is so concerned with what happened while we were designing." Suarez spoke with a pronounced Latin American accent. "We pushed one another to do better and, when we were satisfied, we all left. Valentina was alive. We went to the elevators. We got off at our respective floors. We said goodnight to one another. We smiled because we had stretched our imagination." He turned and indicated the designs with his chin. "Look at those. Have any of us ever done better work?"

Until that moment, the women had, as a group, avoided looking at the spheres. Lee addressed them while seated with her back to the wall. No one turned back to study the crime scene closely; no one wanted to be visually reminded of the grisly death of someone they had worked with just a few hours earlier.

Now, they turned and glanced, but quickly turned back. There was a general consent that everyone's design was worthy of a gold medal.

Helen Weiser spoke up. "Ms. Zhukova kept razzing the other

designers, but she reserved her nastiest comments for Tomás. She said he was a hack amateur with only one trick up his sleeve and kept calling him 'our token man'. She was unrelenting."

"Is that true?" Lee asked, looking at Suarez.

Suarez again shrugged. "I have worked with Tina on many occasions," he said. "It was her style to keep everyone around her off their game by throwing out gratuitous insults. I have long since learned that she did it as a matter of competitive advantage. It wasn't personal. It was trash talk, like in basketball or football."

"But she kept after you all night long," Weiser said.

"And I am used to people like her," Suarez said, this time curtly.

"Speaking of football, isn't this all a matter of watching video footage?" Thomas asked. "I saw the video of that jerk player who beat up his girlfriend on an elevator. Doesn't every hotel have something like that? If there was a camera by the elevator you would know what time we went up to our rooms. If anyone came down later, you'd know that too. There's probably one trained on the corridor leading to the ballroom. You see who went in with Tina, and you arrest them."

"Real life isn't like television," Alvarez said.

Lee tapped him on the side of his leg. *Don't say anything else.*

"This has been very useful," Lee said. I have just one more question: are the ladders you see in the ballroom in the same location you left them a few hours ago?"

Everyone again glanced back at the center of the ballroom. One by one, they all agreed the ladders were where they last remembered using them.

"Thank you," Lee said. As everyone began to rise she added, "May I assume the three designers have those rolling carts with glue and scissors and such in them?"

The designers nodded.

"Would anyone have an objection to my detective inventorying the contents of your cart?"

Lee thought she saw a look of surprise pass across the faces of both Kirk and Suarez. But the three all shook their heads. They had no objection.

Phillips tapped Lee on the shoulder and whispered, "If the assistants are also entered, they'll also have a cart even if they didn't bring it to the ballroom last evening."

Lee nodded. "Are any of you who were assistants doing designs tomorrow?"

All three women nodded.

"May we also inventory your carts?"

"Knock yourself out," Thomas said. The other women only nodded and murmured assent.

Lee gave Jason instructions to have a Forensics team collect the six carts, and to locate the one used by Zhukova. "Then you need to catch me up on what else you've learned."

Turning to Phillips, Lee said, "Liz, you need to go with the Forensics team and tell them what everything is used for. Make certain the inventory calls everything by its right name. I know it sounds like make-work, but I've never heard of so many potential murder weapons being carried around by so many people in one place at the same time."

* * * * *

Fifteen minutes later, Lee and Alvarez were in the hotel's security offices, looking at banks of monitors.

"This is insane," Lee said, looking at the images.

At 4 a.m., when elevators should have been empty, they were crowded. Lobbies that were normally deserted were instead a hive of women and a smattering of men. Hundreds of floral designers had responded to wake-up calls and, in a thirty-minute period, descended to the main lobby where they took cabs or waiting cars to travel to the Flower Market.

Worse, the lobby cameras were designed to look at people

coming off of elevators, using the check-in kiosks, and entering or leaving the main doors. No camera captured anyone turning off for the escalator to ascend to the mezzanine. Further, the two cameras on the mezzanine level pointed solely at the elevator banks serving the floor. No one got on or off those elevators between 3 a.m. and 5 a.m.

On guest floors, the cameras again focused on spotting people getting on or off the elevator. Stairwells were uncovered as were the bulk of the corridors.

"With time, we can isolate for Zhukova," Alvarez said. He was relieved that Lee's frustration matched his own when he first viewed the early morning footage.

"Time is something we don't have a lot of," Lee said grimly. "The hotel is worried about sexual assaults and room robberies. A murder in a ballroom was not what they had in mind when this system was designed."

"So what do we do?" Alvarez asked.

Lee drummed her fingers on the console desk. "Barring getting lucky with those carts, we interview until we have a motive. Then we'll know what we're looking for. I suggest I start with Zhukova's assistant, and you make certain the techs have thoroughly gone over Zhukova's room. There was no purse at the crime scene. Assuming her purse is in her room, check it for any PDA or cell phone and get it analyzed. Then have a talk with the M.E. and see if she found anything interesting."

Chapter 5

Ludmila Karachova sat in her bed with a white hotel bath robe wrapped tightly round her thin body. Her eyes were red, and she hugged her knees to her chest. She and Lee had been speaking for fifteen minutes and had painstakingly covered the basics of Karachova's and Zhukova's relationship: Karachova, who was fifty-two, had accompanied Zhukova around the world for the past seven years. There had been a time a decade earlier when Karachova was the teacher and Zhukova the student. But as Zhukova's skills and creativity became evident, Karachova became her assistant. Until they began traveling together, Karachova had seldom been out of Russia and never to America. Now, her passport bore the stamps of two dozen countries including multiple and lengthy trips to the United States.

They had also covered some sensitive but necessary ground. The designers' cart, which had come back with Karachova to her room, had been taken away by the forensics team. Lee studied Karachova's face and body language as the cart was placed in a large plastic bag and carried out of the room. There had been a tensing of Karachova's shoulders and a look of apprehension on her face.

"I am suspect?" she asked.

Lee spoke soothingly. "We have no suspects. We're at the very beginning of an investigation and, right now, we're just trying to gather all possible clues. That is why I am talking to you. But we are talking here, in your room. Not in a police station. I need information if I am going to find out who killed Valentina."

"I not be much help," Karachova said. "My English is still not good. Valentina say I talk English like peasant girl. But she give lectures. I only place flowers and buy for her. I have no need for much English."

"The women who were doing designs last night and this morning all said Valentina was upset about something. Do you have any idea what that was?"

Karachova shook her head. "She moody person, like many creative designers. Last night not different."

"So, she was always prone to temper tantrums?"

Karachova looked at Lee, perplexed.

"She always shouted and got angry?"

Karachova nodded. "She wanted all designs perfect. She study what other designers do. If they do very good, Valentina must do better. She angry at me. Not put flowers where she want. Think I buy not good flowers at market."

"Was any of it an act?"

Karachova paused. "You mean show?" There was an imperceptible nod of her head. "She use English words: 'psych out'. Valentina say she 'psych out' competitors with moods. Last night she try to 'psych out' German and man designer. They very, very good. 'Psych out' not work so well. Valentina get more angry. She yell at me. I tell her design is best. She say not good enough."

"Ms. Karachova," Lee lowered her voice to almost a whisper. "Was Valentina meeting anyone this morning? Did she plan to be back in the ballroom after everyone else left?"

Karachova began crying, wrapping her arms more tightly around her knees. "She tell me to get good night sleep. She apologize for shouting. She say check design in afternoon. Make flowers fresh. She go shopping. She meet no one."

"What did she do yesterday – before you and she began creating your design?"

"She always have schedule. She meet friends, she have lunch. She have many friends in America."

Lee made a mental note to make downloading whatever address book was in Zhukova's room a priority. "Do you know the names of any of those friends? Especially anyone here in

Boston?"

Karachova again shook her head. "She live own life. I just do flowers with her."

Lee made one final press. "Ms. Karachova, someone killed Valentina this morning. That person may have been a floral designer. Do you know of anyone here who may have had a reason to want to harm her?"

Karachova looked up at Lee, her eyes red and her face tear-stained. There was a puzzled look on her face. "You not understand," she said. "Many people not like Valentina. They…" she struggled for a word and failed to find one in English. "*Revnivyy*. Valentina better designer. Valentina pretty. Valentina have good family. Valentina have all things people here want."

"Everyone was jealous of Valentina," Lee said.

Karachova nodded and mouthed the word silently. "Everyone jealous. Jealous people kill Valentina."

* * * * *

In Valentina Zhukova's room, Alvarez sorted through the clear plastic bags into which he had placed anything that looked of interest from among the dead woman's belongings, coming back to the one holding the plain black plastic device. Fearing fingerprint or other contamination he did not take the object out of its bag but, rather turned it over to observe it from all sides.

It was a phone or PDA of some kind, but it was unlike anything he had ever seen. The device was nearly an inch thick and about four inches by six inches. The screen occupied less than half the available surface area. It had a keypad with Cyrillic letters. The back side of the phone featured a light sensor easily three times the size of one on current-model phones. Fifteen-year-old BlackBerry's had a better form factor, Alvarez thought.

Russians, he had read, spent huge sums to get the latest iPhone and Galaxy models. This one was not the product of Apple or Samsung and, in fact, bore no manufacturer's insignia, only a metal plate with a serial number stamped on it.

Everything else in the purse – indeed, everything else in the room – bore the hallmark of someone who was prosperous, style conscious, and had ready access to Western goods. This phone was the one thing that was out of place.

Lieutenant Lee told me to get the phone analyzed, Alvarez thought. *The Boston PD's tech lab is more than a decade out of step with current technology. They'll probably fry the phone just trying to turn it on.*

Alvarez had a thought. An old college friend at Google in Mountain View. A friend with likely unlimited access to information about Russian phones. Alvarez took out his own phone and took close-up photos of the device from every angle. He added a quick note asking for information and sent it off. He noted the time stamp: 7:35 a.m., which would be 4:35 in California. He'd give it a few hours, then phone his friend.

* * * * *

In a large conference room provided by the hotel, Liz Phillips identified objects pulled one-by-one from seven carts.

"That's florists' tape," she said. "It sticks even when it is wet. Designers use it to tie together multiple pieces of floral foam in arrangements." A tech entered each comment into a laptop which then printed out a label that was affixed to a photo of the object.

Phillips quickly realized that the carts were filled with potential murder weapons. It wasn't just the aluminum wire; every designer carried an array of ultra-sharp knives that were used to make quick, clean cuts on stems going into an arrangement. Phillips' own cart contained an icepick which she used to make holes in rigid plastic. She had once worked beside a designer at a show who pulled out a hypodermic syringe to inject water into an orchid tube.

Wooden picks used to attach ornamentation, scissors and needle-nosed pliers could easily become lethal in the right hands. Even a kenzan could impale someone or be used as a bludgeon. Four of the seven carts contained craft wire identical in color and gage to what had been used to hang Valentina Zhukova, and six of the seven contained wire in other colors.

As she inventoried the carts and called out their contents, Phillips also tried to think of things that were missing. While no two designers kept exactly the same tools, the presence of one kind of tool usually meant a corresponding one was somewhere in the box. The cart belonging to May Wattanapanit, the Thai designer, had no X-Acto knife, a common flower stem cutting tool, and the other knives in her cart seemed ill-suited to creating the swift, fine cuts that ensured flowers would continue to soak up water. Where was her flower-cutting knife? She called the seemingly missing tool to the attention of the crime scene tech, who made an appropriate entry in his computer.

Valentina Zhukova's cart was meticulously neat, as though her assistant had spent half an hour putting everything back into its proper place before retiring for the night. Phillips' own cart was always a throw-together hodgepodge. Zhukova's cart appeared to carry the full complement of design tools, and Phillips noted that everything appeared to have been washed before being put away. The contents of Phillips' cart were washed only when she became disgusted by what she sometimes found at the bottom of a tray.

Eva Kirk's cart showed a Teutonic obsession with order, with foam cutouts for each tool, no matter how small. On the cart's second layer was an assortment of knives. Three were expensive, German-made Henckels kitchen knives that showed the hallmarks of long use though their blades were honed to a fine edge. A fourth utensil, more like a steak knife, fit neatly in the foam cutout space but looked less cared for. Carrying multiple knives for specific uses was common among designers. In Phillips' own cart was a once-cherished bread knife that was now used just for cutting floral foam. She could not imagine consigning Henckels cutlery to a florist's cart, but then wealthy Germans likely had very different sensibilities.

Tomás Suarez's cart was a jumble of tools and design aids. Unlike the other designers he had made no effort to clean or organize its contents upon his return to his room. Oddly, there were two partial spools of purple craft wire; no other cart had more than one. There were also more knives than seemed necessary, many of them with short, very sharp blades. Why would someone have so many?

The cart belonging to Kathy Thomas, one of the local assistants, yielded five knives, two of them with short blades of the kind that was likely used to stab Zhukova. Her cart also contained a length of purple craft wire thirty feet long. Phillips had heard Lieutenant Lee say that approximately ten feet of wire had been used to hang Zhukova. A full spool was forty feet…

Phillips pushed these thoughts out of her mind. The notion of one designer murdering another was ludicrous on its face. And she knew the three local assistants. None of them seemed capable of killing anyone. The vision of a few hours earlier was etched in her mind: three stab wounds plus hanging. This was not a spur-of-the-moment act; it was premeditated. The murder *must* have been committed by someone outside of the floral design world.

At the Northeast Garden and Flower Show, she had been able to assist Lieutenant Lee – to the extent that she was any help at all – only because she was familiar with the judging protocols followed by that particular event. Every show, though, was different; every show's rules evolved to meet a specific set of circumstances. She knew absolutely nothing of the workings of the International Floral Designers Alliance. She was a volunteer like everyone else; pushing staging into place one day and shepherding wealthy, pampered ladies through flower markets the next. *Was that just a few hours ago?* she thought.

She was pulled out of her reverie by a question from the forensic tech. "What's this, ma'am?" he asked.

"It's called a pick," Phillips said. "You twist the wire around something that otherwise wouldn't stay in a block of Oasis. You push the sharp end of the stick into the Oasis."

* * * * *

"This is all unofficial," said Lois Otting. "I need at least twenty-four hours to get you anything that I'll stand behind, and if you go arresting anyone based solely on what I tell you here, I'll take you off my Christmas card list so fast your head will spin."

Lee and Alvarez were in a basement room of the New England Medical Center, the home of the Boston PD's Medical Examiner. The smell of the room was overwhelmingly of antiseptic, and the room temperature rivaled that of the chilly outside air.

The pale body of Valentina Zhukova lay on a table, face up.

"First off: time of death," Otting said. "We did an internal temperature reading at 5:37 a.m. Based on that and the ballroom temperature, we placed the time of death at between 3:45 and 4:30."

"As to how she died: the first two stab wounds – the ones in the back – were non-fatal," Otting continued. "The knife went in about four inches. It was very sharp and very pointed and about a half-inch wide. Both wounds went into muscle but didn't hit any arteries. It caused a lot of bleeding, but you wouldn't see blood spray from those kinds of wounds."

Otting pointed a scalpel at the chest wound. "Same knife, but this one was either lucky or done by a pro. It was done within, say, thirty seconds or so of the wounds to the back. Straight into the heart. Death wasn't instantaneous but her heart stopped within a few seconds, and the killer knew that he or she had finished the job."

She pointed to the neck abrasions. "The hanging was entirely post-mortem. Someone was trying to make a point."

"What about the angle of the knife," Alvarez asked.

Otting nodded. "Based on everything I can see, she was standing, and she was attacked from behind. Zhukova is five-eleven, the angle of the knife indicates her attacker is less than that;

maybe as short as five-two. Maybe even my height. The fatal thrust was delivered sitting or kneeling over her. It went straight in, four inches." Otting circled the skin around the wound with her scalpel. "No hesitation marks. One plunge. Like I say, either the perp knew what he or she was doing or was very lucky."

"How about strength?" Lee asked.

"Very sharp knife," Otting replied. "You wouldn't have to be strong to make those wounds. Just have a strong stomach for blood and someone dying in front of you."

Alvarez asked, "Could Zhukova have been on a ladder?"

Otting started to say something but then stopped. She was silent for perhaps thirty seconds. Finally, she said, "Damn." Otting walked to the end of the autopsy table. "Yes. Not definitely, but she could have been on a ladder. In which case, your perp could be six feet four for all I know. It would also explain why those first two wounds are in the back." Otting smiled. "We're going to make a Detective out of you, young Alvarez."

As they left the Medical Examiner's office, Lee and Alvarez drove by the Flower Market on Albany Street. As many times as Lee had driven this route she had never noticed the drab, block-long rectangular structure set back from the street by parking and truck loading docks.

"Pull in," she told Alvarez, indicating the entrance to the Flower Market parking lot.

They walked inside where, on either side of a central corridor, wholesale florists stacked boxes of flowers of every description and color. The dense displays went back fifty feet on either side of the corridor and ran two hundred feet.

The market, she had been told, opened at 4 a.m. Now, at 9:30, the selling day was winding down toward a noon close. Groups of buyers like the one Liz Phillips had led that morning were still carrying armloads of blooms.

Lee went inside the first wholesaler's display area. A hundred boxes of multicolored roses tightly packed fifty to a rectangular box greeted her. Another display showed enormous Fuji chrysanthemums in pale colors. At least she recognized the roses and mums. Some flower displays bore names but for the most part it was expected that the buyer knew what they were paying for.

The sight of the mums snapped her mind to another issue; one she had successfully avoided thinking about all morning. Matt's 'charm offensive'.

Five weeks earlier, Lee failed to arrive in New York on Saturday morning for a weekend getaway with Matt, her boyfriend of six months. Lee's frantic texts explaining the circumstances – she was investigating the murder of the Executive Director of the New England Botanical Society – were met with silence or, worse, terse replies that indicated Matt was having a fine time with his old college classmates. But on Sunday night as Lee was boarding a flight as part of her investigation, her cell phone rang. Matt had returned home, expecting the two of them to have dinner together. Lee had heard only the start of Matt's tirade before turning off her phone. She assumed the relationship was finished and was surprised that she felt a sigh of relief.

For two weeks she heard nothing from Matt. Then, three weeks ago, a single red lily arrived at her office with the message, "*I was stupid. I am stupid. Forgive me, Matt.*" When she got home that night, a bouquet of chrysanthemums awaited her. The card read, "*From a guy who is only beginning to realize how stupid he is. You have a career and sometimes that career has to come first. Forgive me.*"

The flowers arrived for a week, then came the call, carefully left on her apartment's answering machine at a time Matt knew she would not be home. *"I'm a better person when I'm around you. We have too much in common to let it end over my stupidity. Can we have dinner?"*

They had dinner two nights later, and Matt seemed a changed man. He asked all the right questions and deflected any questions about himself. It took two more dinners for Matt to get around to what was probably the reason for the change of heart.

They were at Little Q, a Mongolian hot pot restaurant in Chinatown. Matt had just pushed half a dozen thin pieces of chicken into the steaming broth.

"You know, my parents are celebrating their thirty-eighth wedding anniversary in April."

In Chinese numerology, thirty eight was 'triple prosperity'. Being married twenty five or fifty years meant little to those of Chinese descent. Thirty eight was the Big One. Big party, all your friends and business associates. Lots of presents. Even more pressure on the children.

"That's great," Lee had said, suspecting what was coming next.

Matt nudged the chicken from one side of the bowl to the other, looking for the perfect boiling spot. "I was hoping you might come out to San Francisco with me for the party."

So that was it. Matt, the Number One Son, the product of five thousand years of Chinese son-worshipping culture – brushed only superficially by just over a century of more recent acquaintance with American sensibility – was expected to produce a proper girlfriend for the occasion.

Matt had rarely spoken of his parents. He was thirty two years old and head of quantitative analysis at the largest hedge fund in Boston. He had degrees from Carnegie-Mellon and Wharton. His year-end bonus – the triggering event for that New York trip back in February – had probably been for at least half a million dollars. But if Mom and Dad commanded his appearance at their anniversary party, he would be there even if the financial world was coming unglued.

"What date is it?" she had asked.

Matt pulled out a piece of chicken and tested its color. "April 11. They're taking over the Oriental Pearl for the occasion."

Yes, that was it. That's what this was all about. A command performance from Mom and Dad. Matt would have been expected to plan the event, which he would not have done. Instead, he would have turned the project and his American Express Black Card over to his dutiful older sister with her two perfect children in their perfect Marin County home. Everything had probably gone swimmingly well until Mom raised the magic question: *Who will you be bringing with you?*

Which was Mom-speak for, *We assume you will have a marriageable young lady on your arm and, by 'marriageable' we mean Han Chinese, at least two college degrees, between the ages of twenty-eight and thirty-two, never married and in an acceptable professional career.*

Lee fit the bill except for the 'acceptable professional career' and Matt would have finessed that with something about her using the Boston PD as a launching pad for something eye-catching…

"Lieutenant?"

Lee snapped out of her reverie.

"Is there something about the mums?" Alvarez asked. "Do you have an idea about the case?"

Lee shook her head. "I was thinking about something else." Then she added, "Let's get back to the hotel."

* * * * *

Alvarez was getting out of his car when his phone buzzed. He looked at Caller ID. *Sarah Kane.* His old friend at Google.

He tapped the 'connect' button. "You got my photos." Alvarez looked at his watch. It was a few minutes before 10 a.m. which meant 7 a.m. in California.

"No, I'm not fine and thank you for asking," Kane said. "You and your damned phone."

"Maybe we both need to start over," Alvarez said. "Hi, Sarah. Thanks so much for calling…"

"You have a genuine Russian-government-issue Federal Security Service – that's the successor to the KGB – phone," Kane said. "Current model; in the field for less than two months." In a lower voice, she added, "I had to tell them I got it from you."

"Them?" Alvarez said.

"The FBI." She paused. "Yeah, maybe I need to start over. A group of us were pulling an all-nighter here. I'll tell you what it's about when the app hits the street next month. Anyway, I needed a diversion and saw your photos. I passed them around to the group and someone suggested we use some image recognition beta software. I plugged in your photos and got a hit in about a quarter of a second, which we all thought was cool. Three minutes later, I got an email warning me I was about to be contacted by the FBI and, sixty seconds later, my phone rang, which is kind of creepy because my phone and email account aren't linked. I hit one of their triggers, apparently. I also found out more about the FBI…"

"Sarah, what did you tell them?"

"I told them you had emailed me a group of photos and that you're with the Boston PD. You're still with them, aren't you?"

"Yeah," Alvarez said. "I'm a Detective as of about eight months ago."

"Cool," Kane said. "How did you get the Russian phone?"

Alvarez paused. "It's related to a case I'm working. I can't really say anything more."

"There's a boston.com story about an unidentified woman being found dead in a hotel," Kane said. "And a guy in Watertown arrested for… is that part of Boston?"

"Sarah, I really can't say anything right now. When did you get the call?"

"Five, six minutes ago."

"I'll call you as soon as I can talk. It's really KGB issue?"

"The genuine article, although it isn't called the KGB anymore. From what I read, you don't want to do anything to upset it," Kane said.

"It'll explode?"

"More like it will wipe itself clean. I'll send you the link."

Lee heard 'KGB' and 'explode', tapped Alvarez on the

shoulder and gave him a quizzical look.

"I'll talk to you later," Alvarez said to Kane and ended the call.

* * * * *

"We just opened a hornet's nest," Alvarez said. He then explained that he had found Zhukova's phone in her room and, because it didn't look like anything he had ever seen before, he sent photos of it to a friend, and what his friend's search had triggered.

"KGB or Federal Security Service or whatever you call it," Lee said. "Exactly what we need. The FBI and the State Department looking over our shoulder. Or taking over the case."

"Do you think it's possible?" Alvarez asked. "That Zhukova was Russian intelligence?"

"It makes sense in a weird sort of way," Lee replied. "You're the one who told me Zhukova is the granddaughter of a revered figure back in Mother Russia. She would be a natural recruit. As a floral designer she gets to travel the world, and no one questions why she's in Western Europe or the U.S."

"*I Spy*," Alvarez said.

"I spy what?" Lee asked quizzically.

"An old TV show my parents used to watch and then made me watch on VHS tapes. From the sixties. Bill Cosby and Robert Culp. They were professional tennis players. That was their cover to be spies."

"Jason, sometimes you remind me of John Flynn, and that's not necessarily a good thing."

"But if she was a spy that blows the suspect list wide open…" Alvarez said.

"I don't think so," Lee countered. "From everything I can see, Zhukova was killed with floral designer tools and hung with florist's wire. If someone came here from the intelligence community to kill her, they would have used a gun or a blow dart or whatever spies use to kill one another these days. Polonium? I read something about that…"

Alvarez's phone chirped. He looked at the Caller ID and then up at Lee. "That didn't take long."

Lee's phone also rang with the distinctive theme from *Dragnet*. "The Captain," she said. Why do I think these calls are about the same thing?"

They each retreated a few steps to take their calls with some degree of privacy.

Chapter 6

Liz Phillips sat in an overstuffed chair near the IFDA Registration tables and pondered why she was still at the hotel. She had provided a quick tutorial on the language of floral design and sat with crime scene technicians as they inventoried the contents of seven carts. Her Pakistani delegation had their flowers. Lieutenant Lee had told her to stay close by. Well, she was staying close. And she felt useless.

She listened to the conversations swirling around her. English was in the minority and many of the English speakers had what she thought of as 'colonial' inflections. She heard French and Spanish but also many languages that were opaque. What was common to the conversations was a sense of excitement. These women – with a handful of exceptions those present were women – were genuinely looking forward to the day.

A woman stopped in front of her.

"I recognize you. You were at our interview this morning, yes?"

Phillips looked up. It was the German designer. She rose to her feet.

"I am Eva Kirk," the woman said. "And you are…?"

"Liz Phillips."

"You are also a Detective?"

"No, no," Phillips shook her head. "I'm just a…. volunteer. I know Lieutenant Lee slightly and she needed someone to explain floral design."

"Your Lieutenant Lee seems very young for such an important job."

Phillips only smiled.

"She also did not ask the right questions," Kirk said.

"What do you mean?"

It was Kirk's turn to smile. "I know Fraulein Zhukova was not genuine. She is not a world-famous floral designer. She is…" Kirk mumbled to herself, searching for a word. "*Der Hochstapler…*"

"An imposter?" Phillips offered.

Kirk's face showed surprise. "You speak German?"

"I was a physics major in college. Not understanding German wasn't an option. But it doesn't mean I speak it."

"*Was sage ich jetzt?*" Kirk said, smiling.

"You're asking me to tell you what you're saying right now."

Kirk nodded. "Yes, Fraulein Zhukova was an imposter. And I know this because, just as you understand German, I understand Russian."

"Valentina Zhukova said she was an imposter?" Phillips asked, perplexed.

"No, of course not. It was the way that she and her assistant spoke to one another. When I spoke to the American woman assisting me, I would hand her a stem and say something like, 'place it just to the right of the yellow one' or, 'no, a little higher'. When Fraulein Zhukova and her assistant spoke, the assistant would say, 'now hand me the white flower' or 'no, the other one'."

"Ludmila Karachova is the designer," Phillips said. "Valentina Zhukova was just there as the…"

"*Puppe*," Kirk said, nodding.

"A puppet," Phillips agreed.

"And a very angry *puppe*," Kirk added. "*Ausfallend.* Fraulein Zhukova called her horrible names. 'Stupid cow', 'peasant'."

"Why didn't you say this when Lieutenant Lee interviewed everyone?" Phillips said. "I don't think anyone else knows anything about this."

Kirk was silent for a moment. "Do you wonder why I understand Russian?" She appraised Phillips for a moment. "You and I are of similar age. More than fifty, less than sixty, *Ja?* I grew up in the DDR; what you called 'East Germany'. While the good little *Jungen und Mädchen* in Bonn and Frankfurt were playing music and learning English, we in the DDR were being *indoktriniert* – indoctrinated – into how to be good little *Kommunisten* including half day classes in *Russischen* ."

"Your family didn't go west after the war?"

Kirk gave a rueful smile. "My family had lived in Leipzig for hundreds of years. They could not imagine life elsewhere. They were very prominent. By the time they knew what the *Russen* had in mind, it was too late and my family, or what was left of it, was not allowed to leave. Forty-five years later came *Wiedervereinigung*. Reunification. Freedom. I never again had to speak a word of Russian. I hope never to again."

"But the police need to find who murdered Valentina Zhukova. You could have said something this morning. You still can."

Kirk shook her head slowly. "You had to be there. The East was not a place for helping the police. The *Stasi*, the *Vopos*, the *Geheimpolizei*. So many different kinds of police, each one worse than the other. We have been part of the West for almost twenty-five years. Meeting Lieutenant Lee this morning brought back feelings from half a lifetime ago: fear."

"I think I can understand that," Phillips said.

Kirk nodded. "But I told the truth that, last night, something was troubling Fraulein Zhukova. She was nervous, and that added to her anger."

It was Phillips' turn to be silent for a moment. "Is it possible that Zhukova went too far last night? I can't imagine being in Ludmila Karachova's position year after year; having the talent but having to hide it. Could she have snapped?"

Kirk looked at her blankly.

"*Berserker gegangen*."

"Ah," Kirk said. "One insult too many. Yes."

"But why the charade?" Phillips asked. "If Ludmila Karachova is a gifted designer, why not let her do her own designs? I know Zhukova was supposed to be very attractive, but floral design is about creativity, not looks. Could it be that Karachova's English is poor? Then use a translator. It doesn't make sense…"

Phillips touched Kirk's arm. "You need to tell your story to the police. This is very important information that I'm certain no one else at this conference knows. I hate to think that Zhukova's own assistant might be responsible, but this is crucial evidence…"

"I should have told my story this morning," Kirk said. "You are correct. If you understand why I did not say anything, then perhaps Lieutenant Lee will also. Do you know how to get in touch with Lieutenant Lee and will you go with me?"

"Lieutenant Lee gave me her card," Phillips said, reaching into her purse. "She may even be somewhere nearby."

* * * * *

Lee and Alvarez, nearly finished with their questions of Eva Kirk after forty-five minutes, eyed one another. Lee could see excitement in Alvarez's face; the kind of anticipation Lee had often felt when she first made Detective. It was an anticipation fueled by equal parts adrenaline and weariness from too many hours on the job and it was dangerous. Lee had learned to keep such anticipation under control because 'easy' answers were too often wrong ones.

Two gigantic pieces of the puzzle had snapped into place with hours of one another. Because of Alvarez's discovery in Zhukova's room, they knew that Valentina Zhukova was Russian intelligence. Now, they were hearing from a plausible source that Zhukova's cover as an internationally prominent floral designer depended entirely upon the cooperation of her 'assistant', Ludmila Karachova.

In theory, this German floral designer had just handed them their first major break that pointed to a plausible suspect. Zhukova was abusive toward Karachova. *Karachova could have killed Zhukova.*

Lee feared narrowing the field of suspects too quickly. She wanted to see Lois Otting's medical report. She wanted to see what Forensics got out of the pools of blood on the floor.

When she had that physical evidence in hand, she would conduct a one-on-one interview with everyone associated with the case, and do so at the crime scene. Only by seeing how each person reacted could she begin to rule suspects in and out.

She especially wanted to see Tomás Suarez's reaction. He acknowledged he and Zhukova had worked together many times. He had apparently been subjected to blistering attacks by Zhukova Tuesday evening, yet he had brushed off any resentment Wednesday morning. Victims almost always knew their murderers.

She noted he, alone among the designers and assistants, had not even glanced around to see the crime scene when he said that everyone had done exceptional work that night. Not wanting to see the spot where someone was murdered could be a sign of distaste for the sensational. It could also be an indication that he already knew what the scene held.

Alvarez, as intelligent as he was, still had a patrolman's mentality: every piece of evidence was crucial, especially if you were the one who uncovered it. Lee knew that it was the overall mosaic that counted. Perhaps Eva Kirk's volunteered information was the key to the case. But she would decline to reach that conclusion until she had followed every plausible lead.

Chapter 7

 "Miss Karachova, we need to review some of the information you provided us this morning."

The interview – interrogations were now always 'interviews' – took place in a small hotel conference room commandeered by the Boston Police. Next door was a makeshift evidence room containing the contents of Valentina Zhukova's hotel room as well as seven carts and the design tools they held.

Ludmila Karachova was now attired in clothing seemingly identical to what she had been described as wearing the previous evening. A below-the-knees skirt the color of oatmeal was topped by a shapeless tan sweater in indeterminate fabric. With Karachova's pale coloring and short-cut brown-flecked-with-gray hair, she seemed to fade into the chair in which she sat.

Is this a perfect disguise? Lee wondered. *Is this a woman whose role in life is to not be noticed? Is this a sign that says, 'Pay no attention to this person. She is of no interest to you.'*

Karachova was visibly frightened. Her hands shook and her eyes were wide. She did not want to be here. The question was, Lee thought, does she know why she is here?

"First," Lee said, "have you thought of anything that you did not say this morning that might be helpful to us as we look for Miss Zhukova's killer?"

Karachova gave Lee a perplexed look.

"Have you thought of anyone who might have wanted to harm Valentina?"

Karachova's eyes began to fill with tears. "People jealous of Valentina." She pronounced it 'yell-us'.

An act, Lee concluded.

Lee pulled a photo from a folder and slid it across the table. It was of Zhukova's mobile device. The original had been taken away by three FBI agents, who placed it in a case guaranteed to be impervious to any signal intended to deactivate it.

"Do you recognize this?"

Karachova's mouth formed an 'O'. Lee could sense Karachova's mind was racing.

"Is phone of Valentina."

"Do you have one like it?"

Karachova shook her head. "Mine not so nice. Common phone."

"May I see yours?" As they were speaking, a crew of techs were combing Karachova's hotel room. The warrant included the personal effects in Karachova's purse, but Lee did want to frighten her – yet. Better to ask politely.

Karachova reached into a brown shoulder bag that appeared to be made of plastic. From it she pulled a phone and handed it to Lee. It was a cheap Nokia phone, multiple generations removed from anything trendy and certainly not issued by any self-respecting intelligence service.

Lee pointed to the photo on the table. "Do you know why Miss Zhukova carried that phone?"

Karachova's face showed pain. She knew. Every line on her face screamed that she knew exactly why Valentina Zhukova carried such a device.

Lee leaned forward in her chair. "I want you to start over. I want you to tell me about how you came to work with Miss Zhukova and who she saw while she was in the United States this trip. And, if you have the quality of English that I suspect you possess, I ask that you drop the 'poor peasant girl' act and let's converse normally."

Lee leaned back and crossed her arms.

* * * * *

"Back in the day of the Soviet Union, I was assistant manager at the Flower Cooperative in Leningrad," Karachova began. "I was in charge of doing flower arrangements for the families of party officials. When everything changed, I found myself with a skill that was suddenly in demand. I helped the Flower Cooperative adjust to a freer market, including flying in the kinds of flowers we had only seen in books. In the course of a few years I studied floral design in Amsterdam, London and Geneva."

"I opened the St. Petersburg Academy of Floral Design and taught the bored wives of the newly wealthy how to design with flowers. I had a stellar reputation and a clientele that reached into every aspect of Russian life. Then, one day – just about eight years ago – I was approached by the FSB – the Russian intelligence service – and asked to do a favor."

"Then, as now, when the FSB asked a favor, you didn't refuse. They wanted me to make an expert out of one of their agents – Valentina Alexandrovna Zhukova. Though I had never met her, I knew who she was. She was like a movie star. She was the granddaughter of one of the few people everyone in Russia can agree was a hero. I knew she was one of Putin's favorites but I had no idea she was FSB."

"I spent three months teaching Valentina everything I knew and, at the end of that time, she put on a show for an audience of some of my customers. She didn't get it. She had learned the mechanics but she had no eye for flowers or for design. The FSB told me to start over. We worked together for six more months. Valentina was bored the whole time and made no effort to improve. She was like a spoiled child."

"I told the agent it was hopeless. Valentina was never going to be a floral designer. She needed a different cover. I thought that after nine months of trying unsuccessfully, my role was at an end. I thought I was free and everything would go on as before. But the FSB had different ideas. Three weeks later, I was told that I was to become Valentina's 'assistant' and accompany her. I would be the designer, but all credit would go to her. I would write the lecture, she would deliver it. And that is the way…"

"Why would you agree to such an arrangement?" Lee asked.

"Because they are the FSB. You do not refuse the FSB."

"But you had friends," Lee pressed. "Powerful friends. Friends who could tell the secret police to back off."

Karachova was silent.

"You were going to let the FSB ruin…"

"They knew my secrets," Karachova said in a near whisper. "They threatened me. They would ruin my life and the lives of those I love."

"Your family?"

Karachova shook her head. "No. They knew I am… different. They knew the name of my lover. And in Russia, many sins can be forgiven, but being different is not one of them. I would lose everything dear to me, especially her."

"That is the way it has been for seven years. I am the plain, stupid peasant girl assistant and Valentina is the beautiful, gifted designer."

"You are not part of the FSB?"

Karachova gave a small laugh. "I am not FSB material. I am their pawn."

"Everyone says Valentina was being… very cruel last night," Lee began. "She taunted the other designers; made fun of their arrangements to their face."

"It is what she does," Karachova replied. "She is very competitive."

"Even though the arrangements are really yours?" Lee said.

Karachova nodded. "After so many years she believes they really are hers. She wants the top award mostly because she does not want someone else to get that award."

"Was she being especially cruel to any particular designer last night?"

Karachova was quick to answer. "The man designer. Tomás? He has beaten me…" She paused and smiled, "…Beaten Valentina for top award several times in prestigious competitions. Valentina knew he would be there last night and she kept criticizing him and his design. Her comments were very biting. He could do nothing right."

"How did he react?" Lee asked.

Karachova shrugged. "He said very little. He did not yell back or ask her to stop. But I could tell that he was very angry inside. The look on his face told me that Valentina's hurtful words got to him."

"And the other designers?" Lee asked. "The German and Thai woman?"

"Valentina has designed against May three or four times and Valentina always got a higher award. The German woman, Eva? Valentina did not know her. She made comments to them, but not nearly so many as to Tomás."

"Valentina was also cruel toward you." Lee said, stating it as a fact.

"Last night was no different than any other time."

"This is the way she has treated you for seven years?"

"Mostly" Karachova involuntarily touched her hand to her face. To Lee, it was a signal that what was to follow was not to be trusted. Karachova also leaned away from the table, another 'tell' that a lie was coming.

Karachova continued. "I liked Valentina. When she was kind to me, she was very kind. She even gave me presents. Although that was also usually when she wanted something." Karachova's gaze had wandered to a large color photo of the Public Garden on the wall behind Lee. "She became more cruel over the years. Especially as she convinced herself she was really that gifted designer."

"A person can take only so much abuse," Lee said.

"Are you asking me if I killed Valentina?" Karachova now sat erect and looked directly at Lee. "No, I did not. I accepted my fate a long time ago."

"Have you contacted the Russian Embassy to tell them Valentina is dead?"

"No." Karachova spoke the word without hesitation or emotion.

"Wouldn't that be expected of you?"

"I'm certain that is true," Karachova said. "But the moment I tell them, a clock begins a countdown. I will be told to return to Russia immediately. When you told me of Valentina's death this morning, a great weight was lifted from me. For the first time in eight years I am free. I want to enjoy that freedom for as long as I can."

"Well, you couldn't leave even if you wanted to," Lee said. "You are a person of interest until we can clear you, and you are the only person here who knew Valentina well. I'll have to ask you to surrender your passport. You shouldn't leave Boston until we make an arrest, not that any airline would sell you a ticket without a passport. So you may as well call them and get it over with."

Karachova did not protest the request to surrender her passport. To the contrary, she rummaged in her purse for a few seconds and passed it to Lee without comment, a passive look on her round face.

Lee took the passport, Burgundy red with gold lettering, and placed it on the table between them. "Did you know Valentina's schedule?" Lee asked. "In particular, did you know it for yesterday?"

"She was always very secretive about who she was meeting," Karachova said. "She did everything through her phone with people in Moscow and St. Petersburg. She told me where she was going or where she had been only if she thought I needed to know."

"But something was upsetting her last night?" Lee asked.

Karachova nodded. "I think she was mostly angry that we could not just do the design in an hour and be done with it. Because of all the people in the ballroom with us she could not leave me to do the design and then explain it to her afterward. She had been gone all day and, I think, had plans for the evening. She was late arriving at the ballroom. So, yes, she was upset. But she was upset in the way that a spoiled child is irritated when it is told that it cannot have a sweet."

* * * * *

Lee sat alone in the conference room, drumming her fingers on the polished table. She was very good at telling when people were lying. She looked for the telltale signs: the perspiration, the crack in the voice, the tiny hesitations and the failure to keep eye contact. She could also tell when someone was following a script. Her judgment was that Karachova had lied at times to protect herself, but that much of what she had said was truthful.

Lee thumbed through Karachova's passport, with its multiple stamps from U.S. ports of entry as well as the U.K., France, Germany, Switzerland and Italy. Her surrender of the document had an eerie quality to it: an air of resignation on the woman's part. Had a police officer made the same request of Lee, she would have demanded the presence of the most senior officer available. She would not have complied until she was provided a detailed receipt and a Xerox of the passport and every page inside it.

Karachova had simply and wordlessly acceded to the request. Maybe it was a Russian thing; perhaps, in Russia, such requests were commonplace.

The exchange sharpened Lee's awareness that, in Ludmila Karachova, she was dealing with a very different culture. It was one which, if film, television, and books were to be believed, all authority was to be distrusted and truth was a function of convenience.

Lee's interview with Karachova showed that truth had many

shades of gray. As soon as Lee had shown Karachova the photo of the FSB phone, Karachova had dropped the 'peasant' act. She had spoken matter-of-factly and with a command of English appropriate to someone who had traveled widely in English-speaking countries for two decades.

Even though asked at multiple points in the conversation, Karachova had volunteered little detail about Zhukova's state of mind. This was a woman whom she knew intimately. Where had Zhukova been all day? Why was she late? What did they talk about when Zhukova first arrived? Karachova could have offered those details as a sign of good faith. Instead, Lee would have to find the information elsewhere, confront Karachova with it and see how she reacted.

Still, Karachova had also faced the question of her innocence directly. There was no attempt to hide or obfuscate.

But there was also a lack of curiosity. Neither in their first meeting in Karachova's hotel room or this one did Lee tell Karachova how Valentina Zhukova had been murdered. Not everyone asked about details but most people did.

Three kinds of people did not want to know how someone was killed. The first were people who were squeamish. Telling them that someone was stabbed and then strung up would give them nightmares. The second kind were those to whom the details were unnecessary because a death was a death. The third kind did not need to be told because they already knew. And they invariably did not ask because they had committed the murder.

Chapter 8

Alvarez felt his fingers tighten around his cell phone and willed himself to loosen his grip on the device before he broke it.

He had dealt with the FBI twice in his career. Those earlier encounters had been brief and most decidedly non-confrontational. The ones today seemed to go on forever. The people with whom he was dealing also possessed a superior, dismissive attitude that bordered on the obnoxious.

It had started with the call from the New York field office. Did he have in his possession an oblong black device with Cyrillic lettering? Had he attempted to activate the device? Had he sent photos of it to one Sarah Kane? Why had he chosen to send photos in the first place and why to Sarah Kane? Did he consider contacting the Boston FBI office? Why hadn't he considered doing so? Had he been in contact with the Russian Consulate office in New York?

That had led to a second call just minutes later from the FBI field office in Boston. He was asked the same questions. This time, he was left with three directives: first, the device was to be continually in his secure possession until picked up by an FBI team. Second, he was not to attempt to turn on the device under any circumstances. Third, neither he nor anyone from the Boston PD was to communicate with the Russian Consulate.

He had sat through the interview with Eva Kirk, the German designer, with the device casually slipped into his suit jacket pocket. When three FBI employees –an agent and two technicians – appeared a few minutes later, he retrieved the device from his pocket. The three gasped in horror, almost in unison, when he reached into his pocket and pulled it out.

"You were to stay with the device in a secure area!" the agent among the trio screamed.

"No, I was told to keep this in my possession," Alvarez had replied calmly. "No one said anything about locking myself in a room."

One of the techs opened a cooler-size box from which he took a second box and, from the second box, a third. The paperback-book-sized device went into the smallest box, which was then sealed. The smallest box went into the medium box and, this time, all three FBI employees signed the seal. That box went into the cooler and, again, three signatures were required on the seal.

"Is that for protection against electromagnetic pulse?" Alvarez asked, indicating the cooler.

"That's none of your concern," the agent replied. "And if this has been compromised, it's your ass that's going to be hanging out."

"There may be data on the phone that I need for an investigation," Alvarez said.

The reply was a contemptuous shrug.

Now, an hour later, he was recounting the story of finding the device to a third caller. The same questions; the same answers. But then a new voice broke in. Someone who had apparently been listening in the background.

"Detective Alvarez, this is Aaron Hirsch with the Cyber Division in Washington. First, may I call you Jason?"

"Why not," Alvarez replied coolly.

"Jason," Hirsh said, "I know police protocol says to just bag and mark evidence, give it to the tech team, and they throw it in an evidence locker. You didn't do that. You saw a device that didn't look like anything you had ever seen before. But instead of bagging and tagging or, worse, turning it on to see what it did, you reached out to find out what it was."

"People could argue that you should have reached out to us, but we don't advertise what we're looking for. Your friend at

Google happened to post the photos to a site we monitor. Here's what I want to say: you did good. We've seen very few of these devices. We just got this one into our lab a few minutes ago. If we're very lucky, the Russians didn't send out a kill signal and, if they did, we got it insulated before they did."

"If I did well, then you can repay the favor," Alvarez said. "We have a murder investigation and a paucity of information to work with. We need to know what you know about Zhukova. And if you've been watching her, we need to know where she was since she arrived in Boston."

There was silence on the other end of the phone. After several moments, Hirsch said, "You understand there's every probability that the FBI is going to take over this investigation."

"What on earth for?" Alvarez asked, incredulous.

Another silence, then, "Because of who she was. She's Federal Security Service. You don't just murder a Russian intelligence officer. We're already developing theories about why she was killed…"

"So you won't give us any background on her beyond what we already know. You've got a dossier on her and you won't let us read it." Alvarez tried to contain the anger he was feeling.

More silence. Then, "What do you really need?"

Alvarez replied quickly. "We need the high points. The summary. And we need to know what she's done since she got to Boston. Because you apparently think this was some 'spy versus spy' killing. I think it may have had nothing to do with her being an intelligence agent."

There was a long silence. Then, "Give me half an hour."

* * * * *

"This is unofficial," said Aaron Hirsch. It was forty minutes since their last conversation.

"We understand," Alvarez said, with Lee nodding in the background, listening with her ear next to Alvarez's cell phone.

"You will probably get notification in the next hour that the FBI is assuming responsibility for the investigation."

"We understand that, too," Alvarez said.

"Then here goes," Hirsch said. "Valentina Zhukova was one of the better FSB operatives. Good enough that we didn't catch onto what she was doing until two years ago, meaning she had a free run of the West for five years because no one ever thought of a floral designer as a Russian intelligence officer. She has a network of contacts in the US and Europe. She debriefs her contacts, collects their intelligence, and hand-carries it back to Russia."

"Here's the principal thing that our people say about her: one of the things that made her so successful was that she made no attempt to fade into the background. She was a Russian zealot, proud of her heritage and dismissive of everything else. Russia could do no wrong and those who disagreed were idiots or, worse, out to thwart Russia's rightful role in history. It's probably why she escaped our notice for so long. The best agents tell you what you want to hear. She was 'my country right or wrong' except that Russia was always right."

"We know she saw two people in Boston. She had a late lunch with Ryan Bratt…"

"The talk show guy?" Alvarez asked.

"Yes, you know him?" Hirsch said.

"He's the most conservative guy on Boston radio," Alvarez replied. "What would he be doing having lunch with Zhukova?"

"I can't comment," Hirsch said. "The meeting was in a restaurant; there was nothing clandestine about it. Zhukova also paid a visit on one Laurie Parkinson. She's a professor of economics at Boston University."

"Can you comment on her?" Alvarez asked.

"No, I cannot," Hirsch replied.

"Anyone else?" Alvarez asked.

"That's what we saw. She was back in the hotel at six. And

never went back out."

"Could anyone have gone in to see her after 3 a.m.?" Alvarez asked.

"We're pulling security footage and will run it through facial recognition. But this is going to be our investigation, Detective Alvarez. I read you what I did as a courtesy."

With the exchange of a few pleasantries the conversation ended.

"What do we do now?" Alvarez asked.

"'We' don't do anything, Jason," Lee said. "You've been on the job for thirteen hours straight. You need to go home and get some rest. And, like your friend at the FBI says, we may get bounced off this case at any moment."

"What are you going to do?" Alvarez asked.

Lee paused. "I think they're being fools, so I'm going to keep investigating until I'm told to stop. We saw the body in place. That wasn't the carefully planned assassination of a Russian agent. There was nothing cold or calculated about it: that was done by someone who was angry. And the hanging was post-mortem."

"The perp is someone associated with IFDA," Alvarez said.

Lee nodded.

"And if the FBI says they're taking over the investigation?"

"Then, officially, they're in charge and we're just clearing up loose ends," Lee said.

"Then I don't need to point out the discrepancy to them," Alvarez said.

Lee cocked her head. "Discrepancy?"

"Hirsch said Zhukova was back at the hotel at six. Karachova says she didn't get to the ballroom until after 6:30. It wasn't that she went back to her room to change; she was wearing clothes appropriate for going out. I think she met someone in the hotel for up to half an hour. Find that person and we're a step closer to solving the crime."

"When we worked together on the Grainger-Elliot murder, you did some fantastic things with that computer of yours," Lee said. "Do you think you can pull a few more tricks out of that thing? Get me everything you can on Zhukova, of course. And, if it isn't taxing your computer prowess, can you run cross-checks on all of the designers and assistants we spoke to today? I'm especially interested in Suarez."

Alvarez smiled. "I'll see you bright and early tomorrow morning, Lieutenant."

* * * * *

The call to Lee came half an hour later but, by that time, she had scanned ten cameras worth of footage between 6 and 6:45 p.m. Lee had watched as Zhukova entered the hotel at 6:07. She had encountered three people in the lobby. The first two resulted in air kisses even as Zhukova's body language showed she had neither the time nor the inclination for such pleasantries.

The third was anything but pleasant. At 6:14, a woman, a head shorter than Zhukova, had an argument with the Russian. The encounter began uneventfully but quickly escalated. It ended with Zhukova giving a dismissive wave of her hand at 6:25 and heading toward the escalator.

The problem was the angle and the distance. There was a lone camera looking into the lobby and it was some thirty feet from where the confrontation took place. The woman's back was to the camera and the event took place in one corner of the frame. When the confrontation ended, the woman went off frame and Lee could not locate her in other camera views. Lee asked security for a screen grab of the two women.

As for 'the call', it was as expected. The FBI 'disliked' getting involved in local law enforcement investigations, but the 'intelligence ramifications, resource requirements, and need for an international perspective' tipped the decision toward taking over from the Boston PD. Her Captain was part of the call, so there was no pretending it hadn't happened.

The galling part was a brief lecture by one of the FBI participants on Lee's failure to detain Ludmila Karachova instead of just taking her passport. "She knows more than she's telling you and all the Russians have to do is put her in a car and drive her to New York. She can be on the next Aeroflot flight, passport or no passport. But leave it to us; we'll have her in custody before the end of the day."

Oddly, there was no specific demand that the Boston PD cease their investigation. The FBI would take control of all evidence collected to date as well as of Zhukova's body. Anyone who contacted the Boston PD with information was to be referred to the Boston field office. But no one ever said, "Stop trying to solve the murder."

Minutes after the FBI call, Lee heard directly from the Captain.

"It wasn't my idea," he said.

"I didn't think it would be," Lee replied.

"The FBI is a squirrelly outfit," the Captain said. "They have near infinite resources to throw at an investigation, but they're also political as hell. They're talking to, quote unquote 'the highest levels of the State Department' on this one. I have no idea what that means, but my gut feeling is that it isn't good."

He continued. "They didn't come right out and say anything I could hang my hat on, but I get a strong sense that they already have an idea of who did this. And we both know when that is the mindset going in, bad things happen."

"So, what I'm telling you is, keep working. You're going to have a lot of impediments including, I'm afraid, shutting down the crime scene and having no access to the forensics you collected this morning. Think of it as a handicap, not as a game-ender."

It was, as far as Lee was concerned, all the permission she needed.

Chapter 9

"I was hoping I hadn't missed you."

Liz Phillips looked up from her coffee to see a well-dressed, tall, slender woman speaking to her. Instinctively, Phillips rose to her feet. The woman was silver-haired and had a tanned face that indicated she lived somewhere that was warm and sunny year round. The soft gray pants suit was exceptionally well-tailored and the silver jewelry achieved the hard-to-manage feat of being both understated and eye-catching.

Phillips had accepted the invitation for lunch in one of the hotel's restaurants from Kathy Thomas with some reluctance. She no longer belonged here; her 'translation' work for Lieutenant Lee was complete and, after she brought Eva Kirk and her story to Lee, there had been no request to stay around for further assignment. For the past forty-five minutes Phillips and Thomas had enjoyed a pleasant meal, though Thomas did most of the talking.

Phillips knew the woman standing beside their table was the one whose face graced the inside front cover of the IFDA program book and whose visage appeared on numerous signs throughout the hotel. This was Winnie Garrison.

Garrison glanced down at the table, from which luncheon plates had been cleared and now only coffee cups remained. She nodded at Thomas. "I'm sorry I'm late. This is turning out to be one of those days that will live in infamy." Turning to Phillips, Garrison said, "If you're free, might Kathy and I have a moment of your time? I'm…"

"Winnie Garrison," Phillips said, nodding. "And I think we're just finishing here."

Phillips looked at Thomas, who had a sly smile on her face. *So this was a set-up*, Phillips thought. *But why?*

"We'll get a lot more accomplished if we're not interrupted," Garrison said. "I'm up on the eleventh floor, if you can spare a few minutes."

A few minutes later they were in a three-room suite, the rooms packed with boxes of design material and signs. Garrison lifted a box of brochures off of a table and indicated two chairs. She then walked over to a bar and opened a bottle of water, which she poured into a glass. She indicated a bottle to Phillips and Thomas, each of whom shook their head.

"It took me a while to find out who you were, Ms. Phillips…" Garrison began.

"It's Liz," Phillips said. "Only the bank tellers call me 'Ms. Phillips'."

Garrison smiled. "And I'm Winnie. The only person who ever calls me 'Edwina' is my husband, and he does that only when he's angry." She sat at the table, looking at the bubbles in the glass. "I have been in a state of shock all morning. Until today, I had never seen a person who had been murdered, much less someone whom I both knew fairly well and had spoken to less than twenty-four hours earlier."

Garrison took a sip of the water. "I offered to find Lieutenant Lee someone to navigate the treacherous shoals of the floral design world, and she instead immediately called you. It turns out that you were down at the Flower Market. May I ask how you happen to be acquainted with a police lieutenant?"

"I am Chair of Landscape Judges at the Northeast Garden and Flower Show," Phillips said. "I was there back in February when Lieutenant Lee was investigating…"

Garrison snapped her fingers. "I remember reading about that! The Executive Director, floating face down in an exhibit. Horrible!"

"I was in the right place at the right time," Phillips said. "Or maybe the right place at the wrong time. Lieutenant Lee needed someone who could explain show procedure to her. She more or less grabbed me off the floor. I received a very nice card and a note from her, but never expected to hear from her again, and I didn't. Until this morning."

"I asked around about you," Garrison said. Indicating Thomas, she said, "Kathy, here, tells me you're president of a very active club, went to Flower Show School, you're part of Judges Council. She also says you're smart and energetic. I can't imagine why the Committee didn't draft you when we were planning IFDA Boston."

"I don't really move in those circles," Phillips replied. "I go to Judges Council and listen to the lectures and watch the demonstrations. A lot of people are talking Federation politics. It isn't my thing." She looked at Thomas. "Sorry, Kathy."

Thomas shrugged. "If the shoe fits…"

Garrison laughed. "They are a Machiavellian crowd, aren't they? What do people say about academics? 'The arguments are so vehement because the stakes are so small?' It's the same thing in the garden club world. Except that in the garden club world, a few very hard working people can accomplish a great deal."

Garrison took another sip of her water. "Liz, Kathy and I asked you up here for two reasons; both of them selfish. We'd love to know everything you've heard about what happened to Valentina, although Kathy says that you are probably the least gossipy person ever to have placed a stem in Oasis. I ask because, ultimately, I'm responsible for having brought Valentina here, and I want to help any way I can to find out who killed her."

Garrison continued. "The second reason is, while it's very late in coming, we would like to recruit you to help us with the conference. Over the past few days I've seen that a number of my erstwhile associates believe their jobs were done when the banners went up. I desperately need someone – a *lot* of someones, actually – who aren't afraid to get their hands dirty, who know Boston, and who can both give and take orders with equal ease. Based on what Kathy – as well as several of your friends – told me, you are such a person."

Phillips blinked. *Me?* She thought. "My cat never got her seconds," was all she could say.

Garrison laughed again and then said, "*'Who says that I am the queen of my castle? My cat is the queen, and I am her vassal.'* I have no idea where I heard that, but it sounds so appropriate. By all means, go feed your cat. But bring back a couple of changes of clothes."

Garrison continued. "With regard to the investigation, Kathy told me about Lieutenant Lee's questioning of everyone this morning, and Eva Kirk sought me out to tell about what she overheard. I believe you were present when she spoke with Lieutenant Lee and Detective Alvarez."

"Then you know almost everything I know," Phillips said. "I helped the crime scene people go through the design carts of everyone who was in the ballroom last night. They were using a spray and a black light to look for blood, so I suspect that Lieutenant Lee believes that a designer's knife could have been used in the stabbing."

"We carry an amazing number of potential murder weapons with us, don't we?" Garrison said. "Based on what Kathy told me, I gather Valentina was upset about something, more than a little cranky, and up to her usual tricks trying to intimidate the competition."

Garrison took a drink of water. "The part I'm having trouble accepting is Eva's assertion that Valentina Zhukova was a fraud. That she didn't do her own design. That her assistant…"

"Ludmila," Thomas offered. "The mousy little woman."

"Right. Ludmila Karachova," Garrison said. "Kirk said she understands Russian and that Karachova was asking for specific flowers. Valentina was just handing her the flowers Ludmila asked for and complaining that it was all taking too long."

Garrison shook her head. "I've sat through two lectures and demonstrations by her in the past year. Each time, Valentina read from a prepared text and Ludmila did designs. Occasionally, Valentina would look over at Ludmila and say something in Russian and Ludmila would nod and answer back. But why would she do such a thing? It makes no sense."

"All I can tell you," Phillips replied, "is that Lieutenant Lee and Detective Alvarez listened and took it very seriously. It seemed to fit with something else they knew. Detective Alvarez said, 'It ties back to the phone.' I don't know what that means."

"Kirk also offered up the observation that Valentina continually verbally abused Ludmila," Garrison said. "Called her things like a 'stupid cow' and 'peasant'. Kirk said that a person could take that kind of abuse for only so long before they snapped."

"Why would anyone agree to such an arrangement?" Garrison wondered aloud. "It's horrible. If Ludmila has been the design genius behind Valentina, then *she* is the Queen of Negative Space. I wouldn't put up with it for a heartbeat." Garrison looked up at Phillips. "Then there's a good chance that Ludmila could have committed… Oh, that's terrible. It makes no sense. Why would Valentina be 'fronting' for Ludmila? And why would Ludmila hide her talents like that?"

"Let me ask you a question," Phillips said. "You know many of the people who are here. Did any of them dislike Valentina?"

"'Dislike' or 'hate'?" Garrison replied. "You don't murder someone you 'dislike'. You avoid them. You don't return their calls or emails. You look past them in a room full of people. Give them the thousand-yard stare. I would think it would take a burning hatred to kill someone."

Garrison paused, collecting her thoughts. "Your Detective Lee asked me that question this morning and I think I said something about professional competitiveness but that ours was a collegial group on the whole. With a few hours to think about it, I would revise those thoughts slightly. Valentina was… abrasive. It wasn't that she went out of her way to grate on people; it's just the way she was."

Garrison continued. "You've heard of ugly Americans? Valentina was an ugly Russian. She wasn't a communist; she never made comments like that. But she was a rabid nationalist. She said the dissolution of the Soviet Union was the greatest travesty of the twentieth century. And Russia never did anything wrong. She toed the party line completely. You couldn't be with her in a social setting for more than fifteen minutes without those sentiments being voiced. As a result, a lot of people found her annoying and drifted away as soon as she climbed on her soapbox."

"I think of the reaction of people like Zara Jretnam," Garrison said. "You'll meet her tomorrow. A lovely lady who lost a sister on the Malaysian Airlines flight that was shot down last year. She took that death very hard. At a conference in London in October, I heard Valentina say, with a perfectly straight face, that Vladimir Putin was returning from a trip to Venezuela and that the Ukrainian military believed they were shooting down Putin's plane and fired on the Malaysian Airlines flight instead. Zara was with me. She just left the room and avoided Valentina thereafter. I had a sense there may have been some kind of showdown afterwards, though."

"But avoiding her was how people dealt with Valentina's views. I have friends who are rabid Democrats or rabid Republicans. I admire them as people and ignore any attempt to drag me into their political discussions. I think Valentina was one of the most gifted designers of our time – though this revelation about Ludmila doing all the work certainly shakes that foundation. I had no truck with her 'Russia forever' fervor and joined another conversation."

"I've tried to think of anyone who would hate Valentina just because of her views. We have no one here at IFDA from the Ukraine. I could imagine that would certainly touch a nerve. Latvia? We have four Latvians here. Russia certainly makes menacing noises toward the Baltic. China? That relationship certainly blows hot and cold but, if I were Russian, I would be more wary of China than the other way around."

Garrison paused. "I realize I've gone on. Liz, go home, feed your cat, and pack a bag. We'll talk more about this later. By Sunday evening, you'll be so tired of me that you'll never want to see me again, but I promise you that you won't be bored."

* * * * *

Victoria Lee checked her phone. The time was 3:15 p.m. She had sent Alvarez home with the charge to use his computer skills to good advantage. The more pressing question was what Lee would or could do with her own time.

The makeshift evidence room had been cleared of everything the FBI wanted. The balance – including all but one of the design carts – was in a corner of the room with a note asking the Boston PD to return the items to their rightful owners. Lee made a note to ask Winnie Garrison to collect and return the carts. She noted that the one that had been taken away for further analysis belonged to Ludmila Karachova.

Lois Otting had called to say that she had turned over her notes and physical evidence to an FBI agent and that Zhukova's body had been removed. Should she do anything else?

I am totally screwed, Lee thought to herself.

She was an investigator with no leads and no evidence. Everything about the crime pointed to it having been done by someone at IFDA, but the closest thing she had to evidence was a photo of Zhukova in a heated argument with someone – and only the back of that person was visible.

What could she deduce from the photo? The other person was a woman and was a full head shorter than Zhukova, who was five-ten. So the woman in the photo was five-two to five-four, and that included short heels. The woman had dark hair worn shoulder length. That was the extent of the 'distinguishing features'. A dark raincoat or trench coat obscured all information about her weight or body shape.

I told myself I wouldn't do this anymore.

Lee again took her phone out of her purse. She scrolled though contacts and tapped a number that, until three months ago, had been at the top of her 'contacts' list.

John Flynn had been her partner for five years. He had single-handedly turned her into a Detective, giving her the education that no classroom could ever provide. He had been more than a mentor; he had been the one person in her life in which she could have absolute confidence. Three months earlier, when she had been promoted to Lieutenant, he had announced his retirement. He had, he told her, no desire at age fifty-six to break in someone new, nor to start fresh in any of the high-profile police units that were his reward for bringing along Lee.

Solving the murder of St. John Grainger-Elliot had been his last case and even that was unofficial as Flynn was nominally on desk duty, clearing up case files awaiting the formal paperwork on his retirement. His retirement party had been three weeks earlier.

Flynn picked up on the second ring.

"So how's retirement?" Lee asked.

"I don't think it's going to work out," Flynn replied. "I guess I'm not ready for fishing and shuffleboard."

"You're coming back to the Department?"

"No. Too much history. I'm thinking about suburban work. They love us old fogeys. We work cheap, we already have health insurance, and we're never going to be part of their pension obligation."

"You've taken a job?"

"A couple of irons in the fire. One-man-band Detective for a town. It'll give me a place to go."

It'll give me a place to go, Lee thought. That had always been the unspoken part of Flynn's life. He was married, but he and his wife apparently lived completely separate lives. Three weeks of living under the same roof had proven to be too much.

"I need your help," Lee said.

"Does this have anything to do with a woman found dead in a hotel ballroom?"

Lee told him everything. Every detail, including being chastised by an FBI agent for not detaining Karachova.

"I feel like I ought to just hang up the investigation and let the FBI screw it up on their own. I've got nothing to work with," Lee said at the conclusion of her story.

"You've got more than you think," Flynn said. "First, go back to the footage – assuming the Fibbies didn't take the masters – and see who else walked by. I'll bet you at least a couple of dozen people passed by during that conversation and will be able to identify who Zhukova was arguing with. Second, find out who is a no-show at this wing-ding. If it was someone inside and it was planned, they may have come in, done the killing, and decided not to stick around to be questioned. That's the sort of thing young Alvarez can do faster than you. Third, think beyond Zhukova and look at her family, especially her husband. You said he's in the Russian Army? That may figure into this. And fourth, watch *The Manchurian Candidate*."

"The what?"

"*The Manchurian Candidate*. The original one, with Laurence Harvey and Angela Lansbury. Not the god-awful remake. That's the worst film Meryl Streep ever made. Apart from *The French Lieutenant's Woman*."

"I hate it when you talk in film metaphors," Lee said. "Jason did that this morning. You probably taught him to do that in just – what? – four days?"

"Film metaphors are very useful tools," Flynn said. "If you have time, go back to the Richard Condon source material, but you probably don't have the attention span right now. Angela Lansbury is this incredibly manipulative woman who is married to a Joseph McCarthy-type figure. She's president of half a dozen super-patriotic organizations. In reality, she's a communist and working for the Russians. Anyway, she's willing to sacrifice her own son to get what she wants. In the end, her son shoots her, and then himself."

"How is that supposed to help me?" Lee asked. "Who is the Angela Lansbury character supposed to represent?"

"It's supposed to help you by taking your mind off the case for a few hours," Flynn replied. "You've been at this for ten hours straight. But the movie may help you in another way: we've had close to twenty-five years to forget about the Cold War. Valentina Zhukova was part of a new Cold War, and that makes everyone's motives suspect. You seem to have taken Ludmila Karachova's 'I'm innocent' speech at face value. She seems like a hell of a suspect to me. I'd also dig deeper into Suarez's background. I think you're right that his reaction to that initial interview was all wrong."

"So I need to be paranoid to solve this murder?" Lee asked.

"Vicky, you are far and away the smartest person working for the Boston PD." Flynn said. "You have the best innate grasp of procedure of anyone on the force. You have a mind that balances logic and intuition in a way that is amazing. Just keep in mind that motive is everything in a case like this. Stop trying to solve the crime for a few hours and let that amazing brain of yours do its thing."

Lee closed the call and smiled.

* * * * *

Jason Alvarez arrived at his Charlestown condo to find his wife, Terri, with their four-year-old daughter, Abby, in the kitchen. "Should I count this as being home really early from a day shift or really late from a night shift?" his wife asked. She was smiling as she asked the question, and that was good. But then the news had been good for several weeks on the subject that mattered most to them: their daughter's health.

Abby had been born with the genetic mutation that caused cystic fibrosis. Worse, the symptoms of the disease appeared earlier in Abby than in most children. Seven weeks earlier, Abby had been accepted into a trial for a pair of experimental drugs, Ivacaftor and Lumacaftor, that held out the promise of decreasing both the frequency and severity of the congestion that built up in her lungs.

Abby's response to the drug regimen had been sufficiently positive that, for the first time in years, the Alvarez family held out hope that life could be 'normal' insofar as two adults with concurrent work schedules could ever be normal. Ever since their daughter's diagnosis, Terri Alvarez had taught school by day while Jason Alvarez pursued his police – and now Detective – career on the 'graveyard' shift. Five days a week, it meant that Jason slept while Terri was at work and vice-versa.

"Lieutenant Lee wants me in tomorrow morning," Jason said. This led to a discussion of drop-in daycare. A few months earlier it would have set off both an argument and a scramble to notify Terri's school that she would be absent for yet another day.

What remained unclear was Jason Alvarez' next career step. He had made Detective the previous October, a joyous step up the law enforcement ladder that turned anodyne when he learned that his assigned partner was the dreaded Vito Mazilli. Mazilli was a slug of a man who held his job by dint of seniority and civil service rules. Alvarez was to the point of asking to go back on foot patrol when he and Mazilli were called to the Harborfront Convention Center at 3:30 a.m. on a Saturday in February to respond to a call of a dead body at the Northeast Garden and Flower Show.

Three days later, Alvarez had impressed the entire Boston PD chain of command with his computer and database management skills. He had been told – no, *promised* – that his skills were recognized and would be rewarded.

Now it was April and, each evening, he reported to West Broadway to share a car or a case report with a man who offered him neither challenge nor education. His shift commander counseled patience.

Alvarez retired to the tiny room they used as a home office. He began plugging search terms into his computer and was rewarded with articles about Valentina Alexandrovna Zhukova which, with the aid of Google Translate, were rendered into serviceable English. The information in those articles led him on additional searches. A search of the IFDA website led to a registration list and those names, too, were fed into a database, together with a highlighted search for information on the designers and assistants that had worked with Zhukova that evening.

Three hours later, he was convinced he could go back to Lieutenant Lee in the morning armed with information with which to launch a fresh investigation.

Chapter 10
Thursday, April 9

Vicky Lee awakened at 4:30 a.m. with a pounding headache that, half an hour later, had been only partially subdued by three Excedrin chased by two cups of coffee.

Netflix offered only the remake of *The Manchurian Candidate* and so she had dutifully found a streaming service that offered a fuzzy feature-length version of the 1962 original that was chopped into a dozen installments. The film would periodically freeze, either to allow some server in Tasmania to refresh and buffer content from another server in Turkey, or else to allow Nigerian con men to upload Trojan horses onto her computer or ransack her brokerage account.

Lee came away with an appreciation of Cold War paranoia and an intense dislike of Angela Lansbury. She also realized that she had been far too quick to dismiss Ludmila Karachova as a suspect.

Lee also concluded John Flynn had been correct in one other, major respect: she needed time to clear her mind and to allow her subconscious to begin assembling known facts into a logical framework. She wondered if the film choice had been some spur-of-the-moment invention; one intended to send her on a scavenger hunt with a lone goal of directing her attention elsewhere. She knew she dared not ask him and, if he brought up the subject, she would lie and say she fell asleep before she could act on his advice.

An hour later, in her office, she confronted the first sign that today would not be one of business as usual. Taped to the laptop in her office was a printout from the Associated Press, the headline of which read, '*PUTIN ASSAILS FBI OVER MURDER OF RUSSIAN TOURIST IN BOSTON*'.

The article, in turn, showed how the death of a spy could be twisted into an indictment of one law enforcement agency in particular and an entire country in general. Russian President Putin, the article said, was 'carefully following' the 'unspeakable murder' of a 'friend who freely shared her love of flowers with the world'. Putin went on to decry the 'lawless streets' of America. The FBI, for its part, said only that it was 'investigating the circumstances' of Zhukova's death. Both sides ignored the spy angle as well as Zhukova's illustrious grandfather.

At the bottom of the printout, someone had written *'glad it's not your case?'*

Lee folded the article and placed in it a jacket pocket.

* * * * *

Jason Alvarez awakened at 5:30 a.m., slipped out of bed and went to his home office. He checked his databases and was satisfied at the extent to which blocks of data had filled in forms. His attention, though, was drawn to a blinking red icon at the bottom of the screen. He tapped the screen and an article followed. The source was the English-language version of *Rossiykaya Gazeta*, Russia's largest daily newspaper and one owned by the government; the successor to *Pravda* as the official organ of government propaganda.

GRANDDAUGHTER OF MARSHAL ZHUKOV BRUTALLY MURDERED IN AMERICA, read the headline.

This is not going to be good, Alvarez thought, as he sat down to read.

The bloody body of the granddaughter of Marshal Georgy Zhukov was found this morning in a hotel amphitheater in the American city of Boston, Massachusetts. In addition to multiple stab wounds, Valentina Alexandrovna Zhukova had also been hanged with a wire noose. There is credible evidence that the murder may have been orchestrated by the American government.

Mrs. Zhukova, 41, was an internationally acclaimed flower arranger and had been invited by an international body to exhibit her designs at the organization's biennial convention.

The outraged Ambassador to America, Sergey Ivanovich Kislyak, said the horrific slaying went beyond the casual murders that are a regular occurrence in cities there. "While tourists are never safe on the streets of America, this killing was especially gruesome. We believe Mrs. Zhukova was specifically targeted because she was a Russian citizen."

Mrs. Zhukova has often been described as "President Putin's favorite flower arranger," and the President issued a statement of regret. "While we cannot be certain that this murder was perpetrated by the American Government, we have strong evidence that officials of the Federal Bureau of Investigation had a hand in it. We know this because they have already launched a propaganda campaign to discredit the reputation of Valentina Alexandrovna."

A Kremlin source said the American Military remains humiliated that Marshal Zhukov reached Berlin weeks ahead of American troops and captured the city of Berlin.

"It is a well-known fact that American forces were stalemated by the Nazi Wehrmacht a hundred miles from Berlin," the source said. "American generals begged Marshal Zhukov to delay his Berlin offensive. Mindful that Nazis could escape during a lull in the fighting, Marshal Zhukov pressed ahead and captured Berlin while American forces were still days away. Seventy years after that triumphal Russian victory, the American military still seethes at being bystanders to the final surrender of the Nazis."

"It is not beyond imagination that the American military may have exacted their revenge on one of the few living direct descendants of Georgy Zhukov," the source said.

The story went on, recounting tales of killings of tourists and FBI surveillance of foreign nationals in the United States. It was first-class propaganda, Alvarez observed. Everything was innuendo and backed by links, however improbable, to real-life events.

What was missing, though, was any additional reference to a 'propaganda campaign' against Zhukova. Alvarez surmised that it was a placeholder: in the event that the FBI named Zhukova as an intelligence operative, that allegation would be swept into the 'propaganda campaign' thread of the story.

The other salient fact missing in the article was any reference to Zhukova's husband, Yuri Soldatov. Soldatov was a Colonel in the Russian Army. He was also the second-in-command at the bland-sounding "Department of Special Technical Measures", the Russian military's unit to develop cyber-warfare capabilities and carry out attacks.

The unit did not formally exist; rather, the Russian government's officially stated plan was to establish a defensive cyber security agency within two to three years. In reality, the unit had been in existence since 2006 and was a growing threat. It was not yet in the same league as China's Peoples' Liberation Army Unit 61398, the vast Shanghai-based cyber warfare agency, but China was clearly Russia's model.

As Alvarez scrolled through the data collected overnight, he kept returning to the immediate subject at hand: finding someone with a motive. It had to be personal. It had to be longstanding. You did not kill someone and then hang them postmortem unless you truly hated this person.

He was nearly finished with his review when one item caught his attention. He read the synopsis and clicked through to see the supporting material. Lieutenant Lee had asked him to check on the designers who worked with Zhukova that evening. It turned out that one of them, Tomás Suarez, had quite a temper.

Alvarez heard movement outside the tiny office. It was Terri. She poked her head in the door and said, "Coffee?"

Alvarez smiled and nodded.

* * * * *

Liz Phillips awoke to unfamiliar rumblings around her. Individually they were small noises: a heating duct blowing warm air, water running through pipes to feed a shower, footsteps outside the door.

Phillips listened and realized she seldom was awakened by anything other than light coming in through a small gap in the curtains in her bedroom at home. The heat – hot water in a baseboard – came on at 6:30 and was always silent. There was never the sound of water because her bedroom at home was specially insulated from such intrusions. And the only time there was the sound of footsteps was when David was home. Sarabeth had been married two years now and had not been back to Boston since Christmas.

David. She sat up in a panic. The bedside clock read 5:53. Exhausted, she had not called him last night. When he was on the road – as he was most weeks – their custom was a goodnight call at 10 p.m. and a wake-up call at six. He would have called their house phone last evening and gotten only an answering machine.

Phillips opened her purse and found her cell phone. No missed calls. David had assumed she was out and did not want to bother her. She dialed his cell phone. He answered on the first ring.

"I missed you last night," he said.

Phillips laughed. "My life has been turned upside down in the past twenty-four hours." She gave him a ten-minute synopsis of Wednesday's events. At several points David interrupted with questions. He was always a good listener.

"Anyway, I've had my second moment in the law enforcement sun, but that's done," Phillips said. "Now, I get to put out fires at a floral design convention with a bunch of ladies who make us look like paupers."

"Keep your eyes open," David said. "You're in a unique position."

"But I never even met the woman," Phillips said. "To be honest, I never even *heard* of her, and everyone acts like she was the most important floral designer who ever lived."

"All the better," David said. "You have no preconceptions. Just look and listen."

She ended the call and looked around the impersonal hotel room. *Keep your eyes open*, her husband had said. *First, I have to know what I'm looking for.*

The room phone beside her bed rang. The clock showed 6:18.

"Liz, how soon can you be downstairs? We've got our first crisis of the day."

Chapter 11

The crisis was real enough. Sometime during the night, the FBI had ordered the Convention Center Plaza Grand Ballroom sealed for the duration. No one was allowed into the room for any reason. Mitsy Fairchild – it seemed to Phillips that every second person on the IFDA Committee seemed to have a name that ended in '-itsy' – declared herself "through with the whole damned thing" and stormed out of the meeting taking place in the hotel's catering office.

Winnie Garrison waited until Fairchild was out of sight. "It's my fault," she said, matter-of-factly. "I asked her to chair the banquets committee. I thought it would be a matter of choosing menus and taking care of special meal requests. A plum job to create a grateful and generous benefactor."

"Yesterday morning you moved everyone over to the Westin," Phillips said.

"And this morning, the Westin says they're fully committed for the next five days," Garrison replied. "We had the ballroom for seven events over the next four days, starting with breakfast at 8:30."

"And there will be up to eight hundred people per event," Phillips said, making certain the number was right.

The hotel's Banquet Manager was on a speakerphone. A young woman whose lapel tag said her name was 'Aurora' and that she was the 'Event Manager', sat mutely, a terrified look on her face.

"We have no liability in this," the male voice of the Banquet Manager said. "This is *force majeure*. In fact, there's an issue of the hotel's lost income arising from our inability to rent the space." It was not a defensive statement. To the contrary, he seemed to be attempting to set the tone for what would follow.

Phillips watched as Garrison's eyes rolled.

"Why don't we save that discussion for a different time and place?" Phillips said. "For right now, we need to feed breakfast to eight hundred people. Your kitchen is presumably already preparing that food, is that right?"

The Banquet Manager allowed that the raw materials were on hand.

"What is the hotel's total banquet capacity?" Phillips asked.

"We don't have another room for eight hundred," was the response.

"That wasn't the question," Phillips pressed. "Taking out the ballroom, what's the meeting room capacity?"

"We don't serve meals in most of those rooms," the Banquet Manager said.

"Liz just asked you a very reasonable question," Garrison said. "What is the capacity?"

"A thousand, but six hundred of those seats are taken starting at 10 a.m."

"Fine," Phillips said. "We'll be out of them by 9:30."

"You don't turn over a room in half an hour," the Banquet Manager said. "These rooms are already set up for morning meetings."

"Which means you already have four hundred spaces that aren't spoken for," Phillips said. "As to the others, you'll have to scramble. If you need to put us on hold for a moment while you make those arrangements, we'll understand."

"I said I can't do it," the Banquet Manager said. "*Force majeure.*"

"My husband is a senior partner at Ropes and Gray," Phillips said. "If you don't do this, he will explain to you, in court, the limitations on claims of *force majeure*, and Aurora here will join Winnie and me in testifying to your complete intransigence on the matter. You have the ability to meet the letter of your contract with us by other means. That you find it *inconvenient* to meet those

88   *MURDER IN NEGATIVE SPACE*

requirements is not a defense. I suspect it will cost you and the hotel in legal fees and damages a very large multiple of what you fear it will cost you in staff overtime to handle our breakfast. My husband, on the other hand, will consider the time Ropes and Gray devotes to the lawsuit *pro bono* work for a worthy organization."

"I never said…"

"Here's what we're going to do," Phillips said. "We're going to release you from your contract for everything after dinner this evening and, if we can find an alternate space for tonight, we'll release you from that as well. But you're going to move heaven and earth to feed eight hundred people at 8:30 using every hotel meeting room you have available. And the hotel is going to provide the staff to help us direct people to the correct rooms. Is that acceptable?"

There was silence on the other end of the line. Then, "Give me ten minutes."

"In ten minutes, you'll give us the seating capacities of the rooms you'll be using so we can divide up the delegates," Garrison said. "I'll be in my room. And you better tell the business office to be open as well because we'll need copies of everything."

"I can't believe I'm doing this," the Banquet Manager said.

"Ten minutes," Garrison said. "I'm in room 1101."

Walking to the elevator, Garrison said, "Kathy Thomas said your husband was some kind of a management expert. He does that for Ropes and Gray? My husband talks about them."

Phillips smiled. "It was the only law firm name I could think of. David – my husband – says, 'when all else fails, bluff'. He once groused that a company was trying to use 'force majeure' to get out of a contract commitment. I remembered what he said to *that* company's CEO and repeated it. And that banquet manager never intended to not accommodate us for breakfast. He just wanted to corner us into agreeing to pay for the expense the hotel will incur – and for us to feel grateful that he was willing to do anything at all.

We cut him off before he could propose 'his' alternative."

"And what will this cost the hotel?"

Phillips shrugged. "If the hotel is a union shop, which it almost certainly is, probably fifteen extra people at twenty dollars an hour for two hours. Six thousand dollars, give or take."

Garrison laughed. "Liz, I expect you and I are going to get to know one another a whole lot better before this week is over."

* * * * *

Phillips walked by the ballroom entrances, where yellow tape now warned that this was a prohibited area and that entry was forbidden. But no one guarded the doors; that would apparently come later. And so she walked in.

The room was now cleared of all tables except those nearest to the four spheres. The ladders were still in place. She made a careful circle around the area. The one section of carpet underneath one of the designs – presumably Zhukova's – was still missing. The FBI apparently believed that there were clues to be discovered in adjacent portions of the carpet, the ladders, and tables.

She also examined, for the first time, the four designs. 'Hanging designs', she knew, were one of more than fifty styles of accepted floral designs; though the hanging designs with which she was familiar generally were a small fraction of the size of the ones in front of her.

Flower Show School had taught her that large designs were not just small arrangements scaled to a different magnitude. The choice of floral material was necessarily different and designers needed to balance close-up viewing against seeing the design from a distance. But the fundamental elements did not change: line, form, space, texture, pattern, light, size and color.

Looking at the sphere above the cut-out carpet, Phillips thought, *If this was Zhukova's design, it is stunning.* Blocks of colors swirled and repeated using varying floral combinations. She had been called 'The Queen of Negative Space' and the use of negative space – areas that called attention to themselves by the absence of floral material – was dramatic. Because of the voids, the color areas were all the more vivid. Zhukova had indeed been a master.

Because everything had stopped when Zhukova's body was found, the names of the designers had never been appended to any signage. Because Phillips had been present at their questioning, she knew the names of the three other designers but, if she had ever seen photos of their creations, their names had not registered. All four were excellent; crafted by designers whose creative skills far surpassed her own.

But being a floral design judge was also a matter of intuition. All manner of care was taken in a competition to ensure that judges did not know the names of the designers whose work was being judged. But judges inevitably spotted details that were 'tells' for certain designers, such as a tendency to use a specific flower or color. Sometimes, a design's 'mechanics' – the behind-the-design system that held up an arrangement – could be a clue to the identity of the person who created the work. Judges were supposed to view designs from a point set down by the rules of the show; typically, three feet directly in front of the design.

Phillips was under no such constraints and so she examined each design closely and from all sides. Intuition told her that one of the designs had been put together by a person with an Asian sensitivity. It might also be that the person was a Master of Ikebana, a distinctly Japanese school of floral design that had many adherents outside of that country. But the design also had a certain sensuousness to it. This design, she decided, belonged to May Wattanapanit, the Thai entrant.

A second design used especially bold splashes of colors; making maximum use of those flowers where breeding and genetic manipulation had yielded hues seldom found in nature. The design also had a bold rhythm than seemed to pulse with life. Phillips decided this was from Tomás Suarez, the New Yorker by way of

Argentina.

Phillips acknowledged in her mind that she could also be completely wrong. Having never seen a design from any of these people, she could be dealing with cultural stereotypes that, in turn, would turn out to be completely wrong. Still, she pressed on.

The third design, interestingly, also used bold colors and negative space, though in a narrower palette and with a more restrained hand. There was more color blocking and more use of smaller flowers that facilitated more intricate patterns. But the overall effect was one of order. This design, Phillips decided, belonged to Eva Kirk. A Teutonic mind would think in terms of order, embellished by flourishes.

Which left the design with the circle of missing carpet beneath it. This was, by default, Valentina Zhukova's work. It was beautiful; *voluptuous* was not too strong a word. Swirls of flowers merged into pools. *Marc Chagall*, Phillips thought. She had seen an exhibit of the artist's work at the Met a few years earlier. Chagall was Russian. As was this work.

Four beautiful designs by four masters of the art.

But she also saw that in less than a day's time, these works of floral art would be all but unrecognizable. Flowers needed to be watered and Oasis, especially in a hanging design, was a poor water reservoir for stems cut to very short lengths.

Had there been no murder, assistants would have watered each design twice a day, all the while looking for and replacing fading flowers from vast buckets of blooms held in a cool room.

Already, Phillips could see in each of the designs some flowers that were beginning to fade or discolor; irises that were closing and wrinkling, roses that were starting to blow. In a major standard flower show, a visitor on the last hour of the last day would still see a design that looked as fresh – or nearly as fresh – as the morning it was created. This morning, less than thirty hours after the designers placed their final blooms, Phillips knew she was probably the last person who would ever see these designs in anything remotely resembling their original incarnation. The FBI was interested in clues to a murder, not in "flower arrangements".

She took out her phone from her purse and began taking photos of each design. She was not certain why she was doing so; she knew only that by tomorrow morning, there would be nothing but brown, desiccated spheres to show for all the time and energy that had gone into these works of floral art.

* * * * *

Vicky Lee felt the visceral surge of pride that came with prying open a crack in an otherwise impenetrable case through sheer intuition and legwork.

She had positioned herself next to the main elevators with her iPad showing a frame of the encounter between Zhukova and a second woman. To everyone who would pause to listen to her, Lee would ask, "Do you recognize these two women?" If they stopped, Lee would show a few seconds of the video and ask the question again.

Several women and at least one man readily identified Valentina Zhukova.

The twenty-second person who viewed the video supplied the name of the other person in the frame.

Zara Jretnam. The incoming Chairman of IFDA. The Malaysian woman to whom Zhukova had defiantly dismissed any hint of Russian complicity in the death of Jretnam's sister.

Lee did not stop with one identification. She kept at it for another hour until she had uncovered multiple witnesses who had seen and heard some part of the exchange between the two women, could place the time of the event to within a few minutes, and could describe each woman's apparel and accessories.

Each witness told a similar story and, by piecing together the disparate fragments, Lee was able to create a twenty-minute-long timeline – albeit with gaps – that told of a chance encounter that featured an escalating volume on Jretnam's part coupled with merciless ridicule on Zhukova's.

One woman claimed to have spent ten minutes with Jretnam after the encounter, attempting without success to calm her. Jretnam, the woman said, instead grew angrier by the minute.

Lee now had the names and contact information for each potential witness. She was about to turn it over to Jason Alvarez to do detailed interviews when her phone chirped with the tone for an unknown caller.

"This is a courtesy call only," Special Agent Ken Grimes told her, and then repeated that phrase eight or nine more times in the course of a five minute conversation.

"The Russian woman, Karachova, has disappeared," Grimes said. "She apparently walked out through a loading dock sometime last night. While we believe you should have taken her into custody as soon as you discovered she was more than a 'peasant assistant' and had full knowledge of Zhukova's espionage activities, we also acknowledge that part of the blame lies with some interdepartmental snafus over who was supposed to do what and on what schedule. But you – and by 'you' I mean the Boston PD as well as your team – are to conduct no search for her. If you somehow become aware of her whereabouts, you are to contact the Boston Field Office but take no further action. Is that clear?"

Lee said it was perfectly clear.

"Also as a matter of courtesy, we want you to know that we are very close to an arrest in the case," Grimes said.

Lee asked for any information that the FBI might share as a courtesy.

"We have high-level intel suggesting that this had everything to do with Zhukova's husband, Colonel Yuri Soldatov. There's a power struggle within the unit of the Russian Army to which Soldatov is attached. It's an oligarch thing, people wanting a piece of the action. We think a pro took out Valentina Zhukova to send a message to Soldatov to back off."

Lee had to stop herself from laughing.

"So some Russian billionaire wants an Army Colonel to 'back off' and, to make the point, dispatches a professional hit man to sneak into a hotel so he can stab Zhukova twice in the back with a small knife, then turn her over and stab her in her heart, and then hang her with a piece of floral wire?"

"Yes, ma'am," Grimes said.

"You don't find that explanation just a little bit far-fetched?" Lee asked.

"Russia is a complicated country," Grimes said. "We trust our intel. And this is just a courtesy call. Don't try to apprehend Karachova under any circumstances. She may have been a witness."

The 'call ended' icon appeared. Lee stared at her phone for several seconds, trying to parse the conversation of which she had been a part. Could the FBI really be so stupid? Or was she being fed a deliberately false story to throw her off her own investigation?

Her phone chirped again. This time, the tone was a snippet of 'The William Tell Overture'. The caller ID said Jason Alvarez.

"We need to meet," Alvarez said.

"And have I got a story to tell you," Lee replied.

* * * * *

Five minutes later Lee and Alvarez were comparing notes in the Convention Center Plaza's coffee bar. Alvarez gave Lee printouts detailing that Zhukova's husband was highly placed within cyber intelligence, and articles showing that the Russian propaganda machine had quickly seized on her death to point fingers of blame at the U.S. Government and that President Putin was aware of events.

"It *is* a complicated country," Alvarez said. "I sometimes think these people want their Czar back. All the palace intrigue, the incessant spying, the willingness to buy into conspiracy theories.

And they still have one foot in the nineteenth century: billionaires that come out of nowhere because they happen to have friends in high places. Is it conceivable that some Russian tycoon could have ordered Zhukova's murder? Maybe. But the MO is all wrong. This was a killing done out of passion; not cold blood. Even the FBI isn't that stupid."

Alvarez continued, pulling out multiple sheets of paper and several photographs. "If we're looking for someone who knew Zhukova, felt he was pushed around by her and had the temper to do something about it, then we need to get to know Tomás Suarez. Suarez was a big-deal floral designer in his native Argentina. He immigrated to the United States in 2000, ultimately settled in New York, and had been very successful here ever since."

Alvarez turned the first sheet. "The question is, why did he emigrate? The answer is that he had some big legal trouble in Buenos Aires. And, by trouble, I mean twenty years in a Latin American prison kind of trouble."

Lee made a time-out 'T' with her fingers. "You can't get a green card with a conviction," she said. "You probably can't really even get a tourist visa."

"Pre-9/11, and a family with money and connections," Alvarez replied. "Here's what happened: Tomás owned a very fashionable flower shop on an equally fashionable street in Buenos Aires. A gift from Mama and Papa. A competitor opened a shop across the street. The next thing you know, the new shop has a rash of broken windows. The police investigate but have nothing concrete."

"The new shop prospers and starts cutting into Tomás' wedding trade, which is huge in that part of the world. More broken windows but, this time, the other owner is ready. He has hired thugs to hunt down the thugs hired by Tomás. This is a very Latin American thing. When they do, Tomás retaliates by torching the competing store owner's car and, a week later, the store itself."

"This time, the police make an arrest. Tomás is charged with arson and attempted murder – a night watchman was in the store at the time of the arson. Then, just before trial, all charges are dropped. Tomás closes his store. Three months later, he has set himself up or, more likely been set up by his parents, in Washington, D.C. Two years later, he's in New York."

Alvarez concluded. "The police reports said Tomás had a really nasty temper. He especially said, according to one newspaper, that no one insulted him and got away with it."

Lee nodded. "Well, he certainly learned something from the anger management classes. He hides it very well. We will talk to him today. Excellent work."

"Which brings us to Zara Jretnam," Lee said, tapping the screen of her iPad. "For her, this conference has to be a nightmare. Her sister's plane was shot out of the sky by Russians, and the biggest Russia booster in this flower arranging universe is here as the star of the show – and Jretnam was part of the small committee that invited her. Last evening at six o'clock, they bumped into one another; passed in the hallway. My guess is that one of them said something – probably Zhukova – and that got it started. Twenty minutes later, they both left angry and upset. We know Zhukova got to the ballroom and had to be talked down by Karachova. We know that Zhukova was still upset hours later. And we know that, for some reason, she went back to the ballroom a few hours later and then she was dead."

"How do you want to approach it?" Alvarez said.

"You get the witnesses' statements and talk to Suarez," Lee said. "I'm going to fill in the rest of Jretnam's background before I talk to her."

Chapter 12

Liz Phillips collapsed into a chair. Breakfast was over, eight hundred delegates had been fed, and Phillips felt as though she had personally served every one of them. Some people readily understood that the ballroom was not available and sensed that a few people had gone to a tremendous effort to make possible a semblance of the original schedule. But others were incensed that not all members of their country's delegation could be accommodated in the same room and demanded their rights.

Every person and delegation that offered even the mildest protest was told by the hotel staff pressed into duty to "talk to the blonde lady in yellow." There were times when she tried to deal with six people simultaneously. A few cursed her in languages where the words were foreign but the meaning crystal clear.

It was *breakfast*, for crying out loud.

She had twice needed to contact the Banquet Manager and each of those calls were answered with a viciousness that was a product of dealing with a man who had been beaten by a woman, and being beaten was costing him money. "Would your husband like to come down and take the coffee temperature, *honey*?" was one of the few profanity-free taunts she had endured.

"You look like you need either a drink or a shoulder to cry on," a voice said.

Phillips looked up. It was Winnie Garrison, hands on her hips, smiling.

"Congratulations, Liz," Garrison said. "*You* pulled this off. Not me, not anyone else on this so-called committee. It was a first-class heroic effort, and it worked."

"Now we have to worry about dinner," Phillips said.

Garrison shook her head. "While you were handling this crisis,

I found us places for every meal except dinner Sunday. We're going to be fine, thanks to you."

"Then what's next?" Phillips asked, unsure if she wanted to hear the answer.

"I thought you might like to design this afternoon," Garrison said.

Phillips shook her head. "I'm not registered."

"Not a problem," Garrison said. "I've got at least two dozen cancellations and no-shows. I need to fill those slots. I can give you your choice of miniatures, armatures…"

"It's a wonderful offer, Winnie, but I'd rather just help."

"Then here's what I prescribe," Garrison said. "From now until at least three o'clock, this place is going to be deserted. Everyone's going to be at the Convention Center designing. Go upstairs and curl up in your room for a few hours." She leafed through a stack of pink and yellow sheets and selected four of them. "When you're back on your feet, see if you can find the hotel's Lost and Found department. I've got a couple of people who are convinced they've lost earrings, computers or the Crown Jewels. See what the hotel needs to retrieve lost property and let me know this afternoon."

"Where are you going to be?" Phillips asked.

"I'm doing a floor design," Garrison said. "A designer from Australia called Monday to say her prized brood mare is about to drop a foal that she's convinced has been bred to win the Perth Cup. She says seeing a thoroughbred through the delivery is worth missing a flight. Imagine that." Garrison smiled broadly.

"I'll take your advice," Phillips said. "Sleep, then Lost and Found." She allowed herself to yawn. "Definitely sleep."

* * * * *

Jason Alvarez felt his foot tap the floor. It was an involuntary reflex, one he had noticed only since he made Detective. His foot tap matched a rise in blood pressure and metabolic activity when he heard the elements of a case 'clink' into place.

He had now interviewed eleven women and he had created a computerized timeline that fit their stories into a continuous narrative. At 6:14, Valentina Zhukova was walking toward the escalator to the second floor when she passed Zara Jretnam. The subsequent encounter would never have taken place except that Zhukova said something as the two passed one another. Jretnam immediately whirled around and replied, "You cannot possibly mean that!"

Zhukova had smiled; one observer called it a 'smirk'. She had hooked Jretnam. There had followed a litany of gratuitous abuse: the inability of the Malaysian government to find one aircraft over the Pacific had led it to quickly blame Russia for shooting down a second airliner. Russia was the scapegoat for the ineptitude of Malaysia's airline industry. Everyone "knew" that the Ukraine government had set out to shoot down Vladimir Putin's plane as it returned from Venezuela, but that poor training and quick trigger fingers had instead sent missiles toward the Malaysian airliner, which in any event had no business being over 'patriot-held territory'.

"Your sister is dead because of Ukrainian stupidity," two witnesses heard Zhukova say. And the same two witnesses heard Jretnam reply with considerable calm, "You can lie until the end of eternity, but it does not change the truth. Every day you cannot acknowledge that truth is a day my sister's soul is tormented."

The retort set Zhukova off on a tirade against 'Western conspiracies' intended to keep Russia under its collective thumb. The fall of the ruble, the precipitous decline in oil prices, domestic inflation, German sanctions, and even the death of a French oil executive sympathetic to Russian interests were all actions coordinated in Washington and London. "Your sister was a pawn," Zhukova said at least twice.

Eleven minutes later, Zhukova had made a dismissive gesture

to Jretnam. The Russian was bored with the discussion and headed toward the escalator to the Mezzanine level and the Grand Ballroom.

Jretnam, though, felt as though she had been assaulted. She was short of breath and visibly agitated. Friends – or at least acquaintances who sensed the mental ordeal Jretnam had undergone – sought to console her. One suggested tea; another dinner. But with Zhukova's departure, Jretnam began to regain her strength and, with it, an anger that had been suppressed during the exchange.

"She cannot be allowed to broadcast such blatant lies," Jretnam had told one witness. "She has no right to speak of my sister that way. She must be stopped."

She must be stopped….

Alvarez pushed the two women who had been part of that conversation. "Did she say how Zhukova must be stopped? Did she say she would stop her?"

Both witnesses shook their heads. They agreed Jretnam had said, "She must be stopped." And they agreed Jretnam had gone no further in her statement.

You can't take that to a jury, Alvarez thought. *I need more.*

But he also now had multiple eyewitness accounts of Zhukova gratuitously badgering someone. After hearing these accounts, a jury would be unlikely to convict Jretnam for anything beyond manslaughter absent a full confession.

Alvarez's final interviews with witnesses had been conducted at the Convention Center rather than the hotel. There, attendees were assembling in three bays of the massive building; collecting flowers and hauling carts filled with the tools of the floral design trade.

These women's willingness to help Alvarez were the foundation of a case against Jretnam. It would be up to Lieutenant Lee to get Jretnam to implicate herself, and for the FBI to supply any physical evidence found at the murder scene.

But Alvarez had also conditioned himself not to be lulled into a false sense of success. There was at least one incongruous element to the case that – at least for the moment – required a leap of faith: judging from the video, Zara Jretnam likely stood an inch or two over five feet. Her raincoat hid other elements of her physique but her short stature made dealing with a dead body problematic.

Jretnam could have killed Zhukova but, short of an adrenaline-fueled burst of strength, how did she manage to hang a woman who might have outweighed her by fifty pounds?

If Jretnam was the killer, there was a strong likelihood that she did not act alone.

* * * * *

Two hours after her conversation with FBI Agent Grimes, Victoria Lee still seethed at the implication that she was somehow responsible for the disappearance of Ludmila Karachova. And the notion that Valentina Zhukova had been killed as a warning to her husband went beyond strained credulity. Nothing in the crime scene gave any indication of a professional's involvement.

The one-sided conversation kept replaying in her head, pushing out the task at hand: learning everything she could about a *real* suspect. She rose from the chair in which she had been sitting for two hours. For ten minutes she stretched, did windmills and rotated her neck. Secure behind the locked door of the conference room, she ran in place and did jumping jacks.

Only when she felt her heart racing and her muscles tiring did she go back to the conference room table and begin looking at the neat rows of stacked papers. She slowly circled the table, looking at but not reading the sheets on the top of each stack.

Lee did not believe in Chinese superstitions – nor superstitions from any culture. The statue of Guan Gong – a kind of patron saint of law enforcement – sent to her by her parents upon her promotion to Lieutenant, had not only been promptly opened (a superstitious person would have waited several days to open such a package), but had been promptly consigned to a closet.

But she did not consider to be a superstitious act her own ritual of physically circling evidence nor doing strenuous exercise before doing so. It was simply a ritual. A way of clearing her mind before shifting gears from the accumulation of information into the assessment phase. And, in this instance, pushing out the toxic memory of the call from Agent Grimes.

On her next pass around the table, Lee took a pile of papers at random, found a different chair that had been pushed to the far side of the room, and sat down.

This pile told the horrific story of the death of Jretnam's sister. Alya Jretnam was a pediatrician and was returning from a medical conference in Amsterdam. Newspaper articles spoke of her being from a 'prominent' family and that in addition to her thriving office practice, she was also widely known for her appearances on Malaysian television to speak on child health and disease prevention.

Alya Jretnam was also the mother of two teenaged children and there were photos of those children at memorial services. Jretnam's body had never been recovered, adding to her family's anguish. Her husband had traveled to the Ukraine and the Netherlands seeking permission to search for his wife's remains. The Ukraine government had promptly given its assent. The rebels controlling the crash site refused entry at gunpoint.

Grief. Loss. Inability to reach closure, Lee thought. It was a powder keg of emotions that could tear apart any person. And then toss in a match in the form of Valentina Zhukova. She could imagine the words that were thrown around by Zhukova. The look on Zhukova's face in the surveillance video was one of contempt. While Lee could not see Jretnam's face, she could see the reaction in Zhukova's. Zhukova was *enjoying* inflicting pain. There was more than a hint of a smile after each barrage of words. The woman was a monster.

Lee retrieved another stack of papers and found yet another chair. This one was about Jretnam's role in the International Floral Designers Alliance. Four years earlier she had more or less single-handedly convinced IFDA's steering committee to hold the biennial event in Kuala Lampur. The event would confer honor on the city and country and draw in thousands of visitors.

The Malaysian press, or at least the English-language newspapers, did not show much interest in the financing of the event. But two or three articles written at the time of the announcement spoke of Zara Jretnam as being the event's 'benefactor'. It appeared quite likely that whoever hosted IFDA also ended up footing the bill for it, or at least fronting the expense money with the hope that fees and sponsorships would recoup that investment.

A third pile was retrieved. This one dealt with the Jretnam family. It was large and influential. There was shipping and banking and ownership of firms that supplied materials to the nation's semiconductor fabrication and assembly industry.

It was all, of course, privately held and the families – there appeared to be three or four – never gave interviews about themselves. But *Malaysian Business* estimated the family's businesses to be generating in excess of two billion dollars a year in revenue and *Forbes* placed 'R. Jretnam' midway in its ranking of the country's forty wealthiest people with a net worth of $218 million.

Zara Jretnam was a woman who could afford to put on a world-class flower show.

Lee carefully reviewed the other stacks but they all pointed to the same conclusion. Jretnam was a wealthy woman whose passion was floral design. She could indulge her passion without wondering how it would be paid for. She had enticed IFDA to put on its next conference in Malaysia and, to prepare for it, she had become Winnie Garrison's 'apprentice'. For the past two years she had traveled the world, attending meetings and planning sessions.

Then, on July 17, 2014, her world had come crashing down in an act of terrorism. And the anguish of losing a sister had been exacerbated by the continuing presence of a Russian designer who seemed to revel in mocking Jretnam's loss. The unanswered question was whether Zara Jretnam had snapped after that lobby encounter.

It was time to answer that question.

* * * * *

Detective Alvarez sat with Tomás Suarez in the hotel conference room. Suarez was a handsome man who looked younger that forty, though that was the age on the information sheet in front of Alvarez. Suarez accentuated his Latin good looks and winter tan with an aquamarine jacket and tropical pink dress shirt. To Alvarez, the look was more South Beach than New York.

Alvarez had planned to conduct the interview in the ballroom but had been turned away by a hotel security guard who made it clear that even Boston's Chief of Police would be denied entry to the room. Only the FBI could grant entry and they made clear there were no exceptions.

And so he had to make do with the conference room. There would be no forcing Suarez to stand where Zhukova had died; none of the power of place that worked so well in other cases.

"Tell me about your previous encounters with Valentina Zhukova," Alvarez asked.

Suarez seemed ready for the question. "We were in the same class five times over the past seven years. Philadelphia, Chelsea, Berlin, Milan and Barcelona. I took firsts three times, she won gold once. In the eyes of the judges, I was clearly the better designer."

"Was she as nasty seven years ago as she was Tuesday evening?" Alvarez asked.

Suarez cocked his head. "No, seven years ago she was almost

normal. The strangest thing about her was always keeping that drab little assistant with her to do the 'dirty' work. It was almost as though Valentina was too important to actually put stems in Oasis."

"When did she change – start badmouthing the designers around her?"

"There was always some of that," Suarez replied. "But after I took firsts in Philadelphia and Barcelona and she settled for seconds, I became 'the enemy'. It has been non-stop ever since."

"Did she ever get to you?" Alvarez asked.

Suarez tapped his head. "Focus. She became part of the background noise. I tuned her out."

"She called you a kind of one-trick pony," Alvarez said.

Suarez laughed, showing teeth that had been artificially whitened. "Which is kind of droll coming from someone whose stock in trade is color blocking and negative space. But yes, she called me a one-trick pony, one-hit wonder, and a couple of other things. Doesn't stop me from winning, though."

"You weren't always so casual about strong competition." Alvarez made it a statement.

For the first time, color showed in Suarez's face. "You'll have to be more specific, Detective."

"Buenos Aires. Recoleta. Avenida Libertad… Is that sufficiently specific?"

Anger spreads over Suarez's face and his hands tensed on the conference room chair. Through gritted teeth he said, "You are talking about something that happened a very, very long time ago."

"You torched a competitor's store. And his car."

"Those charges were dropped for lack of evidence," Suarez said. "It was an unproven allegation."

"I note you don't deny it," Alvarez said.

"And so it follows I'm capable of a rather gruesome murder? *Te ves como un hombre inteligente. No seas estúpido, Detective. El chico latino moreno no siempre es el culpable.*"

Alvarez understood. It wasn't an insult. It was a plea to look beyond stereotypes; 'the swarthy Latin guy isn't always the guilty party'. "You must have some idea of who would have killed her," he said.

Suarez was silent for perhaps thirty seconds. Then he said, "Don't think I haven't asked myself that question a dozen times. I keep coming back to that assistant of hers. Zhukova was throwing insults around that ballroom all night long and, yes, I received more than my share. But she saved the worst ones for that poor, drab assistant. Some were in English but most were in Russian. You didn't have to speak the language to know she was being cruel. And the worst part was that Zhukova seemed to be getting some sick pleasure out of doing it."

The interview ended. Alvarez asked that Suarez make himself available after hotel video was re-checked.

Afterward, Alvarez made notes. Suarez hadn't been stupid enough to deny what he had done in Argentina; that would have set off alarms. He was a man who had to work exceptionally hard to control his anger. And, what had happened to Valentina Zhukova had been done in anger. Suarez wasn't off the suspect list. He was just in abeyance pending the pursuit of other avenues.

* * * * *

The floor of the Boston Convention and Exhibition Center was a swirl of color and motion. A bird's eye view from one of the catwalks that crossed the hall floor showed a geometric array of some 800 individual pedestals arranged in long, straight lines of twenty, like-sized units. Some pedestals were less than a foot on a side. A dozen pedestals, scattered around the floor, were like enormous chairs each fifteen feet high at the back. Several dozen were round and some were yin-yang creations with two pieces of differing heights. The common denominator was color: each pedestal was painted the identical dark grey.

And at each station there was a man or woman – but usually a woman – surrounded by buckets of flowers. The buckets spilled into aisles creating their own swirls of color. Discarded flowers or cut pieces of them littered the floor.

Eight hundred designers were competing in forty entry classes, meaning an average of twenty entrants each per class. No one designed in secret because each entrant was in plain sight of everyone else. And while there was competition there was also cooperation. Tools were readily loaned and returned, extra hands were provided while 'mechanics' – pieces of plastic, metal or wood that supported an arrangement but that were designed to be invisible to the viewer – were adjusted or tightened.

Lee surveyed the activity and appreciated the energy if not the talent of the participants. These people had traveled thousands of miles to participate and to be in the company of like-minded enthusiasts. For the rest of the week they would socialize and sit through lectures and demonstrations. This morning and afternoon was their one opportunity to show off their skill and creativity, after which their finished product would be on display to the public as well as to one another.

Lee noted that the design process was not continuous. Participants would periodically step away from their work. Some went to the long refreshment tables set up around the perimeter of the Convention Center floor, there to pour cups of coffee or tea and take a plate of the pastries provided. Other people would simply wander, pausing to take photographs of other designers' work in progress. Some designers drew clutches of admirers and Lee wondered how a train of thought could be maintained with such distractions.

Near the front of the floor of the vast hall was an area where tall and large designs were being created on square raised platforms, each eight feet on a side. While just a foot or two of space separated most pedestals in the Convention Center, the floor designs provided ample room to appreciate the work from all sides.

Winnie Garrison worked in the second row, the third pedestal from the end.   In the center of the pedestal a wooden superstructure taller than Garrison rose and sprouted arms pointed at odd angles.   Four flower buckets surrounded Garrison, who would periodically place greens or flowers on the structure, then remove them.

Lee descended an escalator to the floor of the hall and went to where Garrison was working.

"I came here with a finished design in my mind," Garrison said, shaking her head slowly while appraising the skeleton of her work. "I am just beginning to see how wrong that design is. I fear this is going to be a very long and possibly frustrating day for me."

"Could we find a place to speak for a few minutes?" Lee asked.

"The farther away from here the better," Garrison replied. "I definitely need to clear my head."

They settled on the coffee bar at the Convention Center Plaza which, with most of the hotel's guests at the Convention Center, was nearly deserted.

"In our first meeting, you mentioned Zara Jretnam," Lee said.

"My understudy," Garrison replied, nodding. "She'll manage the next show in Kuala Lampur."

"Have you interacted with her yesterday or today?" Lee asked.

Garrison's face showed sudden concern. "This is about Tina's murder?"

"I'm following a great many leads," Lee replied. "This is just one loose end. Did you see her yesterday or today?"

Garrison cocked her head, thinking. "I pulled the entire staff together yesterday morning to tell them what had happened. I know Zara was at that meeting."

"Did she react in any special way to the news?"

"Not that I remember," Garrison replied. Then she looked at Lee. "You wouldn't ask that question if you didn't suspect her…"

Lee shook her head vigorously.   "The two of them had a

confrontation in the hotel lobby Tuesday evening...."

Garrison grimaced. "I heard about that. Tina was apparently vicious. She could get that way for no good reason. At least as far as I could tell."

"You spoke with her about it?"

"Someone told me Zara was very upset. But she seemed to have recovered. I mean, I don't recall any unusual reaction when I broke the news."

"But you saw her again yesterday?" Lee asked.

"Two or three times – very briefly. Zara's specific job at the conference is to coordinate speakers and other special events. Most of those events would have been held in the ballroom. I made certain Zara was aware of the new venues."

"And she never mentioned Valentina Zhukova?"

"No. She was doing her job, and very efficiently, I think."

"I'd like to speak to her," Lee said. "Can you arrange that?"

Garrison pulled her phone from her purse. She scrolled through a list of names and tapped one.

"Zara, can I pull you away from whatever you're doing?" There was a pause. "It's important. Can you come to the suite?" Another pause. "Ten minutes is fine."

Garrison tapped the 'close call' icon and placed her phone back in her purse. She looked for and found a room access card which she handed to Lee. "Room 1101. I can get another key from the front desk. But you're wasting your time. Zara didn't kill Tina."

"I didn't say she did," Lee said.

"You found out that Tina was taunting Zara and that Zara was upset afterwards," Garrison replied. "I know Zara. She couldn't have done.... She couldn't have done what I saw in the ballroom. That isn't the kind of person she is."

"Then our conversation will be brief and cordial," Lee said, then added, "I have to follow all leads."

* * * * *

Alvarez filled in Lee while they waited in Garrison's suite. "Suarez checked all the boxes," he said. "He didn't make the mistake of denying what happened back in Buenos Aires, but he said he's a different person. He even tried to sweet talk me in Spanish."

"And you believed him?"

"I want to circle back to him when we know more."

At that point they heard Jretnam's knock at the door.

"Let's do it," Lee said.

From the surveillance footage, Lee had surmised that Jretnam was an inch or two over five feet tall and so, coupled with a preconception of 'Malaysian', Lee expected to see a thin woman with delicate features.

Instead, the woman who stood at the door had an athletic build. Jretnam appeared to be in her mid-40s, with jet black hair and expensive makeup. She was attired in a navy blue cashmere sweater and charcoal slacks.

"Winnie Garrison asked me to be here," Jretnam said. Her English had a lilt to it.

Lee introduced herself and Alvarez. "We have some questions about the death of Valentina Zhukova. We won't take much of your time."

Lee did not sense wariness on Jretnam's part, only confusion that the woman had been summoned for a meeting, and that two policemen were there instead.

"I don't think I know anything that can help you," Jretnam said.

"Perhaps not, but we're speaking with everyone who had contact with Ms. Zhukova," Alvarez said. He indicated the two sofas in the suite's living room.

"You encountered Ms. Zhukova in the lobby Tuesday evening," he said. "Can you tell us what happened? How you happened to come to speak with her?"

A look of dread came over Jretnam's face. "That was a horrible evening."

"Did you speak to her first or was it the other way around?" Lee asked.

"I had spotted her twice since I arrived," Jretnam said. "Even though she was one of my speakers, I had made up my mind to avoid her. She has…. views…"

"She was an ultra-nationalist Russian," Lee said. "We've already heard that."

"My sister died on Flight 17," Jretnam said.

"We also know that," Lee said. "Your sister's death was a tragedy, and we are very sorry for your loss," Lee said.

"I had decided that I would not speak to her. I gave her the schedule by email…"

"Why would you not want to speak to her?" Alvarez asked.

"Last October I encountered Tina in London," Jretnam said. "It was the first time I had seen Tina since my sister's death. Tina said something to me about my sister dying because the Ukrainian government was trying to shoot down the Russian president's plane. I just got up and left the room. But the next day, Tina… trapped me. Got into an elevator with me and then started on this tirade."

"She knew your sister was on that flight before the two of you met in London?" Lee asked.

Jretnam nodded. "It was as though she had been waiting for me. She started this diatribe about the Malaysian government joining the U.S. and the Ukraine in trying to hold Russia responsible for firing the missile. I pushed every button on the elevator trying to get off. But Tina physically blocked the door. I finally shoved her out of the way…"

Lee and Alvarez looked at one another.

"You didn't see her again after that encounter," Alvarez said.

"I left London a day early just to be certain," Jretnam said.

"But you met her again Tuesday evening," Lee said.

"I was going out to dinner with friends. She was – I think – coming in. She saw me before I saw her; otherwise I would have done something to avoid her. When she passed me, she grabbed my arm and said something like, 'Your sister died a fool's death. I hope you're happy.'"

"What did you say in response?" Lee asked.

"I ought to have broken free and walked out of the hotel," Jretnam said. "But ever since that time in London in October, I had been telling myself that I ought to have confronted her. Told her I knew she was lying. And so Tuesday night, I did. I said that in her heart, she knew the truth and that she was just trying to avoid feelings of guilt."

"And that set her off," Alvarez said.

"It was the wrong thing to do," Jretnam said. "For more than ten minutes she hit me with everything in that 'everyone is trying to blame Russia' mind of hers. At first I tried to tell her where she was wrong. But that just made her angrier. When she saw that I wasn't protesting any more, she started getting very personal. The look in her eye was horrible. Finally, I think she must have gotten bored because she just said something in Russian and left."

"Friends saw what had happened," Alvarez said.

"They tried to comfort me," Jretnam said.

"You told your friends Tina had to be stopped," Lee said.

"She was a horrible person."

Lee and Alvarez again looked at one another.

"What did you do next?" Lee asked.

"I went to my room. I skipped dinner. I threw up. I cried. After a few hours I cried myself to sleep."

"Did you go out Wednesday morning to buy flowers?" Lee asked.

Jretnam shook her head. "I have too many responsibilities to also design. After that encounter, I wouldn't have had the strength."

"But you were awake when the designers were going to the flower market?"

"No," Jretnam replied. "I had a wake-up call for, I think, seven o'clock. When I went downstairs, everyone was already talking about Tina being dead. Winnie called everyone together to give us the official news."

"So, between three and five in the morning, you were asleep in your room," Lee said.

"Room 1022," Jretnam said.

"You have no roommate," Alvarez said.

Jretnam looked surprised by the question. "No. I… would not want to share a room."

"Can you think of anyone who would want to kill Ms. Zhukova?" Lee asked.

Jretnam paused. "She was not always like this. When I first met her, she wanted to be friends with everyone. But with each passing year she became more… more like she is now – or was before her death. I cannot think of anyone who was her friend. She was talented and so people excused her behavior. But that tolerance had limits. There would have come a point – and perhaps this IFDA conference was that point – when people would say that working with her was too hard."

Jretnam looked first at Alvarez, then at Lee. "You are wondering if I killed Tina. I acknowledge that I likely had more motive than anyone here. And I realize that I do not have an alibi, as you call it."

She continued to shift her gaze from Alvarez to Lee and back again. "But I did not kill her, though in a private moment, I will allow myself to take pleasure in knowing that she will no longer torment me or anyone else she may have terrorized."

Jretnam continued. "You are obliged to bring the person who did this to justice. I understand. But I do not know anyone here at this show, aside from myself, who suffered for being with her.

Please keep searching. But please know that, when you find that person and place them on trial, I will stand up in a court of law and tell everyone of my own encounters with her and what an evil person she was. I owe that to my sister."

"Ms. Jretnam," Lee said, "can I presume you brought with you one of those floral design carts?"

"I did," Jretnam said.

"Would you have objection if we make an inventory of the cart's contents?"

Jretnam suddenly looked very ill at ease.

"Why do you wish to do this?" she asked.

"We are looking for clues to the death of Ms. Zhukova," Lee said. "We have asked many people for permission to inventory their carts."

"Do you not need – what is it called? – a warrant to search someone's property?" Jretnam asked.

"Only if the person does not give permission freely," Lee said, keeping her voice both friendly and even. "So far, of the seven people we have asked, no one has declined."

"And if I do not give you permission, you will get one of these warrants?" Jretnam stared directly into Lee's eyes.

"We will," Lee replied, leaving out the possibility of an extensive delay that might accompany such a request or the distinct possibility that a judge would decline to issue a warrant.

Jretnam sighed. "Then I imagine my refusing would only delay the inevitable and cause you to view me with even greater suspicion than you do already."

"We are only looking for answers, Ms. Jretnam," Lee said. "It is not our intention to harass you."

"Then search my cart. It is in my room, in my closet. It has not been touched since my arrival in this country."

"Detective Alvarez will accompany you to your room to retrieve it," Lee said. "We will keep it only long enough to inventory its contents."

When Jretnam and Alvarez had left Garrison's suite, Lee found Liz Phillips's cell phone number.

"Liz," Lee said when Phillips answered, "I need one last favor from you."

Chapter 13

Liz Phillips awakened with a start. How long had she been asleep? The clock by her bedside said 2 p.m.

After inventorying the contents of Zara Jretnam's cart with Detective Alvarez making notes on what she found, Phillips had planned to lay down for half an hour. Instead she had slept four hours.

Great way to make a good impression, she thought.

The four slips of paper were on the nightstand and, for the first time, she read them.

Caroline Macdonald Rm 854 gold Cross fountain pen trash can?
Aimi Nakata Rm 422 iPad w/ Hello Kitty cover restaurant?
Adede Oyenusi Rm 909 Carrera y Carrera gold cuff room service tray?
Olivia Smith Rm 638 gold hoop earrings trash can?

How on earth could people throw fountain pens in a trash can, Phillips wondered, *or leave a $5,000 gold cuff on a room service tray? Were they so wealthy that they didn't notice, or care?*

From the hotel operator, Liz learned that the hotel's Lost and Found office was located two floors below the lobby level.

* * * * *

A gold-colored badge on her bright red blazer said her name was Francine Leilani. She appeared to be in her late twenties, though her Polynesian heritage provided her with the smooth, glowing skin that frequently made even much older women appear youthful on anything except detailed inspection. Her demeanor, however, said that she was trained to be courteous but to also be skeptical.

"If someone calls and says they left a pair of gloves in the restaurant or glasses on a room tray, we tell them to come right down," Leilani said. "Or, better yet, we scan the shelves, match the description, and send the missing item back to its owner without their ever having to make the trip down here."

Leilani continued. "If the object is expensive and we don't have it, we ask that the person report it to the group they're a part of – and almost everyone who stays here is part of a convention group."

Phillips asked why the hotel requested the additional step.

"Insurance claims," Leilani said, matter-of-factly. She held out one of the slips. "'Carrera y Carrera gold cuff'. Very expensive and very unique. If this person left it on a room service tray, the staff member collecting the tray would have turned it over to us immediately. If a maid saw it in the corridor or in a room following check-out, her instructions would be to make a special trip to bring it here. We drill that into every person we hire. But the cuff isn't here."

Leilani continued. "It is conceivable that Ms. Oyenusi somehow left it on the tray and that some guest walking down the corridor spotted it and pocketed it. But I don't think so."

Leilani and Phillips had been talking across a counter. Leilani beckoned Phillips to come through the door to her side of the counter. Leilani typed 'Adede Oyenusi' into her computer. Immediately, an information page appeared showing the woman's check-in and planned check-out dates, together with the information that her home was in Lagos, Nigeria.

Then a second window appeared.

"This is a list of items Ms. Oyenusi has reported lost at various hotels over the past two years," Leilani said. "Hotels share the information and we, in turn, share it with insurance companies. I am sharing it with you because Ms. Oyenusi will complain to your group that she lost a valuable piece of jewelry while at your conference and that the hotel was unable to locate it. She will blame the hotel and she will blame you."

"What we want to make certain of is that you understand that the item was almost certainly never lost," Leilani continued. "Our staff are not thieves; they do not pocket valuables that guests inadvertently leave behind. That's what I need for you to understand about our procedures, including the lengths we go to for our guests."

Phillips was going to explain that she had no role in managing IFDA, but thought better of it. Instead, she pointed to the slip of paper with the gold hoop earrings that the owner believed found their way into a trash can.

Leilani typed the name 'Olivia Smith' into her computer. The same information page appeared, showing that Ms. Smith had traveled to the IFDA conference from Auckland, New Zealand. The insurance window was blank.

"Olivia Smith isn't trying to put something over on an insurance company," Phillips said.

"I agree," Leilani said. "But let's take a walk."

The two women went out a service door from Lost and Found and down a short corridor. Leilani opened a door and the two were immediately engulfed by the din of mechanical equipment and a slightly sour odor, offset by disinfectants.

"This is the triage room," Leilani said, raising her voice to be heard over the clanging of the equipment. "We bring in the contents of every room's trash can, as well as those from conference rooms and even the public spaces throughout the hotel. We never know when something valuable is going to turn up."

Behind her, a man in white coveralls was emptying black trash bags onto a conveyor belt. Three feet away, two women wearing gloves, hairnets and masks pulled at the mass of tissues, paper and whatever else was on the belt. Paper went into one bin, cardboard into a second and plastics went into a third. Little was left from that first sorting.

"This much is basic recycling," Leilani said, still shouting. "All hotels are required to 'go green'. There was a time just a few years ago when everything went, unsorted, into trash trucks to be hauled away. That's ancient history."

Five feet on, a similarly clad woman examined what remained. She cleared overlapping items and periodically plucked things from the conveyor line which she put into one of two bins.

Leilani walked to one of the bins. From it she took a handful of forks and spoons. "This alone pays for what goes on in here," she said. "How people manage to throw hotel towels, cutlery, glasses and even china into their room trash is something for psychologists to ponder. But if we didn't do this, we'd have to charge you ten or fifteen dollars more per room. It's that pervasive."

She then picked up and brought over another bin.

"This is what goes to Lost and Found," Leilani said. She pulled out a man's dress shirt, a woman's blouse, coins, and hair brushes. "If clothing or toiletries aren't claimed, they go to the Pine Street Inn or another homeless shelter where they will get put to good use." She then pulled up a round, heavy object. "I wonder what this is?"

"I can answer that," Phillips said. "That's a kenzan. Floral designers use it to get stems to stand up straight in an arrangement. I wonder why someone would have thrown it into the trash?"

Leilani shrugged. "I've been here eighteen months and I've learned there is no accounting for human nature. It may have fallen into a trash can by accident or it may have been carelessness. Will someone claim it?" Leilani tossed the kenzan into the air, feeling its heft.

Phillips pondered the question for a moment. "They're expensive – thirty dollars or so – but most of the people at IFDA don't have to worry about money, I suspect."

"We've got all manner of things that might be useful in flower arranging," Leilani said.

"Fine, but how about Olivia Smith's earrings?" Phillips asked.

Leilani looked at the slip. "Let's see if they've turned up."

The two women walked back to the Lost and Found office. This time, Phillips remained on Leilani's side of the counter. A side room held shelves five feet high on either side of a ten-foot-long office.

"Look at all of this," Phillips said, astonished by the breadth of items. There was jewelry, briefcases, Swiss Army knives, sunglasses, and mascara and lipstick tubes, among hundreds of other items. Everything was arranged according to 'likes' – cosmetics in one plastic bin, sunglasses in another, and knives in a third.

"Two sets of gold hoop earrings," Leilani said, reaching into a bin and spreading its contents onto the counter. I think Ms. Smith is going to get lucky. I'll call her and ask her to come down and make an identification."

"She's probably designing right now," Phillips said. "You may want to try later on in the afternoon."

"And here's Hello Kitty," Leilani said, picking up an iPad from a stack of three in one of the cubbyholes. She tapped the screen and Japanese characters appeared. "Would you like to return this to Ms. Nakata?"

"No gold Cross fountain pen?" Phillips asked, accepting the iPad.

Leilani shook her head. "If it hasn't turned up yet, it's probably in her room, or she left it in a restaurant. We hold things for ten days. Then we give them to a charitable organization for disposal. At least some good comes out of it."

Phillips took a last look at the shelves of unclaimed items. "Absolutely amazing," she said.

* * * * *

Victoria Lee walked back to the Convention Center and again viewed the activity from the balcony above the main floor. There appeared to be no completed designs as far as she could tell. The activity, though, seemed to be less frenetic. There was less socializing and more work going on. Winnie Garrison's floor display now sported dozens of flowers and greenery, and Garrison seemed to be satisfied with her plan because flowers no longer came off of the superstructure.

Lee had not ruled out Zara Jretnam, the woman's vehement denial of complicity notwithstanding. To Jretnam, Valentina Zhukova was the physical embodiment of Alya Jretnam's gruesome death, with Zhukova laughing at her grief. For whatever reason, Zhukova had assaulted Jretnam, emotionally if not physically. Whether there had been a second, early morning encounter or Jretnam had gone looking for Zhukova, the motive was there. Lee's task was to find connecting pieces that would put the two in proximity in time just before the murder took place.

Nor could Tomás Suarez be ruled out. There was a longstanding animosity between the two designers and Suarez had once resolved a conflict with violence. She thought back on Alvarez's comments on his interview. What Alvarez had failed to consider was that Suarez's family had bought their way out of a felony conviction. It reminded Lee of the thundering words of a college professor from when she was earning her degree in Criminal Justice: *When a crime carries no punishment, not only is the deterrent to a future crime absent, there is every expectation that the next crime, too, will be free of punishment.*

She would continue to look at Tomás Suarez.

The disappearance of Ludmila Karachova left unresolved the status of a prime suspect. Zhukova's 'assistant' could have been spirited out of Boston by Russian agents, in which case her guilt or innocence would never be established.

Karachova could also be in the custody of the FBI. The call from the FBI agent could have been misdirection; an effort to get Russians looking everywhere except an FBI safe house or holding cell. Karachova would be held in an effort to learn of Zhukova's movements and activities over the past several years. Her possible role in Zhukova's death would be buried in some plea bargain agreement. As had been amply explored in the trial of Whitey Bulger, the Boston FBI field office seemed to have little interest in what crimes its informants committed while under the protection of the Bureau.

Or, Karachova could be simply trying to disappear, either because she had committed the murder or because she had no desire to return to Russia. She did not want to contact Russian embassy officials to tell them of Zhukova's death. Moreover, with Zhukova's demise, Karachova's traveling days were over. It was back to the flower shop and whatever retribution the FSB had in store for her.

Lee had a thought. FBI Agent Grimes had said Karachova had left the hotel through a loading dock, apparently avoiding surveillance cameras. But she couldn't have avoided all cameras. She took out her phone and called Alvarez.

"Jason, I need your help," she said. "Start looking through surveillance footage near Ludmila Karachova's room from last night. I want to know if she left on her own or in the company of someone. Also, did she take anything with her? A suitcase, an overnight bag. Then check her room. You inventoried her belongings yesterday morning. What seems to be missing? If it has been cleaned out, find out by whom."

Lee had another idea. "There are half a dozen shelters within five miles of here. Get a couple of Detectives to show Ludmila's photo to whomever checks people in. See if a first-timer with a Russian accent showed up last night. She can't use credit cards and probably doesn't have a lot of cash so her lodging options are limited."

Lee's phone showed an incoming call. She looked at the name. It was Matt.

"Get back to me when you have something," she said. She

disconnected and tapped the screen to take Matt's call. A phone call was unusual; he usually texted his communications with her.

"Hey," Matt said. "I know this is late, but I'd like to take you to dinner tonight."

"I'm trying to wrap up a case," Lee said.

"It's kind of important and I'll make it easy," Matt replied. "You're at BCEC. How about Legal Test Kitchen or Morton's? Your choice. Please say you can do this."

More of his 'charm offensive', Lee thought. The idea of steaks and the stench of cigars made her nauseous. "LTK," she said. "Can we make it early? Six o'clock? There may be some case stuff breaking."

"Six would be beautiful," Matt said. "See you then." He hung up.

What does he want now? Lee thought. She looked at her phone. Half past three. Well, she would know in two and a half hours.

* * * * *

Liz Phillips consulted a diagram and attempted to orient the schematic with the Convention Center floor. Class 31 – a 'stretch design' – ought to be over *there*. But over 'there' were miniatures. She turned the diagram 180 degrees and began wending her way through the arrays of gray staging, some with backs, and some without. She stepped around buckets of flowers and apologized for bumping into people stepping back to examine their designs as judges would do in a few hours.

Finally, she saw a paper sign that said '31' and, indeed, along a row of 36-inch pedestals with 20-inch by 30-inch tops, were entries she knew to be stretch designs. At station number 11 was a Japanese woman applying a glue stick to a ti leaf.

"Aimi Nakata?" Phillips asked.

The woman turned around. "*Hai?*"

Phillips took an iPad out of an IFDA tote bag. "Did you lose this?"

The woman gave a broad smile and a nod. "You find?" She tapped the screen, which gave a musical response. The look of relief on her face was palpable. "*Domo arigato gozaimasu,*" she said.

"It was turned into Lost and Found," Phillips said, not knowing whether Nakata's English vocabulary extended beyond simple greetings. "Winnie Garrison asked that I return it to you." The last statement wasn't strictly true, but it explained why a total stranger was involved.

Nakata gave Lee a blank look of non-comprehension, then returned to her iPad, tapping various parts of the screen, each time smiling to see that the contents of her tablet had not been compromised.

"She has very limited English, Liz," someone said. "We have even more limited Japanese."

Phillips turned to see who was speaking. It was Helen Weiser, one of the women who had been assisting the designers in the ballroom.

"The police have you returning stolen property now?" Weiser asked.

Phillips laughed. "That's ancient history. I 'interpreted' flower show language for the detective and lieutenant investigating the case. Then Winnie Garrison got hold of me and put me to work. This is Lost and Found duty."

"Then go check Lost and Found and see if they have my common sense anywhere," Weiser said. "We have to be done in half an hour and this design is going nowhere. Put on your judging hat and tell me what I'm doing wrong."

Phillips eyed Weiser's work in process. A 'stretch' design calls for two units of dissimilar size with at least one prominent component connecting the two units. The smaller unit should look like it was pulled out of the larger one. The 'stretch component' is supposed to be imaginative and create what designers call 'dynamic tension' between the two units.

What Phillips could see was that Weiser's two units – each attractive in its own right – faced forward. Moreover, the 'stretch component' looked like an afterthought. It was a carefully trimmed palm frond that arched from one unit to the other. It was graceful, but a judge would likely see it as a perfunctory nod to the category requirement.

"Am I allowed to give advice?" Phillips asked.

"As long as you aren't judging this evening," Weiser said. She gestured around the room. "We've been giving one another advice all day long."

"Well, for starters, your two units look like they're standing at attention," Phillips said. "Do you remember at the Flower Show a couple of years ago, someone had a design that looked like a person was walking a dog, with the dog straining at the leash? It had anthurium in it."

Weiser snapped her fingers. "Gloria Freitas. I remember that one. She got a Tri-Color."

"I'm not saying that one is a person and the other is a dog, but could one be pulling the other?" Phillips asked.

Weiser removed the palm frond and tried her two units at varying angles and distances from one another. She nodded at Phillips. "I see what you mean. Thank you for not just saying, 'oh, it's beautiful like it is'. That's what got me a trunk full of Honorable Mentions." She took out a knife and began shaping a willow branch. "I'm thinking lasso."

Phillips watched her work for a moment. "Do you remember anything else from Tuesday evening? Anything that stands out after thinking about it for a day?"

Weiser continued to work. "What I remember most is how nasty that Zhukova woman was to her assistant, and how she kept eyeing everyone else's designs and making horrible comments." She put down her knife for a moment. "I wouldn't have put up with that for one minute. I have no idea why – what was her name?

Ludmila? – why Ludmila would put up with it. I imagine she gets to travel a lot, but to have that kind of abuse heaped on your head. Count me out."

"Did anyone else seem to notice?"

"I was helping the German woman – Eva Kirk," Weiser said. "Kirk was mildly disappointed that with a name like 'Weiser' I didn't speak a word of German, because she obviously had a lot of things she wanted to say about what was going on. She would eye the two of them – Ludmila and Zhukova – and mutter things. Eva got off fairly easy from Zhukova, as I recall."

"I heard one of the detectives say they were told that Tina Zhukova had those tantrums specifically to throw off her competition," Phillips said.

"Well, it worked," Weiser said. "Ms. Kirk spent as much time watching the two of them as she did designing."

Phillips thought, *That's because she understood Russian.* But that tidbit of knowledge went beyond what was generally known about the case. She didn't want to be viewed as someone who leaked information, and so she said nothing.

Their discussion was interrupted by the ringing of Phillips' phone. She looked at the incoming number and saw an '805' area code. Warily, she answered the call.

"Liz, it's Winnie. Are you still around?"

"I'm on the Convention Center floor," Phillips said.

"Great. We're short a clerk," Garrison said. "Would you be willing to fill in? The *quid pro quo* is an invitation to the judge's dinner. I assume you've done your share of clerking."

Phillips laughed. "If a dozen times is my 'share'. Sure. I just delivered a lost iPad to Aimi Nakata and was wondering what to do next."

"Judges' instructions are at four o'clock," Garrison said. "They're already serving coffee and sandwiches if you're feeling peckish." She gave Phillips a location and panel number. After a pause, Garrison said, "Liz, I want to thank you so much for being here. I've got committee members dropping the ball in so many areas. The first item on my suggestion list for Zara is to make certain she has two or three Liz Phillips – good people with no fixed responsibilities other than to be ready to step in when needed – as part of her inner committee."

Phillips wasn't certain how to respond. She mumbled a reply and said she would be there.

Weiser saw the look on Phillips' face as she returned the phone to her purse.

"I hope it wasn't bad news," Weiser said.

Phillips shook her head. "Good news, I guess. Another assignment, plus an invitation to dinner."

"Some people have all the luck," Weiser said, and continued adjusting her design, smiling as she did so.

Chapter 14

Detective Alvarez reviewed his notes from looking at a dozen security cameras. He was fortunate that, because Ludmila Karachova's room was so close to the elevator, activities at her door were captured by the wide-angle lens trained on the elevator doors. Rooms farther down the hallway were effectively invisible to any security camera.

3:07 a.m. – LK leaves room. Carries small overnight bag. Uses stairs.

3:10 a.m. – LK in shipping/receiving

3:12 a.m. – LK off loading dock. Turns right on D St.

3:44 a.m. – Two men enter hotel lobby, take elevator to 8th floor

3:46 – 3:51 a.m. – Two men attempt to enter LK's room. Unsuccessful.

3:55 a.m. – Two men leave by hotel lobby. Turn left on foot.

So, were the two men there for show? he thought. If they were Russians, intent on seizing Karachova, anyone competent could have defeated a card key system in under a minute. Maybe the FSB had sent incompetent agents. Or, maybe they had intercepted Karachova but wanted to leave the impression she had gotten away, and giving a performance for some hotel security cameras gave credibility to any assertions they might make.

He had gone through her room two hours earlier. It had not appeared to have been searched and, as far as he could tell, Karachova had taken only her purse, a change of clothes and perhaps some toiletries.

But there were other, more interesting videos.

Partly out of boredom but mostly on a hunch, Alvarez had reviewed the lobby security camera footage between 3 a.m. and 4 a.m. on Wednesday. He was looking for specific individuals as they came down the elevator and noting whether they left the hotel immediately or lingered. But he also noted people who came into the hotel. There were cabbies and car service drivers and a handful of late-night returnees.

One person entering the hotel caught his attention: a man wearing a Red Sox baseball cap worn low over his brow to hide his features. He appeared to be about five-foot-ten and he carried a slight paunch under a dark-colored jacket.

The man bucked the outgoing tide of people and rode an elevator to the eighth floor, all the time keeping the top of his cap to the camera. At the eighth floor, he turned right and went down the corridor to what appeared to be Valentina Zhukova's room – it was impossible to be certain because it was at the edge of the camera's field. The man knocked several times and put his ear to the door, listening for activity. He knocked again and listened.

After about five minutes he returned to the elevator and rode it down to the lobby. The elevator stopped at every floor, picking up passengers. At the lobby level the man joined the river of people heading for the doors that led out to waiting cars and the world beyond.

But Alvarez did not see the man go out the door. And, with the dozens of people in the lobby, Alvarez could not be certain the man did not turn off for the escalator to the mezzanine and the Grand Ballroom.

He retraced the man's path through the hotel, looking for the moment in time when he might have inadvertently looked up or passed a reflecting surface.

Alvarez found it thirty seconds into the man's travel through the lobby. With the interior of a lobby store dark, the glass acted as a perfect mirror. Alvarez paused the video and advanced it frame by frame, looking for the best image. He found it: a good, three-quarters shot of the man's face. Alvarez grabbed the screen image and printed it, then tried several enlargements until the digital image pixelated.

The man looked vaguely familiar. Not someone from an APB

or BOLO. But he had seen the face, though he had never met the man.

Damn, Alvarez thought.

He uploaded the image to his phone and mailed it to his Facebook account with the tag, '*Who is this guy?*'

Less than a minute later, his phone beeped.

"Ryan Bratt, dummy."

Alvarez stared at his phone screen. Within a minute he had two more confirmations. One had appended, '*my hero*'. Another wrote, '*and you didn't get his autograph?*'

Ryan Bratt was a long-time Boston *Globe* columnist who had parlayed his column's readership into much larger fame as a late-night talk-show host on a Boston radio station. His stance was invariably and shrilly right wing: deport illegal aliens, armed guards for schools, and get rid of every vestige of Obamacare. In a city and state that invariably elected liberal Democrats, Bratt's show was the refuge for that portion of Boston that refused to go along with 'progressive' policies.

And here Bratt was, knocking on a Russian spy's door at three in the morning.

And Bratt had lunch with that same Russian spy fifteen hours earlier, according to the FBI.

The possibilities were endless. He looked at the time in the corner of his iPad. Just four o'clock. There was still time to accomplish a great deal.

* * * * *

Phillips listened to a litany of instruction that was at once both familiar and foreign. In the standard flower shows she was used to, the judging panel dealt with a class consisting of four designs and awarded a first, a second, a third, and a fourth place. If more than one design showed high degrees of skill and imagination, the judges would point-score the contenders for the first-place 'blue' and give the awards according to the point scores. Phillips had once received a 'yellow' third but with the judges notation that it had scored at more than 90 out of 100 points, or good enough to have received a 'blue' had the competition not been so outstanding.

On this afternoon, though, each class contained as many as twenty entries. According to IFDA rules, three-judge panels could award a 'reasonable number' of firsts and seconds, and that point scoring was not required.

As clerk, Phillips did not have a say in judging. Technically, her duty was to record what the judges agreed on and to make note of the positive and negative comments that would appear on each judging certificate. In reality, clerks sometimes nudged judges in one direction or another by asking for 'clarification'.

She had expected the judges to be drawn from the regional Judges Councils around New England, but was surprised to find the international flavor just as strong as among the attendees. One was French, one was Mexican and the third was from China. They spoke English as their common language, each with a different degree of fluency.

From the moment they went out onto the floor of the Convention Center, though, their interest was in the murder of Valentina Zhukova. Phillips was surprised at how much information – and misinformation – the three women had.

"Garroted with florist's wire and stabbed a dozen times," one woman said.

"I was given to understand she was also shot," said another.

"But it wasn't one of us," the third said. "She was killed by the Russian mafia."

Phillips chose to say nothing; only to listen.

"If ever any designer was setting herself up to be murdered, it was Tina," one of the women said, and the other two nodded assent. "Every time I was around that woman she was asking for trouble. Bad-mouthing the other designs."

"Making little 'changes' to other designs after everyone was finished and gone but before the judges arrived," said another.

"Throwing everyone off their concentration with those tantrums. Making certain she was the center of attention."

"All the while telling everyone about how her grandfather saved the Soviet Union," the French woman said. "He did it single-handedly and got Stalin to go along by sheer genius."

"The apple fell a long way from that particular tree," the Mexican judge offered. "I judged with her once and only once. She was trying to bully us into accepting her choices. When you asked her for a justification, she would look at you and call you a 'peasant', or something that sounded like 'peasant' in Russian."

"Her point scoring was a mystery," the French judge said. "She never offered support for her score. How someone that talented on stage could be so clueless is beyond me."

"And she treated that assistant of hers like a dog," the Chinese judge said. "I always felt so sorry for that woman. Tina didn't want anyone to upstage her."

Phillips absorbed what the women were saying while remaining silent. It was remarkable that they had not heard that Ludmila Karachova was the 'talent' and Zhukova gave empty orders. It would explain why, when judging, Zhukova often made errors and attempted to cover them through intimidation.

It was Phillips' experience that most judges – and especially the Master Judges that were invited to major shows – both knew good designs when they saw them and understood *why* a design was either flawed or did not conform to its class. Judging would have been the one time when Zhukova was without someone to whisper in her ear.

Phillips found herself with an easy job. The women were fair and they agreed on their assessments of each entry. She found herself with ample positive comments and constructive criticism for every design. Moreover, she largely agreed with their choices. They were finished with the first class in just over an hour. Phillips has been part of teams that took that long to judge just four designs.

The panel had a second class to judge: the same stretch designs that Phillips had watched be completed earlier in the day. When the panel came to Helen Weiser's design, Phillips silently tensed up awaiting criticism that she might have inadvertently caused by offering comments.

Instead, the panel was uniform in its praise of Weiser's work and awarded it a 'first'; one of only two in the class.

"You need a constructive comment on this one," Phillips said, one of the few times she had spoken during the judging.

The French judge laughed. "This person understands this design perfectly. Or else she had superb advice along the way."

* * * * *

Lieutenant Lee stood by the main entrance to the Convention Center Plaza Grand Ballroom. A private security guard looked at her identification and listened to her plea to enter but declined to allow her to pass through the closed door.

Frustrated, Lee found the entrance to the kitchen service area and made her way to the service entrance to the ballroom. That door, too, was locked but she could at least peer into the crime scene through a pair of porthole windows. The ballroom had been cleared of all furnishings, leaving only the four hanging spheres, one of which now had an even larger section of carpet removed from underneath it. Though empty, the room was brightly lighted.

There was little to see from her vantage point. The flowers in the spheres were wilting. Some had dropped out of their Oasis and spent blooms were scattered on the floor under each of the designs.

If only the flowers could talk, she thought.

She had been taught that every murder begins with a motive. Even in a senseless street shooting where an innocent bystander was hit by a stray bullet fired a block away, there was a reason why the gun had been fired. Determine the reason why the gun was discharged and a suspect will emerge.

Someone had gone into the ballroom and stuck a knife several times into Valentina Zhukova. After she was dead, that someone had taken the precious time that could have been much more productively used to either escape or conceal a body and had instead hung her with a length of wire.

The notion that the killer was a professional was absurd on its face. Guns, and particularly large guns equipped with silencers, were invariably fatal with a single shot. They were the most efficient means of ensuring that a target was dead in a few seconds; and quick, certain death was the goal of a professional.

Further, the hanging was probably not an afterthought. The killer knew that Zhukova was dead. The hanging was intended to send a message. It might be a message of triumph. It might be a warning. It might be retribution.

Every murder has a motive.

Zara Jretnam had a motive. End the torment. Act as judge, jury and executioner to find Russia guilty of causing the death of her sister; with Zhukova as the incarnation of her country. Zhukova had chosen to torment the wrong person.

Ludmila Karachova also had a motive and it, too, was to end the torment. But this was brutality on a larger scale; a brutality that had lasted years. Zhukova had dehumanized Karachova, turning a gifted designer into a colorless puppet. Moreover, the arrangement was sanctioned by the state police apparatus who added the extra dollop of institutional blackmail by threatening the safety of those about whom Karachova cared.

But why here? Why now? Had there been a final blow-up, or was Tuesday night simply the culmination of years of abuse? Lee had investigated such domestic violence. A partner snapped under the cumulative strain and death was the result.

The common element in those cases, though, was the sense of closure on the killer's part that it was over. More than once Lee had entered an apartment following reports of gun shots and found a woman sitting in a chair, smoking a cigarette, the murder weapon on the table beside her. On the woman's face was a look of relief. What lay ahead might be years in jail, but the pain had stopped.

Karachova, though, had denied culpability where human nature might have decreed that a bold confession was preferable. But now she had run. Killers ran. But so did scared people.

Lee's sixth sense told her that she had not yet cast the net widely enough. Perhaps the killer was one of these two women. But there had to be other people with motive.

If only the flowers could talk.

Had the FBI not intervened, she would be parading suspects and witnesses individually through the ballroom to jog their memories. Witnesses frequently recalled additional details. She would be able to note how suspects reacted when confronted with the reality of the crime scene. Cases were sometimes solved when a suspect, standing in the spot where a homicide had taken place, found it was easier to confess than to live with the secret of the crime.

Her concentration was broken by the sound of footsteps. A different security guard.

"I'll have to ask you to leave, Ma'am." His voice was polite, but insistent. "This area is off limits."

Moments later, back in the hotel lobby, her phone vibrated. It was Alvarez.

The excitement in his voice was palpable. Karachova had left her room, on her own, carrying just a few possessions. Ryan Bratt had been in the hotel and had gone to Zhukova's room just before 4 a.m., then disappeared from the view of the security camera.

"See if the FBI is interested in Bratt," Lee told him. "They've gotten serious about shutting us out of this investigation, and I don't want to step on anyone's toes. But if Karachova shows up at a shelter, call me."

* * * * *

Alvarez tip-toed around his discovery of Ryan Bratt as he spoke with FBI Agent Hirsch. Hirsch again thanked him for delivering a still-working FSB smartphone, but declined to say whether the laboratory had retrieved any information from it.

"So you have nothing on the record to tell me about your investigation," Alvarez said.

"My group is focused on the phone," Hirsch said. "I get calls every half hour from people asking if we're in. All we know about the murder is what the people in the Boston field office are saying."

"Which is?" Alvarez asked.

There was a long pause. "It was an independent contractor – a Venezuelan national – hired by Boris Gusinovich, who is part of Putin's inner circle and a big wheel in various government-owned industries. Gusinovich decided he wanted a slice of a cyber-warfare unit that Zhukova's husband runs. The husband…"

"Yuri Soldatov," Alvarez said. "My boss was told that story, but without the other names."

"The Venezuelan landed at Kennedy Tuesday afternoon," Hirsch said. "There are photos of him in Boston Tuesday evening…."

"You don't believe this stuff, do you?" Alvarez asked. "I've looked at every minute of the hotel video. There's no…"

Hirsch cut him off. "Detective Alvarez," he said, "the FBI is very certain of its facts. It will make those facts public on its own schedule. You did a very good thing by recognizing that smartphone and calling attention to it. Don't screw up now."

"And if I have another suspect?" Alvarez asked. "Someone I can actually place in the hotel?"

The line went dead.

Alvarez clenched the phone, his anger growing.

They take us for fools, he thought. *We are idiots who will believe anything we're told.*

And then a second thought gained a foothold. *This is all for the ears of the Russians. They hack computers, they listen to phone calls. This is what the FBI wants the Russians to hear. We – the Boston PD – are the pawns. What we're being told isn't meant for us. It's meant for someone – or several someones – in Russia to overhear. The purpose of all this is to sow doubt in the mind or minds of someone four thousand miles away.*

But then who is investigating Zhukova's murder? Or is this a case that no one wants to solve because the FBI's 'explanation' achieves some greater goal?

If that was true, then it was only Lieutenant Lee and himself who were trying to find the true killer.

Not only was it not a comforting thought, it was a more than a little scary.

Alvarez's phone chimed. He thought it was Hirsch calling back to apologize. Or to instruct him to drop all investigations. Instead, it was an incoming call from a local number.

"This is Detective Dawson out of the South End. She just checked into the Santa Lucia House on Dwight Street. What do you want me to do?" The name was unfamiliar.

Alvarez noted the time: 4:20 p.m. "I'll take it from here, Detective," he said. "Thank you."

'She' would be Ludmila Karachova. He faced the policeman's dilemma: two suspects fleeing a crime scene, each one running in different directions. Which one to apprehend?

Ryan Bratt didn't know he was a suspect. His radio show began at 9 p.m. and ended at 2 a.m. Bratt could be anywhere right now – asleep in bed, writing his newspaper column or working with the radio show's producer. But at 8:45 p.m. he would be at the radio station.

Ludmila Karachova, on the other hand, was already running. She might stay at the shelter all night or she might sense danger and flee yet again.

Alvarez called Lee.

"Maybe we ought to have this conversation in person," she

said. "I'm in the conference room off the lobby. At least they haven't taken that away from us."

Five minutes later, Alvarez sat beside Lee in the conference room.

"I've been trying to make sense of it," Lee said, agitation in her voice. "My mentor, John Flynn, said when it starts to get too confusing, to go back to the beginning and question your assumptions. That's what I was trying to do except that the FBI has sealed the ballroom to prevent riffraff like us from spying on their betters."

Lee stopped herself. She slowly shook her head. "No. I can't let them get into my head like that." She took a deep breath and started over. "It all comes back to the crime scene. Why in the ballroom? Why not in her room where there would have been no chance of someone walking in on you? Why the knife and why the hanging?"

"You think we're looking at the wrong group of suspects," Alvarez suggested.

Lee sighed. "The ones we have right now certainly have motive. I can't remember when I came across a victim who doled out motives so generously. The woman was a sadist. Worse, she was an entitled sadist."

"Sociopath," Alvarez offered.

"Yeah, sociopath, if you must," Lee said. "And, eventually, sociopaths or sadists come up against someone whose anger or pain reaches a boiling point. And, in that instant, the perp becomes the victim."

"And the idea of a Venezuelan hit man?"

Lee laughed. "The FBI is playing some kind of geopolitical poker game with its Russian counterpart. Does this have something to do with Zhukova being a spy? Maybe. I won't rule it out. But do I see the work of a professional? Not a chance."

"We've both been at this a long time today," Lee continued.

"Put those computers to work tonight. Go talk to Bratt tomorrow morning. I've promised to have an early dinner with someone tonight, but I'll go see Karachova and I'll let you know how that comes out. For now, go home."

Chapter 15

Lee gave both her own and Matt's name to the hostess and was shown to a table. There was noise from the bar but the restaurant was still relatively quiet at this hour. The table at which she was seated, she noted, was in a corner of the room. Had that been at Matt's request?

Matt appeared five minutes later, puffing and apologizing that Silver Line service was 'a joke'.

"You're not exactly late," Lee said. "It's not a big deal."

Matt was a fourth-generation Chinese American. He was the *summa cum laude* product of top engineering and business schools. At 32, he had likely already banked a couple of million dollars, and had that much more hanging on his walls in the form of modern art in his Back Bay condo. He was good looking and reasonably tall.

He was also an impeccable dresser. His dark blue blazer and light blue sweater fit perfectly over khakis, which had a perfect crease despite having been worn all day. His loafers were polished to a high sheen and, she knew because he had told her, those shoes were custom made for him in England.

"Let's have wine," he said with a broad smile.

"One glass," Lee said, holding up a finger for emphasis. "You're done for the day. I don't know when I'll be finished."

Matt chose a white wine, a Montrachet that was probably well over a hundred dollars a bottle. It was, Lee had observed, a 'tell'. When Matt went overboard by ordering the eighteen-year-old Balvenie or a premier-cru wine, something was up.

"Are you packed?" Matt asked as the wine was poured. "I think I'm about half done."

"I don't have the kind of wardrobe choices you do," she said.

"I own seven or eight suits and maybe three pair of shoes."

He looked disappointed. "No special dress for Saturday night?"

"Matt, I've been flat out all week…"

"No problem," he said, giving a dismissive wave of his hand. "My sister Kay will know several great shops within a block or two of the Four Seasons. We can do that Saturday morning."

"Do I get to choose my own dress, or do you have something already picked out?"

He smiled. "Sorry. I'm just getting excited." He reached across the table and took her hand. "This is important. Both my grandmothers are in their mid-eighties. I don't know how many more times…" He shook his head. "Sorry again."

The charm offensive at full throttle, Lee thought.

It was in the middle of the truffled lobster mac and cheese that Matt drew the box from his blazer pocket.

"I called my sister for advice. She's the one who is into this stuff." He placed a small box in the middle of the table. "I'd like you to wear this on Saturday night."

Lee looked at the box, which was dark green and two inches on a side. A ring box, clearly, she thought. But one unaccompanied by either wrapping paper or a satin ribbon. "What is it?" she asked, making no move to touch the box.

"Open it," Matt urged her. "Go ahead."

With a sense of dread, Lee opened the box. Inside was a diamond ring. The stone was enormous. She stared at it, slack jawed.

"Like I said, I called Kay her for advice. She said two carats would be about right. Anything more would be ostentatious. But she said to go for the D-flawless. So that's what I got. So, will you wear it Saturday night?"

Lee stared at Matt, a look of incredulity on her face. But then she started parsing the words Matt had spoken. An idea formed in her mind.

She smiled demurely, "If you are asking me to marry you, the answer is yes."

Matt looked baffled. Words started to form, then evaporated. "Well, I, uh…" Then he said "Sure. If that's what you want." His broad smile looked forced and uncomfortable.

"I think we should set a date right now," she said. She took out her phone and tapped the calendar icon. "Four or five months seems about right. The middle of August. That's perfect." She looked up at Matt. "Here or in San Francisco?"

Matt's eyes were blinking rapidly. "Why the rush?"

"I think San Francisco," Lee said excitedly. "It's easier on both our families. It's just a little over two hours from Vancouver. And for your friends, it would be almost like one of those 'destination' weddings, except they'd never be out of range of Wi-Fi."

Lee tried the ring on her finger. It was at least one size too large. Matt apparently thought she had fat fingers. "We can get this re-sized tomorrow."

Matt had sweat on his brow. "We should take our time…"

"We should call your family now," she said. "If we wait until Saturday, it will upstage their anniversary. I'm definitely calling my mother and father. Do you mind?" She began scrolling through her contacts list.

"Wait, Vicky…" Matt said, wiping sweat from his sideburns.

Lee paused, her finger ready to tap her parent's icon. "You said you wanted me to wear this on Saturday night. Those were your exact words."

"It wasn't…"

She put down her phone and took the too-large ring off her finger. She spoke in a clear, confident voice; the kind she would use with a suspect who had just confessed. "This isn't an engagement ring, Matt. This is a prop. Just like I'm a prop. The suitable Chinese girlfriend. The right age, the right education. Put a sock in my mouth and I might even show the proper deference."

"It *is* a marriage proposal," Matt protested. "Vicky, will you marry me? Just not right away."

"No, it's not," Lee said. "I said the word 'marry' and the look on your face told me the whole story. The ring completes the picture. Perfect Number One Son returns home for Mom and Dad's big anniversary. With the perfect girl on his arm. Well, not quite perfect because she isn't very pretty and she's too educated, but doesn't she look great in that thousand dollar dress and look at that rock on the third finger of her left hand! Number One Son finally wised up and decided to please Mom and Dad. Not to mention two grandmothers who may not have decided how to divvy up the real estate holdings."

The look on Matt's face told her she was uncomfortably close to the truth.

"Did you buy the ring?" she asked. "Or is this just a loan; something you took out on approval with every intention of returning Monday morning? You couldn't even spring for wrapping paper and a bow? I thought stores did that for free, except if it is 'on approval' and they've never seen you before. Or was this an internet deal? Did Amazon give you same day delivery?"

Matt's face was red. He shook his head slowly, trying not to hear what was being said.

"Let's make a deal, Matt. Let's see. You need me for Saturday night. What if I get to keep the ring? What's it worth? Six thousand? No, this is D-flawless. Ten thousand? At what point is it cheaper to call 'Rent-a-Chinese-Date' and rehearse her on the flight out? But then what if she flubs a line? I won't do that. I'm perfect. So, let's see: first class airfare; my own hotel room at the Four Seasons, of course; that thousand-dollar dress; and this ring. Oh, and I promise to be deferential. I'll even ask your mother about baby names, if you want, and I promise to blush"

"I wanted to do it right," Matt mumbled.

"Do your parents' anniversary right, you mean. Matt, you don't love me. I sure don't love you. You asked me to go with you to please your family and I said 'yes' because I thought I might sneak in a flight up to Vancouver afterwards to see my own parents and make them happy. That was selfish on my part but then I live on a public servant's salary and flying is expensive."

Lee rose from the table. She looked around and noticed that every diner in the room was looking in her direction. She was not aware she had raised her voice.

"Matt, that was cruel," she said, loudly enough that nearby patrons could hear her. "What you did was very, very cruel."

And, with that, she collected her purse and left the restaurant.

* * * * *

The No-Name was a vestige of a fast-disappearing Boston. There had been a time when the South Boston waterfront sported half a dozen venerable restaurants specializing in seafood. Jimmy's Harborside, Anthony's Pier 4. They were gone now, victims of changing tastes and the reality that the land they occupied was far more valuable than the business atop that land. Now, that real estate sprouted dull, mid-rise office and apartment buildings and more than a few hotels.

The No-Name occupied part of Fish Pier, itself a remnant of the time when brokers bought and sold trawlers full of cod caught in the fish-rich Grand Banks. Now, the fish business was in decline but the need for luxury condominiums was never higher. Fish Pier might hang on for a few more years but, eventually, the government agency that owned the waterfront would elect to monetize its asset.

Liz Phillips sat at a long table with eighteen women and two men. Four more such tables held eighty additional judges, clerks or IFDA officials. The room buzzed with conversations.

To Phillips' right sat Winnie Garrison. Garrison needed someone willing to listen to a tale of frustration. Sympathy was not required, only the tacit acknowledgement that the story would go no further than the table. Phillips apparently was the ideal listener.

"I had it all worked out," Garrison said, possibly for the third time. "I cannot believe the idiocy of that woman. The Tower Hill Botanic Garden had agreed to take the staging. *All* the staging. They would take all eight hundred pieces even though they really wanted just two hundred of them."

Garrison continued. "And then that birdbrain starts giving it away to her friends. She promised fifty pieces to Newport. Fifty pieces to Philadelphia. Fifty pieces to some group in Texas. Everybody *loves* the staging. They ought to. It cost enough to build. But not all of it. Not the big pieces or the complex pieces. This afternoon she gave the list of what she *hasn't* given away to the person at Tower Hill. What's on the list? The six hundred pieces that Tower Hill didn't want, but agreed to take because they'd get the two hundred pieces they *did* want."

"Now, Tower Hill just told me they don't want any of it, and I can't blame them. So I get to store it, or ship it back to California. Either way, I'm stuck with the bill. I could strangle her…"

Phillips listened, nodding in the right places and offering words of sympathy. She recognized that to run an event of this size required years of careful planning. However, the execution of the plan was dependent on volunteers, some of whom came to the 'Committee' with either an exaggerated sense of entitlement or a personal agenda that might be very much at odds with the one so carefully devised by the people who devoted those years to its planning.

'You can't fire a volunteer' was one of the mantras of the garden club world. As Phillips listened, she glumly realized that, at a certain level, all you could do was vent to someone whom, you hoped, wouldn't turn around and repeat the story to the wrong person.

To Phillips' left was a judge from Florida. A heavy-set woman in her sixties, she was regaling the people around her with tales of far-flung floral design events she had attended. Phillips was listening to Garrison's tale of expensive incompetence when she heard the woman on her left say, 'Valentina'. Now, Phillips strained to hear both conversations while trying to give the appearance of being engaged solely with Garrison.

"…Berlin in – I'm pretty sure – 2008. We were on a bus tour of the eastern part of the city and Valentina was crowing about how her grandfather had restored order after the war and prevented the country from starving."

The woman continued. "Our tour guide stopped her spiel and asked Valentina who her grandfather was. She puffed herself up and said, 'You have the honor to address the granddaughter of Marshal Georgy Zhukov!' Well, the tour guide's face turned ashen. She said, very diplomatically, 'Not everyone remembers him that way, but you are entitled to think of him as you wish'."

"Well, it was like a bomb had gone off on the bus. Valentina started yelling in German, English and Russian that her grandfather was a revered figure and had been given a dozen medals from the East German government, that she had them all on display in her home, and that had it not been for her grandfather, Stalin would have ordered Berlin to be reduced to dust and everyone still in the city killed. She demanded that the guide apologize for – I think she said – 'denigrating the memory of one of history's greatest men'."

"When the guide wouldn't apologize, Valentina started screaming that reunification was the worst thing ever to happen to Germany and that the guide's attitude was proof that the Nazis were coming back. The driver beat a hasty retreat back to the hotel. As far as I know she never apologized to anyone. I know I will never forget being on that bus as long as I live…"

The woman's tales went to other events in other cities and Zhukova's name was not mentioned again.

As they were leaving the dinner, Garrison thanked Phillips for listening. "You have no idea how much pressure there in in this job," Garrison said. "And my biggest fear right now is that Zara is having some kind of nervous breakdown. We start our speaker series tomorrow morning. Zara is supposed to be in charge of that and I have this gnawing feeling that she isn't going to show up."

"If you're willing and able, I'd like for you to shadow her; be there to help her but, in reality, to step in if something happens. Could you do that?"

Phillips was too surprised to say anything other than, "Of course."

"Then come on up to the suite and I'll give you the material you'll need to know what's going on. And, if you're not tired of Lost and Found duty, I have a couple of calls on that, including one woman who seems to have misplaced the world's most expensive emerald ring. And this one isn't from Nigeria."

* * * * *

Lee had been to women's shelters on many occasions during her law enforcement career. Some were shelters in the most basic sense of the word: bare-bones operations that provided cots and a meal. The Santa Lucia House was at the other end of the spectrum. It was one of Boston's oldest shelters, housed in a four-story brick townhouse in the South End. The building was identical to the other townhouses up and down this street, but this one provided refuge. Guests, she knew, were limited to a seven-night stay but, for those seven nights there was safety, a degree of comfort, and counseling. Lee wondered what tale Karachova would have told to gain entry.

Lee showed her ID. "I need to speak to one of your residents," Lee said.

"The House Director isn't here," a woman, clearly a volunteer, said nervously.

"You can call the House Director if you think it necessary," Lee said, using her most soothing voice. "I don't think your guest has done anything wrong, but she may have been a witness to a serious crime. I interviewed her yesterday and I have some follow-up questions." Lee did not flinch at bending the truth on a number of points. Her goal was to get into see Karachova, and that chance diminished if calls started getting made.

The volunteer was listening carefully to Lee's words. She was on uncertain ground. Had a man shown up looking for one of the residents, it would have prompted a call to whomever managed the shelter as well as to the police. Instead, here was a woman police officer. Moreover, she was a Lieutenant.

Lee pressed her advantage. "We can speak in one of the public rooms. You can be present, if that will set your mind at ease."

"Which of our residents is it?"

"Her name is Ludmila. She speaks with a Russian accent."

The volunteer nodded. "Oh, her. Yes."

Lee smiled. "It is important. Please." She pressed her Lieutenant's badge and ID card into the woman's hands.

The volunteer wavered, then capitulated. "You can see her in her room. Let me know if you need anything."

* * * * *

Karachova seemed resigned to having been located. "At least it was by you," she said.

"Why did you run?" Lee asked.

"What choice did I have?" Karachova responded. "I knew it would be a matter of a few hours before the FSB ordered me brought in. I am not so stupid that I believe they would forget about me or leave me alone."

"You need to tell me everything you know," Lee said. "And, this time, I mean 'everything'. This isn't about bargaining. And, you're right. Two men – I presume from the FSB, came to your room a few hours after you left."

Karachova closed her eyes and nodded, perhaps imagining what she had avoided by choosing to leave when she did.

"Remember that I have just one goal here: to catch the person who killed Valentina."

Even if it is you, Lee thought to herself.

"So, let's go back to the beginning. Before each trip – and I would assume, especially a trip to America – you and Valentina had to coordinate what each of you were going to do. You would have an idea of her schedule. You would prepare her for her floral design lecture."

Karachova nodded.

"What did she say about this trip in the days or weeks before you arrived?"

Karachova paused. "She was always excited. Not about the conference – that bored her. She would have contacts she planned to meet, information to gather. She believed, in her heart of hearts, that Americans are stupid. That they are gullible. That they treat everything you tell them as the truth, without questioning anything. She especially believed that many Americans, deep inside themselves, despise their country. They are wealthy but feel guilty that they have money they have not earned. They hate the inequality and they hate democracy."

Karachova continued. "It is not that they admire Russia. Valentina said it is just that these people are willing to give Russia secrets because they believe America is corrupt. This is what Valentina believed and how she found people willing to work with her. She would never deal with anyone who wanted to sell information. She dealt only with those who gave secrets freely to help destroy what they saw as an evil government."

"She saw two people on the day before she died," Lee prompted. "Laurie Parkinson at Boston University, and Ryan Bratt, a columnist and radio show host. Why did she see them?"

Karachova hesitated and looked at Lee. "You will tell this to the FBI?"

Lee returned Karachova's gaze. "I will use what you tell me to catch a killer. I will let the FBI do its own investigation. Why did she see Parkinson and Bratt?"

"They are both informers. Parkinson sees reports written by American government agencies about Russia. She makes copies of them and gives them to Valentina. It allows the FSB to know which people in Russia are passing information to the Americans. Bratt has many influential and highly-placed people on his radio show. He is their friend because he gives them the chance to speak directly to the people. Because they think they can trust him – because Bratt thinks the same way they do – they tell Bratt private things about policy and about other people. Bratt tells these private things to Valentina."

Karachova paused for a moment, as though choosing words. She said, "Bratt was also her lover. One of many. Valentina used sex to make men want to tell her more secrets."

"Valentina's husband knew of this?" Lee asked.

Karachova shrugged. "They were married because it helped their careers. There was no love. Valentina was the granddaughter of the revered Marshal Zhukov. Being her husband meant Yuri was promoted to Colonel at thirty-four. He is one of the top men…"

"I know who he is," Lee said.

"Valentina could only marry a big politician or an important military man. She told me that she married Yuri because Putin was not available. Valentina and Yuri made appearances for the press – the opera, ballet. But it was all for show."

"So, if I told you that some people believe Valentina was killed on the orders of an oligarch to frighten her husband, what would you say?"

Karachova looked at Lee, curiosity in her eyes. "Who would say such a ridiculous thing?"

"It's not important," Lee said. "What did Valentina tell you after completing her design Tuesday night?"

Karachova shrugged. "That she was tired and going to bed. It could have been the truth. Valentina did not always tell me the truth about her plans."

"She said nothing that would have given you any suspicion that something might have happened earlier in the day?"

"She was agitated," Karachova said. "But then she is frequently agitated."

"What were her plans for Wednesday and today?"

"She was going to New York," Karachova replied. "She said she would be back Wednesday night depending on what happened when she saw her FSB people."

"Let's talk about Tomás Suarez," Lee said. "How was he acting Tuesday evening?"

"Valentina hated him," Karachova said. "She may not have not have done her own designs, but she loved having the reputation and hated it when she did not win the top prize. Suarez got a better award at several shows. She worked especially hard at distracting him Tuesday night. She said many terrible things to his face."

"How did Suarez react?"

"I think he was used to her taunts after so many competitions," Karachova replied. "He would not say anything in return. He just kept working. He even smiled. That made Valentina even madder."

"So she no longer had any effect on Suarez?" Lee asked.

Karachova shook her head. "He knew what Valentina was doing. So it no longer mattered."

So, Tomás Suarez was playing his own game with Valentina, Lee thought. *Not a priority for now.*

"Can you think why Valentina would have gone back to the hotel ballroom?"

Karachova paused. "I have asked myself that question many times. She may have received a call from someone. She may not have wanted that person to go to her room. She may have been unable to sleep. Valentina often could not sleep for many nights at a time. Because she possibly would not be back for several days, she may have wanted to admire 'her' design one more time. But I do not know. I can only guess."

Lee thought she heard a hesitation in Karachova's voice in that last response. She was reaching for acceptable answers when there was one that she did not want to divulge. It was time to ask the 'big' question.

"Did you go back down to the ballroom?"

Karachova shook her head and stared at the floor. "No. I did not go back to the ballroom, and I did not kill her. The end of her life is also the end of mine, or at least the life I have been able to lead since I became her 'assistant'. I have only a few dollars. I can run only so far."

"Can you ask for asylum? In exchange for information?" Lee asked.

"I am a pawn." There was sadness and resignation in Karachova's voice. "Pawns do not have the kind of information that gets governments to open their doors. I have a few days of freedom."

She is either one of the best liars I have ever encountered, Lee thought, *or else she is telling the truth.*

Lee pressed her business card into Karachova's hand. "Before you do anything, or if you need help, call me." Lee circled the cell number. "I will answer this number any time of the day or night."

Lee descended the staircase from Karachova's room. In the first floor living room, a woman waited, standing. She was in her fifties and wore slacks and a sweater. Looking at her thick, black glasses, Lee's first thought was *doctor*.

"You are Lieutenant Victoria Lee?" the woman asked.

"Yes."

"May I see the identification you showed Irene?"

Lee handed her the requested material. At the same time, Lee noted the woman's manicured nails. "And you are….?" Lee asked.

The woman studied the card and badge before answering. "My name is Ann Tretis. I'm also a volunteer here. I provide psychological counseling services to our residents. Could we speak somewhere in private?" She indicated a small office with a desk and two chairs.

When they were seated, Tretis said, "Irene called me after you went up. I live around the corner."

"She told me she might have to call the House Manager," Lee said. "Is that your title?"

Tretis gave a quick smile. "Not hardly. I'm a psychologist in private practice. I help the residents get over their trauma. We see a lot of domestic abuse."

"I also see more than my share," Lee said. "But I usually see it right after it happened. But I'm in the middle of an investigation. How can I help you?"

Tretis gave another smile. "It's how I may be able to help you. Our volunteers are very well trained. We teach them how to look for what we call 'markers'; behavior that provides a clue to abuse. And not just physical abuse. Emotional abuse as well. They alert me."

"And she thought she saw it in Ludmila?" Lee asked. "It's no wonder. That woman has been through nine years of hell."

Tretis shook her head. "Ludmila – which isn't the name she gave me – and I spoke earlier. And you're right. She will require a lot of help, but that isn't why I'm here. Irene called me about you."

Lee was dumbfounded. "Me?"

Tretis leaned across the desk. "You're under no obligation to speak with me. But I may be able to help you. As I said, not all abuse is physical. Sometimes it entirely emotional…"

Lee started to protest but Tretis raised her hand and continued. "… and the receiver of the abuse may not even think of it as such. But Irene saw – and I do, too – someone who is a victim of recent trauma. All I ask is that you talk about it."

Lee rose from her chair. "I came here to investigate a murder. I know you mean well, but I can deal with my own relationships. And in fact, I have. This evening. What you see is someone who… ended a relationship that was going nowhere. I'm sorry you were pulled away from your own evening."

* * * * *

Lee did not return to the hotel or the Convention Center. The investigation could wait twelve hours. Instead, she drove home. In her apartment she found the bottle of seldom-drank Scotch and poured two ounces into a glass, her hand shaking as she did.

She would not allow herself to cry. So, instead, she did what she had done so many times before. She reached for her phone.

John Flynn answered on the second ring.

"How's the case going?" he asked.

It was the perfect question, she thought. Not, 'how are you doing' or 'how is it going' or 'so what did a psychologist say to you tonight', any of which questions constituted an invitation to open the floodgate that she was holding back. And so for thirty minutes she gave every detail of her progress, or lack thereof. She detailed what she had learned at her meeting with Karachova. And for thirty minutes more, Flynn asked more questions and offered the kind of logical advice that only a detached observer could see.

"But that isn't why you called," Flynn said. "There's no background noise. You're home and you called before eight o'clock. What's really going on?"

He knows, Lee thought. *He always knows.*

"I may have just made the biggest mistake of my life," she said. "Or done the bravest thing." For ten minutes she took Flynn through Matt's 'charm offensive', leading up to tonight's dinner 'proposal'. She left out only Dr. Ann Tretis' diagnosis of traumatic abuse. When she was done, she braced herself for his reaction.

"Vicky, I'm possibly the least qualified person on the face of the earth to be giving advice," Flynn said. "But Matt is a jerk. Oh, he's a rich jerk and a suave jerk, but he is now and always will be a jerk. That's an opinion I've kept to myself for the better part of six months because it was none of my business. It still isn't my business except that you asked."

"My sage counsel is that you did exactly the right thing, except that you ought to have pocketed the ring – which, by the way, is worth closer to twenty thousand than ten – on your way out the door," Flynn said. "The only way that jerks absorb new information is when something hits them hard in their most tender spot. Twenty grand isn't a fortune to him, but he can't deduct it and, if you had it, he can't spend the equivalent sum on some jerk bauble."

"You also ought to call the landscaper guy," Flynn added.

"What?" Lee said.

"You know who I'm talking about. The landscaper guy from the Flower Show. Give him a call. Ask him out for dinner. Ask him for houseplant advice."

"John, I have no idea of who you're talking about," Lee protested. In truth, she knew exactly who he was referring to.

"I saw the two of you. There was a connection. And he's your type. And he's definitely not a jerk."

"I don't need those kinds of complications right now," Lee said.

"And Matt the Jerk wasn't a complication?" Flynn shot back. "And, by the way, if I ever hear that you went crawling back to him asking for forgiveness, it's the last time I'll ever return your call. And I mean that."

"I thought you said you were the last person on earth to be giving advice," Lee countered.

"I said I was the least qualified. But that's my advice. Call the guy. Or, make sure that Alvarez does the full work-up on this Bratt guy and look for the opportunity timing with the Malaysian woman.

Have him work on Suarez. The guy smells like a walking time bomb. And, when you've done that, then call the guy. But do it."

The call concluded. Lee looked at her glass, which still held half of what she had originally poured. She noted that her hand no longer shook. She poured the remaining contents of the glass carefully back into the bottle.

John Flynn was the brother she never had, the teacher she had never been able to talk like an adult to, and the father in whom she had never been able to confide. He was only a phone call away but she worried that, over time, he would slip away.

She was acutely aware that she had no friends. She had not spoken with childhood playmates since leaving home for college, and had made no effort to keep in touch with classmates from her college years.

Her meteoric rise within the Boston PD left those of her own age and gender suspicious or resentful. Her law school classmates were wrapped up in their own relationships. Even those in her study group appeared to view her as some kind of hyper-intelligent collector of degrees; not someone to be included in some late-night, coffee-fueled off-topic discussion of the world and its ills.

She had met Matt through a dating service. 'Lunch with a Nice Guy' or some such name. Just a meal on neutral turf. She had not specified 'Asian' for her dating preference but noted that all of her matches were Chinese, meaning that white guys took a look at her profile picture and scrolled on. Why Matt had asked her out for a second date was a matter of some conjecture. What they had in common was cultural heritage and, if he bothered to notice, intelligence.

The dates were regular enough to be meaningful but not so frequent to make them a couple. Lee surmised Matt probably had one or more 'Blondies' on his radar. He certainly spent enough time eyeing them when they were together. But you couldn't take a Blondie home to meet mom and dad for their triple prosperity anniversary.   You needed a bona-fide, presentable Chinese girlfriend.

Maybe their entire six months together had been a build-up for that one event. Until Matt's weekend in New York with his buddies and his explosion at finding she had the temerity to put her job ahead of his whims, everything had been – at least from his perspective – perfect. Had it not been for that unplanned breakup, in a week or two he would have broached the trip to San Francisco. There would have been no need for a ring or extra effort of any kind. Hell, she might even have paid her own way out to the west coast. Lee would have blindly fulfilled her part in Matt's role as Number One Son, then been summarily dumped on Monday morning.

Now, he was stuck – unless, of course, it really was possible to hire a model or an escort. Right now, Matt was probably scouring Craigslist, trying search terms like 'pliable/ cute/ demure/ Chinese/ 30-32 years/ quick study'.

Lee sighed and turned on her computer. Nail down the timeline for Valentina and Zara Jretnam. As to calling the handsome landscaper from the Flower Show, she thought, '*dream on*'.

Chapter 16
Friday, April 10

Jason Alvarez read through the online English-language editions of *Pravda* and *Krasnaya Zvezda* and scanned several other Russian publications. The outrage, real or manufactured, over the death of Valentina Zhukova continued to dominate the Russian news. It was clear to the government-controlled Russian press, and thus to its readers, that the CIA and the FBI had engineered the assassination of a living link to the Great Patriotic War. Incredibly, anonymous sources within the American intelligence services professed without a shred of proof that an as-yet-unnamed Russian businessman was behind the cold-blooded murder. The Americans were tracking down a South American assassin-for-hire. *Krasnaya Zvezda* mocked the effort, saying that the reason the person could not be found was that he did not exist.

A *Pravda* correspondent claiming to be writing from the 'frigid, snow-covered streets of Boston', wrote that the local media had been ordered not to cover the gruesome crime. It had certainly been a snowy, miserable winter. However, Thursday's high temperature had been 52 degrees and there had not been measurable snow in ten days. The absence of coverage, Alvarez thought, was the combination of tonight's Red Sox opener against the Yankees in the Bronx, and continuing coverage of some prominent murder trials.

But the Russian coverage of the crime underscored what was impossible to ignore across each of the newspapers he reviewed: a constant drumbeat of rabid, anti-American rhetoric. The United States was responsible for the death of Zhukova, and her murder was a calculated slap at the Russian people. There was no countervailing point of view: the newspapers marched in lockstep, printing only the government's point of view. Alvarez imagined that the television and radio coverage echoed what he was reading online.

Krasnaya Zvezda – Red Star, which was the official newspaper of the Russian Ministry of Defense – used the occasion of Zhukova's death to reprint excerpts of a Putin-era biography of Marshal Zhukov. Alvarez could not help but smile at the re-writing of history.

Through his other readings, Alvarez knew Zhukov's reputation had twice been officially 'downgraded'; the first time by Josef Stalin in mid-1946 when the Soviet Premier feared Zhukov had become too popular among the Soviet citizenry. Zhukov was denounced in a speech to the Central Committee, recalled from his post as Commander of the occupation army in Germany, and relegated to a minor military position in Odessa.

Premier Nikita Khrushchev had restored Zhukov upon Stalin's death and, for several years, Zhukov enjoyed the favors of being a heroic, retired military figure. Ultimately, like Stalin, Khrushchev came to fear Zhukov's popularity and denounced him in 1962. By the time of his death in 1974, Zhukov was living in shabby quarters, all but officially forgotten by the Soviet government.

But when the Communist Party required heroes, and especially when the Soviet Army was humiliated in Afghanistan, Zhukov's star began to rise yet again. With the dissolution of the Soviet Union and the loss of its satellites, the country needed larger-than-life ethnic Russian superheroes, and Zhukov was placed in that Slavic Pantheon, with new statues, new biographies, and television specials.

Alvarez skimmed through the biography noting inconsistencies with non-Russian ones and the substitution of euphemisms for the widespread atrocities that were committed by Red Army soldiers and condoned by its generals in the months after the fall of Berlin. Then his eyes fell on several paragraphs that glorified something called "Operation Ossavakim". In 1946, Zhukov was Supreme Military Commander of the Soviet Occupation Zone, effectively the military governor of what would become East Germany.

"It was Marshal Zhukov's signing of Order 140 in May 1946 authorizing the 'training of qualified workers and retraining of workers for critical occupations' that laid the necessary groundwork for October 1946's initiation of Operation Ossavakim. Zhukov brilliantly understood that reparations for Nazi Germany's atrocities could be more swiftly extracted by transferring to Russia not only the physical equipment that had been developed by Hitler's ministries, but the technicians, managers and skilled personnel, along with their family members and the industrial tools they would operate…"

Alvarez re-read the paragraph. Only in Russia, he thought, could someone be lionized for coming up with a plan to strip a country of its ability to pull itself out of the rubble of war, and then to forcibly deport the people who could have hastened the rebuilding. The Russians picked themselves a hell of a hero.

He plugged the link to the article into the database management system he had created for the case.

Lee had written him a lengthy email summarizing her conversation with Karachova. Alvarez took to heart the reality that, had he presented himself at the shelter instead of Lee, the interview with Karachova might never have taken place. If it had, the circumstances would likely have been very different, with several staff members in attendance, all of them objecting to questions he might ask. The details from Lee's interview also went into the database, where his computer would look for correlations with information available on the web.

Lee's email included the information that, while Tomás Suarez was still a suspect, her conversation with Karachova indicated Suarez had appeared immune to Zhukova's baiting Tuesday night. Accordingly, Alvarez was to focus on Ryan Bratt. The knowledge that he was, in reality, someone who turned over sensitive information to a Russian agent made the talk show host's biography all the more puzzling.

According to multiple sources including his own website, Bratt was the scion of Boston Brahmins who traced their lineage to John Cotton. His parents lived in a house on Louisburg Square, and he graduated with honors from Milton Academy. In four years at Dartmouth he distinguished himself in multiple sports.

He also was one of the editors who founded the *Dartmouth Review* in 1980. The off-campus newspaper quickly established a reputation for very good writing but also very conservative coverage of national and international topics. Following graduation, he went to work for the *Wall Street Journal*, a publication his father doubtlessly read every day but could never have dreamed his son would write for. After ten years in the *Journal's* Boston bureau, he joined the *Boston Globe's* staff as a business editor, but also as the liberal newspaper's 'pet' conservative columnist.

There, he mercilessly tweaked the paper's orthodox liberal editorial positions. Inevitably, that notoriety led to a nightly stint as a talk show host on a minor Boston radio station. Bratt became the antithesis of NPR and a refuge for those Bostonians who shared his arch-conservative views. His voice, in turn, was amplified by web streaming. His acidic commentaries had been gathered into three books that sold surprisingly well.

Bratt had been married three times and was currently single, although he was seen frequently at social events with a local TV meteorologist twenty years his junior. He lived at the Residences at the Ritz Carlton, a glass tower located in what used to be called the 'Combat Zone' but was now simply 'Midtown'.

What would have caused a man with impeccable conservative credentials to leak sensitive information to a Russian agent? It seemed incongruous, Alvarez thought.

The rest of his overnight database search had turned up few items of interest. The Russian government offered fresh claims that the downing of Malaysian Air Flight 17 was orchestrated by the Ukraine Ministry of Defense. The latest 'evidence' was that missile fragments photographed at the crash site bore the unmistakable blue and gold colors of the Ukrainian flag that were known to be painted on the Ministry's surface-to-air missiles. The missile fragments had 'mysteriously disappeared' after European crash scene investigators arrived at the scene.

One item that caught his attention was a brief item saying that New York City police had detained a Venezuelan national and was holding the man for unspecified charges. The arrest had come at the conclusion of a standoff that shut down six square blocks in Harlem and caused traffic backups that affected three boroughs.

Then, a blinking red link appeared. Databases continually updated themselves and intelligent databases used spare capacity to use inferences to cast a net for potentially information; the computer equivalent of playing a hunch.

Alvarez had built his database with the ability to consider information where groups of secondary search terms were present even if a primary one was absent. It was akin to searching for articles about 'hamburgers', and the database offering a result that included the close proximity of the words, 'beef', 'bun' and 'grill', even though the word 'hamburger' never appeared in the article or report.

The link led Alvarez to a short, year-old article in the *New York Post.*

New York State Police at the Javits Center were called Thursday evening to break up a fistfight over flower arrangements.

There, they encountered two floral designers invited to show their skills for the World Floral Expo engaged in a set-to that left one arranger with a broken nose and another with a cut lip. Before hundreds of onlookers, Thomas Sworez and Giovanni Lucciano traded punches and insults over a purported theft of flowers and copied arrangement techniques.

"There were smashed-up flowers all over the place," said an officer who asked not to be identified. "These guys really got into it. We don't get many

calls like this one."

Could 'Thomas Sworez' be Tomás Suarez? Alvarez ran a search for crime reports or a booking record for the date with New York City or New York State Police, but could find no corresponding file with either agency.

If there were injuries – the broken nose and cut lip referenced in the article – there ought to be an official record, yet none existed. As he had done in Argentina, had Suarez bought his way out of an investigation or used his family's influence to remove the paper trail?

Alvarez plugged in further searches: a program for the 'World Floral Expo', an ad for the event, or anything that might link Suarez. If the designer's temper had been on display as recently as a year ago, then there was no way Alvarez would downgrade him as a suspect.

But half an hour of searching yielded no further evidence. Reluctantly and with some frustration, he abandoned the effort and began planning his day. His first stop, without question, would be the Residences at the Ritz-Carlton. There was nothing like waking up a suspect after three hours sleep.

* * * * *

Liz Phillips awakened half an hour before her six o'clock alarm. She felt energized. The Judges' Dinner had been more than just a convivial get-together among a group of globetrotting designers. There was a renewed sense that she could be a vital part of something.

In her adult life Phillips had been a graduate student, a sales representative for laboratory equipment, a wife, a mother and, most recently, a garden club president. She had maintained an orderly life for her family, managed its many moves, handled its finances and raised a daughter who was now married and achieving success in a corporate career in Seattle.

Her husband's decision five years earlier to launch a one-man management consultancy that took him out of town for months at a stretch had shaken the foundation of her self-identity. With her daughter on the other side of the country and her husband home on weekends, if then, Phillips ran a household that consisted of herself and her cat. She was a vital force in the Hardington Garden Club, but that was hardly a mission in life. Her other volunteer work demanded fewer than ten hours each week.

But IFDA was enticingly different. It was a complex, international undertaking. She was still working to gain an understanding of its finances, but she sensed that the budget for the event was several million dollars and that a fine balance and management skill was required to keep IFDA from careening into a loss-making venture. It had hundreds of what her husband, David, called 'moving parts'. The murder of Valentina Zhukova had profoundly disrupted several of those moving parts. Three committee members had effectively resigned on the spot. Zara Jretnam – who would chair the event two years hence – was feared incapable of carrying out her responsibilities here in Boston.

And she, Liz Phillips, had become one of those parts. Forty-eight hours after Lieutenant Lee's call, she had resolved bona-fide crises and become a trusted, go-to person and listening post for Winnie Garrison.

There was also the appealing thought of spending several weeks in Malaysia two years hence, with intervening trips for planning purposes to other international locales. Phillips had to admit to herself that the glamor held a certain allure.

As she lay in bed she went through the paperwork for the day's speakers program. There were nine talks scheduled, each on a different area of floral design. They were a mix of demonstrations and slide-based lectures. Phillips had to be prepared to assume any role that Jretnam played: she might introduce a speaker, ensure that a PowerPoint presentation carried on a memory stick could be transferred to the computer and projection system supplied by the

Convention Center.

She could become the 'wrangler' for the dozen volunteers who ensured handouts were on chairs at the start of each presentation or she could make certain that the flowers for a demonstration had been properly conditioned and that the volunteers dressed in black who silently carried materials on and off stage and knew the order in which those materials would be required.

Swirling through her mind was the unresolved question of who had killed Zhukova. Phillips had silently listened to the conjecture of the people around her at dinner, well aware that she knew more details about the killing than any of her fellow diners. There was the uncomfortable recognition that Jretnam's behavior could be more than just a reaction to the torment Zhukova had caused her on the evening before her death. Jretnam may have caused that death.

Phillips showered and dressed quickly. She was expected in Garrison's suite at 6:30 for her formal briefing. It has been years since she looked forward to a day with such anticipation.

* * * * *

Vicky Lee, too, was awake at 5:30. Hers had been a troubled sleep: the case, of course continued to shape itself in her mind, but the whole debacle with Matt weighed on her conscience. Had she been too hard on him? Despite his title and absurd compensation, Matt had demonstrated time and again that he was not socially adept. He lived in a world of mathematical models and computer code. He needed to reassure his parents that he was living a normal life. The ring had been a stupid mistake on his part, but it was the kind of social lapse that guys made. His error was more egregious because he could afford to spend that kind of money.

Maybe if she had stayed at the restaurant and talked it out with him; explained to him why what he had done was so hurtful…

Her thoughts were interrupted by the chirping of her phone. It was the special ring tone she reserved for her Captain. If he was calling at this hour it had to be serious. She answered the call on the second ring.

"I need you here at 6:30," he said. There was no pleasantness in his voice. It indicated there would be no formalities and 'here' meant his office at C-6's headquarters on West Broadway. She knew better than to ask about the subject of the meeting.

"I'll be there," she said.

"Good," he responded.

The entire conversation had consisted of just eleven words, which was even more worrisome.

Lee went to her bedroom closet. The next skirted suit in line was black. She skipped over that one and pulled out the dark blue outfit she thought of as being for official occasions.

When they relieve me of duty, she thought, *at least I'll look the part.*

* * * * *

The Ritz-Carlton concierge, a white-haired man of seventy who nonetheless wore an impeccable business suit at 6 a.m., was adamant that "Mr. Bratt" accepted no visitors before noon on weekdays. Alvarez was equally insistent that his Detective's shield trumped any claim to eight uninterrupted hours of sleep. After ten minutes and the threat of arrest for impeding an investigation, the concierge agreed to allow Alvarez onto the elevator.

The door on the seventh floor was opened almost as soon as Alvarez's first knock, an indication that the concierge had promptly forewarned Bratt that a policeman was on his way up.

Ryan Bratt was in his mid-fifties, with a full head of thick dark hair that spoke of individual follicle implants and regular visits to a colorist. His face was well tanned, though puffy from having just been awakened. He wore a bathrobe, but the underlying physique was of someone who regularly worked out at a gym.

"This had better be damn good," Bratt said. Alvarez had never heard Bratt's radio show, but the voice was in keeping with someone who understood what radio audiences wanted to hear: a deep baritone that was undeniably masculine.

"We're at a critical stage of an investigation," Alvarez said.

"What investigation?"

"Valentina Zhukova," Alvarez said.

Bratt muttered an obscenity. "Let's talk in the library."

Alvarez thought it odd that a conversation in a private residence needed to be held behind a closed door. Then he saw a door – presumably a bedroom door – open an inch and remain that way. Bratt was not alone.

"Lemme see those credentials," Bratt said when they were seated in the library, the primary contents of which were stacks of Bratt's essay collections.

Alvarez handed over the plastic case with his badge and identification card.

"Alvarez," Bratt said the name slowly. "Mexican?"

"I was born in Baltimore," Alvarez said. "I need to ask you some questions…"

"Your parents came up from Mexico so you could be born here, right?" Bratt was grinning. "Figure about 1984 or 1985?"

"Perhaps we need to have this conversation in an interrogation room," Alvarez said, his voice cold.

"And if we do that, I'll bring my lawyer who will advise me not to say a thing," Bratt said. "Humor me a minute. So where do your people come from?"

"My grandparents emigrated from Cuba in 1959," Alvarez said. "Now, let's talk."

"I was just yanking your chain," Bratt said, handing back the plastic case. "I'm working on three hours sleep here. I'm a lot more sociable around three in the afternoon."

"You had lunch with Ms. Zhukova on Tuesday afternoon," Alvarez said.

"Yeah, yeah. I did," Bratt said. "Where was that? At the Langham. Café Fleuri. Yeah. So?"

"What did you talk about?"

"I wanted her on my show," Bratt replied. "Been trying to book her for more than a year. Her grandfather was Marshal Zhukov, you know. Hero of the Great Patriotic War. She's like, one of just two or three direct descendants. Or was…"

"Had she agreed?" Alvarez asked.

Bratt made a face. "I was getting close. She wanted an 'appearance fee'. I kept explaining that we don't pay guests, but lots of organizations would hear her on my show and they'd pay big bucks to get her as a speaker."

"I would imagine your show takes a fairly hard line on Russia," Alvarez said.

"So you're not a listener."

"I'm on the job while you're on the air." Alvarez kept his voice neutral. "Ms. Zhukova was probably aware that your audience would give her a hard time…"

"I only wanted her to talk about her grandfather," Bratt said, his voice becoming testy. "No politics. Just history. We were on the same side back then. Or don't they teach history where you went to school?"

Alvarez did not rise to the bait. "Did you see her any time after your luncheon?"

Bratt shook his head. "No. I heard about the murder Wednesday afternoon. A real shame."

"Did you attempt to contact Ms. Zhukova after your luncheon on Tuesday?"

Bratt cocked his head. "That's an odd question. I just said I didn't see her. You mean, like, did I call her or text her? I don't know. I certainly don't remember."

"Were you at the Convention Center Plaza Hotel on Wednesday morning at about three o'clock?"

"'For thirty-five dollars and pieces of silver…'" Bratt said. "Simon and Garfunkel. Way before your time. Almost before my time." He laughed. "I would imagine you wouldn't ask that question unless you knew the answer."

"Were you at the Convention Center Plaza?"

"Yeah, I was." Bratt leaned back in his chair and put his arms behind his head. "Yeah, I was. She wasn't home. Or at least she wasn't answering the door."

"You wore a baseball cap and avoided cameras." Alvarez made it a statement.

"Guys are allowed to wear baseball caps indoors," Bratt said. "It's right there in the Constitution. And I'm a guy who doesn't like people coming up to me and telling me how much they like my program. At least not at three in the morning. And, as to the cameras, I have no idea. But apparently someone saw me and recognized me."

"Why were you at her room?" Alvarez asked.

Bratt grinned. He turned to make certain the library door was closed. "Booty call, Detective Señor Alvarez. A booty call." He indicated the living room and bedroom beyond with a nod of his head. "And in yonder bedroom lies a certain very attractive TV weather lady who would be quite peeved if she knew where I was at that hour of the morning. In her eyes, the fact that I was stood up would not be a defense."

"Where did you go after you left her room?"

"I was never in her room so I couldn't have 'left her room', Detective Señor Alvarez." Bratt's tone had become testy. "I knocked on her door. She didn't respond. It meant one of three things: she wasn't there; she was there but she was sound asleep; or she was there, knew it was me knocking, and had changed her mind. My money was on the first two because the third option was kind of depressing."

"This was a regular thing when she was in town?" Alvarez asked. "You and Ms. Zhukova?"

"We found each other attractive," Bratt said. "She always

initiated it. I knew her politics, but I also know a great body when I see one."

"I'll ask the question again," Alvarez said. "Where did you go after she did not answer the door?"

"I take it that this time you don't know the answer to the question," Bratt said. "You gave it away in how you asked the question. You're going to have to work on that. I left the hotel, I came home. I slept alone, unfortunately."

"The gentleman downstairs will be able to vouch for your time of arrival?"

"I probably used the garage entrance," Bratt said. "But I'm sure you can scrounge up some video feed. So, you don't have this case solved?   I heard some Chinese gal is heading up the investigation. God, what affirmative action paragons we are. Asian and Latino. No Anglos need apply for the all-inclusive Boston Police Department."

"Do you have any thoughts on who may have killed Ms. Zhukova?" Alvarez asked.

"I can't offer you even a scent," Bratt said. "I had a very pleasant lunch with her. I tried once again to get her on my show. She promised to listen to the show, and we made a date for afterward to put aside all political hostilities between our two quarrelsome nations and engage in a little mutual, sensual between-the-sheets pleasure."

The interview ended and Alvarez returned to the lobby. The concierge did not remember Bratt returning to the building Wednesday morning. Garage and elevator videos were kept only twenty-four hours so there was no record of the time Bratt returned. His car had not been moved in six days. Residences did not have entry recorders.

Alvarez had declined to go into questions about Ludmila Karachova's assertion that Bratt passed information to Zhukova. That was the FBI's business, and he didn't want to spoil any surprises the FBI might have in mind for him.

Bratt had given all the right answers and given them very smoothly. Moreover, Bratt had attempted to taunt him with ethnic slurs; hardly a smart move by someone with something to hide. It was a performance, of course. And the fact that it was delivered on a few hours of sleep made it all the more impressive. The question was whether it was all rehearsed?

If Bratt was, indeed, part of Zhukova's intelligence network then there needed to be a well-rehearsed logical explanation for their meeting periodically. Bratt had given just such an explanation, and his responses were plausible.

The lone flaw was the timing of his return to the Ritz-Carlton. Why would someone who was not driving a car use the garage entrance? Alvarez resolved to come back to that question when he had more information.

Chapter 17

Lee did not recognize the tall, thin man in the light gray suit but, by his close-cropped hair, non-descript tie, and wire-rim glasses, she guessed that he was FBI.

"Please sit down," said the Captain. With his left hand he indicated the man in the gray suit. "This is Agent Ken Grimes of the FBI's Boston Field Office. I believe the two of you have spoken."

Grimes nodded but said nothing.

Captain Malcolm Riddle was a large, imposing man. Always attired in his formal uniform, he was known to the men and women of District C-6 simply as 'the Captain'. Only his fringe of white hair against his ebony skin betrayed any sense of age. He had been 'the Captain' for probably two decades. Although the antithesis of the archetypical 'Southie' resident, he knew South Boston better than the longest serving patrolmen in the area. No one had ever heard him laugh and seldom had anyone seen him smile.

Lee was silent. She knew it was best to listen and to respond to questions. When an FBI agent was present for a meeting at 6:30 a.m., it was a sign of something very serious.

"Lieutenant Lee, Agent Grimes has requested the BPD to wrap up its investigation in the matter of Valentina Zhukova. And, by wrap it up, he means pull any people you have working on the case, write up your paperwork, and declare the case closed."

The Captain spread his fingers on the desktop. "Upon hearing that request I expressed my strong reservations. The FBI does not tell the BPD what it can and cannot do. He told me his reasons, and I am asking that he repeat them to you, in person. Hence this meeting." He nodded at Grimes.

Grimes took a manila folder from a briefcase and, from it,

extracted an 8x10 mug shot of a bearded, Latino-looking man. He laid the photo on the table.

"This is Ramon Fortunato," Grimes said. "He is currently being held at an FBI detention center in New Jersey. Mr. Fortunato, who has multiple aliases, is a Venezuelan national. He is a contract killer who will work for anyone who can pay his fee, which is usually around $75,000. When working in the U.S. he usually slips into the country via Miami and travels using one of several aliases that allow him to move about without detection."

Grimes continued. "He is a suspect in at least nine murders in the United States and twice that number in Europe. The South Americans lost count years ago. His usual target is someone in drug trafficking but he does not specialize. He goes where the money takes him. Two months ago, he murdered a witness in a case we had been building against a money-laundering enterprise in Revere. He got sloppy; something he rarely does. He left behind DNA evidence and fingerprints."

"We apprehended him last week," Grimes said. "Since that time, he has been doing nothing but talking. He has been a gold mine of information on cartel activities. On Wednesday morning, though, we discovered another use for him and he has agreed to cooperate."

Grimes extracted an 11x17 sheet of paper bearing a color-coded organization chart, replete with head shots.

Grimes swept his hand across the page. "This is the new Russian nobility. These are the friends of Vladimir Putin. He had made these men billionaires by allowing them to run Russia's petrochemical, mining, construction and shipping industries. When oil was $115 a barrel, Putin could do anything he wanted, including invade Ukraine. Today, it is less than half that price and Putin is dipping into reserves to keep his empire afloat."

"Our friends at another government agency believe that the death of Valentina Zhukova can be the event that drives an irreversible wedge between Putin and the oligarchy that keeps him afloat, and that Ramon Fortunato can be the catalyst."

Grimes tapped a photo on the sheet. "Three months ago, Fortunato was hired by this man, Boris Gusinovich, to murder a London call girl who made the mistake of walking out of Gusinovich's house in Kensington with a half a dozen watches worth, collectively, $400,000. Gusinovich, who is closely tied to Gazprom, has a motto: 'no one steals from me'. Fortunato made a clean hit with no evidence left behind, which impressed Gusinovich sufficiently that he bragged about Fortunato's effectiveness to his friends. And that's our opening."

Grimes opened another folder. "For Gusinovich, the crash in the price of oil has meant having to find new ways to make large sums of money. One of the few areas where the Russian government is investing is in its army, and particularly in cyber-warfare. Everyone wants a piece of that pie: supplying computers, office space, padding the payroll with their friends and cronies." He extracted a photo from the folder. "And this is the number two guy in that cyber-warfare unit, the Department of Special Technical Measures. Yuri Soldatov, who also happens to be Valentina Zhukova's husband."

Grimes slid the photo of Soldatov next to the one of Gusinovich and tapped them with two fingers. "If Gusinovich was pressuring Soldatov to give his companies major contracts – something that is entirely likely – and Soldatov was resisting – also likely – then a thug like Gusinovich might well have upped the ante: 'give me the contracts or else'."

Grimes continued. "And, if Gusinovich hired a hit man to kill a woman because she stole some watches, it requires no leap of logic to assume he'd go back to the same hit man to kill Soldatov's wife. These men get what they want. Brutality is part and parcel of their management skill set."

Grimes returned to the organization chart. "If we can pin

Zhukova's murder on Gusinovich, the repercussions would be huge. Putin would immediately purge Gusinovich, who has a lot of friends, and Putin might even very well have him killed. Gusinovich's friends have been riding the gravy train for more than a decade, courtesy of Putin. But Putin is no longer delivering, and now he is vulnerable. It could very well be the end of Putin."

Lee had listened carefully while Grimes spoke, resisting the urge to comment. Now, she saw her opening. "But a killer goes free," she said.

Grimes nodded. "Yes, a killer goes free. But who is that killer and what was the motive? We've followed your investigation. Captain Riddle has shared your reports to him, and we turned over crime scene photos to the psychologists at the Behavioral Research and Instruction Unit down in Quantico."

Grimes found a photo of the murder scene in the Grand Ballroom. "The folks at Quantico say you are absolutely right. This murder was intensely personal. The person who did this acted on a long-standing animus. The profilers say this person has never killed before and isn't very good at it. But they also say the rage is out of that person's system. This isn't the start of a killing spree."

He returned the photo to its folder. "But let's say that the killer was the Malaysian woman who lost her sister on the airplane shot down over the Ukraine. If you arrest her, you've handed Russia a major propaganda victory. Remember that, in Russia, there is no newspaper or television station that is acknowledging that Russian-backed rebels brought down the plane. Every single media outlet toes the official line. And the Russian government will have a field day with Malaysia perpetuating the 'lie' of Russian complicity."

"And if we arrest Ludmila Karachova?" Lee asked.

"Then we're framing an innocent Russian citizen for the wanton lawlessness and deadly violence that permeates America," Grimes replied.

"We're also looking at Ryan Bratt," Lee said. "He was in the hotel at three in the morning. That brings in an intelligence service connection…"

Grimes interrupted her. "Detective Lee, this murder is being pumped up across Russia. Zhukova was Putin's friend and the living legacy of a national hero. And, if it becomes convenient to acknowledge that she was an intelligence agent, that's not a problem for them. Being a spy in the service of Mother Russia is an honorable profession, and a fitting line of work for the granddaughter of the Man Who Saved Russia."

Grimes returned the folders to his satchel. "We've worked through the suspect list, but with an eye to the international repercussions. No matter who you arrest, it always comes out as a victory for Vladimir Putin and a sharp stick in the eye of Russia's enemies. Except for Ramon Fortunato. If Fortunato killed Zhukova, and he did it at the behest of one of the Russian Robber Barons, then everything implodes on Putin. Our friends in that other government agency seriously believe that Putin would start a bloody purge. And, in the end, he might be gone from power."

There was a moment's silence in the room. The Lee asked, "Why should Fortunato go along with this? Doesn't he risk getting a knife through his neck in some lockup?"

Grimes took off his glasses and looked at Lee. "We have Fortunato dead to rights on the one murder, and he can help us put away a lot of bad guys. But he's willing to help on the Zhukova matter for a very personal reason: he has stomach cancer. He is in a great deal of pain. He knows the cancer is inoperable. But what we've promised him is that he will receive the best medical care in the world and that he will be comfortable. And we will keep that promise. His alternative would be to die a very slow, agonizing death."

The Captain spoke. "Vicky, I wanted you to hear this first hand. I do not ask my Detectives to suborn perjury or to whitewash cases, and my first instinct was to tell Agent Grimes to go to hell. But he made some compelling points and I wanted you to hear them. What I want you to know – and what I want Agent Grimes to hear – is that I will support you in whatever decision you make. You are the primary. You decide."

"Before I decide, I want to know who did this," Lee said.

Grimes shifted uncomfortably. "There's an element of time involved. Last evening, we staged a very noisy and disruptive 'manhunt' for Fortunato down in New York. Our plan is to announce the arrest of Fortunato for Zhukova's murder later today."

The Captain shuffled a stack of papers on his desk and found the one he was looking for. "You asked for vacation time from this afternoon through Tuesday evening. It was approved."

"Those plans have changed," Lee said. "I'm not going anywhere."

A look passed between Grimes and the Captain.

"If and when we make our announcement," Grimes said, "it would be better if you're unreachable. We don't want reporters tracking down anyone in the BPD for comment."

"You might want to consider taking that vacation," the Captain said.

"Let's see what happens this morning," Lee said. "You'll have my answer by early afternoon."

* * * * *

Liz Phillips dabbed jam on a croissant and took a quick bite, then returned to making notes.

Phillips had feared that her presence would be seen by Zara Jretnam as a sign of a lack of confidence on Winnie Garrison's part. Instead, the look on Jretnam's face had been one of relief when Garrison introduced Phillips as the person who would be 'assisting' her throughout the day.

For forty-five minutes they covered details of speaker requirements, with Jretnam suggesting the division of duties.

It was the first time Phillips had the opportunity to observe Jretnam closely. The thing that struck Phillips immediately was the woman's athletic build. This was a wealthy woman in a land where hiring help for even the most menial tasks was both inexpensive and readily accepted. The few Malaysian women whom Phillips had met were slender, with thin arms and legs. Jretnam's clothing showed evidence of muscles. When she turned or rose to get something from elsewhere in the room, there was a quickness to her movement. This was a woman who had a gym and used it, Phillips concluded.

But Jretnam was also a woman dealing with worry, sleep deprivation, or both, Phillips thought. Was it long-term grief over her sister's death? Phillips had heard, second hand, about the barrage of verbal abuse Jretnam had suffered from Valentina Zhukova the evening before her death. Were the involuntary tics she saw a continuing traumatic reaction to what had passed between them? Or, was it possible – as it was also whispered – that Jretnam was the person who had killed Zhukova? Was Phillips seeing the emotion of that event?

She thought back to yesterday morning and helping make the inventory of Jretnam's design cart. Like May Wattanapanit, the Thai designer, there had been no X-Acto knife in Jretnam's cart. Phillips assumed it was a missing X-Acto knife because of the need by every designer for a short, sharp blade to quickly and efficiently cut floral stems. No other tool in Jretnam's cart seemed capable of making such cuts, and she pointed out the missing tool to Detective Alvarez.

Could Jretnam have taken a knife from her own cart, placed it in her purse, used it to confront and then stab Zhukova, and then dropped the knife into the nearest trash can?

"Liz?" It was Garrison's voice.

Phillips snapped out of her musing. "Yes?"

"Did you get that about Tony Todesco wanting one-sided

handouts?"

Phillips nodded, but what she wrote on her pad of paper was, *Has an X-Acto knife been turned into Lost and Found?*

* * * * *

Lee returned to her office following the meeting with the Captain and Agent Grimes. She closed the door, sat in her chair, and placed her head in her hands.

This is the culmination of ten years of law enforcement, she thought. *I am being asked to set aside guilt and innocence and allow some 'greater good' to dictate the outcome of a case.*

There was no precedent in her career or in her training. The code of criminal justice was clear: each case required a resolution; a determination of culpability or the reaching of a dead end because of a lack of leads. Further, a determination of culpability required the affirmation of a court of law. Sometimes, the individual or individuals charged with a crime convinced a judge or jury that they were not guilty of the crime with which they were charged.

Here, though, was an entirely new kind of justice, or lack thereof. As soon as the FBI learned the identity of the woman found murdered in the hotel ballroom, wheels began to turn. They assumed 'responsibility' for the investigation with the full knowledge that they would conclude – complete with a confession – that one Ramon Fortunato would take the fall for the murder.

Why, then, had she been allowed to continue her inquiry? The investigation was already compromised and hobbled by the fact that the FBI had control of all physical evidence. The Medical Examiner's office had turned over not only Zhukova's body, but also the notes and tests performed in those first few hours. The Boston PD did not have access to the crime scene. Even if Lee found what she believed to be the murder weapon, how could she match the weapon to the lacerations on the body? And, even if Lois Otting had re-created her notes after she turned over her originals to the FBI, would it have made a difference? Likely not.

The answer had to be that her investigation was intended to be a charade. The FBI probably had some mild interest in learning the identity of the killer but, from the outset, it was pre-ordained that she would fail for a lack of evidence. The FBI would have a confession and could make the physical evidence conform to that confession.

The thought of this made her feel sick.

She thought of calling John Flynn. The time on her phone read 6:53. Of course he was up and awake. But she needed to resolve this on her own. There would be time, later, to talk with her mentor.

For the next hour, Lee worked through three days' notes and files from her other Detectives. When she was caught up she texted Alvarez and said they needed to meet to review the progress on the investigation. He needed to know. He needed to have input. He also needed to hear it in person.

On her way out, she heard her name called.

"Package for you, Lieutenant." The Desk Sergeant handed her a thick business-size envelope.

She looked at it carefully. It bore only her name plus the words, 'please hand deliver'.

OK, she thought.

She carefully slid her finger under an unsealed part of the flap and pulled it open. Inside was an airline ticket; the old-fashioned kind that she had not seen in years. The kind airlines now charged about twenty dollars to issue in order to discourage customers from requesting them.

It was for a trip to Vancouver, first class. Leaving late this afternoon, changing planes in San Francisco. Returning Monday. She looked at the price and gasped at the $4,168 price.

There was a note attached.

I've been a complete jerk. I don't expect you to forgive me, but the least I can do is to help make your weekend a little more pleasant. Please use these with no strings attached. Tell your folks 'hello' for me. Matt.

She noted the change of planes in San Francisco. *Just in case I change my mind*, she thought.

She put the envelope in her purse and set off for the hotel.

Chapter 18

Jason Alvarez listened as Lee spoke, trying to keep emotion from showing on his face. Inside, his mind was racing. It was a mix of anger, frustration and helplessness. He was on a major case; the kind that made careers. He had been, he thought, days away from being asked to use his computer skills full time. All that was now ashes. His work would go into a sealed file. Officially, it would be the FBI that solved the case while the BPD ran out of avenues of investigation and threw up its hands in a collective act of failure.

There was also the fact that a Latino was going to take the fall. Ramon Fortunato's photograph would be everywhere: a scowling Latino hit man. It was just what the community needed.

Alvarez was rarely conscious of his Hispanic heritage. His grandparents had been born in Cuba, his parents in Miami. He learned to speak Spanish as a child and still considered himself fluent though he had few reasons to speak the language apart from instances when other Detectives said, "Hey, Alvarez, come talk to this guy…"

But the notion that he would be a part – even an insignificant part – of a plan to hang a murder on a Latino man because it fit a narrative developed by the unassailable FBI caused resentment he had trouble keeping under control.

Lee sensed what he was feeling. "We don't have to do this," she said. "If we can make an arrest, we have that option. The Captain will back us up."

"And the FBI will throw a couple of hand grenades in our career path," Alvarez retorted. "We lose either way."

"Are you close on anything?" Lee asked. "Anything that might give us leverage?"

Alvarez shook his head. "Plenty of suspects. Plenty of motive. Nothing conclusive. Nothing I'd take to the Captain."

"Anything in that database magic?"

"I chased a lead on Tomás Suarez for half an hour," Alvarez replied. "It didn't go anywhere. Ray Bratt is a guy who has an answer for everything, all of it smooth as silk. And he knows how to push buttons. Called me a 'Mexican' just to throw me off balance."

"Could either of them be the guy?" Lee asked.

Alvarez shook his head. "I don't have enough to go on with Suarez. I think he has a temper control problem and he could have figured out where to find Zhukova. With Bratt, there's the question of how he would have known Zhukova was in the ballroom. We don't have her phone. I could pull Bratt's cell phone records, but that wouldn't cover any burner cells he uses to reach Zhukova."

"Put Suarez on the back burner for now," Lee said. "Go for Bratt's official phone and see if there's evidence of another one. And get back to that computer of yours. That's the one thing we have that the feds don't."

"What about you?" Alvarez asked.

"I'm going to make one more run at Ludmila," Lee said. "She's had a night to think over what we spoke about last evening. My guess is that she had more to say."

* * * * *

Looking down over the exhibition floor from the top of the escalator, Liz Phillips marveled at the overnight metamorphosis the Boston Convention and Exhibition Center had undergone. The floor of the exhibit hall now sported dozens of banners and colorful directional signs. In the two bays beyond the floral exhibits, vendors selling everything from flowers and gardening tools to thousand-dollar embroidered jackets were putting the finishing touches on booths. Above the floor, a massive

"International Floral Design Alliance – Boston" banner stretched for fifty feet. The show would not be open to the public until 9 a.m. but, already at 8:15, a sizeable but polite crowd had formed in the ticketing lobby.

Phillips took an escalator up to the suites of meeting rooms on the eastern side of the building. Until Wednesday, these talks and design demonstrations had been scheduled for the hotel's ballroom. They had been transferred to the higher-cost BCEC facility by Winnie Garrison, though it was unclear whether the difference in cost would be borne by IFDA or the hotel.

A large meeting room had been set up, theater style, for seven hundred. Declining to take the assurances of a twenty-something BCEC services staff assistant, Phillips checked all microphones to make certain they were 'live' and advanced the first half dozen slides of Garrison's 'Welcome' presentation to ensure they fit the massive screen behind her. There was a pitcher of ice water on the rostrum, a pad for making notes and a foam foot cushion that would allow Garrison and subsequent speakers to stand comfortably for extended periods.

Ten minutes after Phillips had completed her pre-meeting check, she saw Garrison enter the room and waved at her.

"Everything looks ready," Phillips said. "All you need now is a crowd."

Garrison smiled warmly.

"I still have some business at Lost and Found," Phillips said. "If there's nothing else you need me for, I'll take care of that and be back before the start of your presentation."

"I'd rather you put that off for a little while," Garrison said. "You can call me skittish or superstitious or anything else you like, but I'd like you close this morning. You seem to be a sort of good luck charm, and sometimes all the advance planning in the world can't take the place of some good, old-fashioned luck. Besides, I can easily pass that assignment onto someone else."

Garrison took her phone from her purse and scrolled across several screens. "More than anything else, I need one very large favor; one that I didn't want to bring up in the meeting this morning. You probably know that Marie Levy's talk at two o'clock was originally going to be Tina Zhukova's slot. Marie graciously agreed to fill in, but I'm as nervous as a cat about whether she's ready on such short notice. She has agreed to do a dry run in my suite at nine o'clock. I would very much like for you and a couple of people whose judgment I trust to be there and give her honest feedback. She knows how to take criticism; she just has to hear it from people who aren't afraid to tell someone that she's going over the audience's head."

"What's her topic?" Phillips asked.

"Hanging designs," Garrison replied.

"Everything I know about hanging designs would fit comfortably on a three-by-five index card with plenty of room for a cake recipe," Phillips said. "You need…"

"That lack of special knowledge is why I need you," Garrison said, taking Phillips' hand. "The other two people there know the subject well enough that they could deliver the talk if they had brought the right presentation. You are the real audience. Seven hundred people will hear that talk this afternoon and, if Marie talks too much about inset beading techniques or structural armatures, five hundred of those seven hundred people are going to walk out the door. I need a lively talk with enough illustrations to let the audience know they learned something."

"I still need to get to Lost and Found," Phillips said.

Garrison gave a look of mild exasperation. "The dry run starts at nine. If you think you can leave now, do what you need to do between now and then, and be back here for the eleven o'clock talk, then you have my blessing. But please be back at eleven." Garrison gave Phillips's hand one final squeeze. "I admire your dedication to a cause you have taken up so recently."

Phillips walked quickly out of the meeting room. Once she was in the corridor, she picked up her pace. Volunteers were now seated at registration tables and designers – a few of whom she recognized – were milling in the halls. She pretended not to hear the handful of calls of her name. Walking as fast as she could, she opened her purse and took out her phone. It showed 8:46.

She took the long down escalator steps two at a time and, for the first time, saw there were upwards of a thousand people waiting to get into the IFDA exhibit. She had to push through the crowd to get out into the loading area, then skirt cars and taxis to reach the hotel. She went down two flights of stairs and made two turns to get to the Lost and Found office.

We will re-open at 10 a.m. said an elegantly lettered sign.

Phillips wanted to scream.

* * * * *

Lieutenant Lee parked in a 'South End Residents Only' space on Dwight Street opposite the Santa Lucia House and placed her law enforcement placard on her dashboard.

A woman Lee had not met before opened the door seconds after her knock. Lee produced her police credentials.

"I'm Sister Margaret, the House Manager," the woman said. She was attired in black slacks and a gray sweater and appeared to be in her early forties. Her red hair was in a neat bob. Lee was led to the same small office where, twelve hours earlier, she had met with Ann Tretis, the psychologist on call. As she was seated, Lee noticed for the first time the presence of a crucifix on the wall behind the desk.

"You caused quite a stir," said Sister Margaret.

"It wasn't my intention," Lee replied. "I needed to speak to one of your residents as part of an active investigation."

Sister Margaret retrieved a copy of Thursday's *Boston Globe* from a desk drawer. The paper was open to a page in the Metro section with the headline, "*Russian Tourist Found Hanged in Hotel*

Ballroom". Lee had studiously avoided reading or listening to any of the coverage about the case.

"I'm going to take a guess that this is the case you're working on," Sister Margaret said.

Lee nodded.

"I thought the fact that she was Russian was too much of a coincidence," Sister Margaret said, nodding. "Before I go further, you need to understand that we don't provide round-the-clock lodgings here. Rather, we ask that, unless a resident specifically volunteers to help with cleaning and meals, everyone must find a place to go from nine until six. We have supporters who provide day jobs – mostly light cleaning – that keep our residents off the streets and provide some pocket money. Others simply go to a library or other public space."

Sister Margaret shifted in her chair. "I tell you this because the woman you called 'Ludmila' left sometime before dawn this morning. As she took her suitcase with her, I doubt she will be returning."

"After you left, Ann Tretis – with whom I understand you also spoke last evening – and Ludmila had a long talk. Those talks are covered by doctor-patient privilege, but Ann gave me some highlights and said I could pass them on to you when we spoke."

Sister Margaret leaned across the desk, her hands folded as though in prayer. "Ludmila believes she is being pursued by agents from her own country as well as by the FBI. Ordinarily, such claims are a product either of an overactive imagination or of mental instability. Your presence last evening made Ann look more closely at Ludmila's claim and found it entirely credible. Ludmila believes she has no choice but to run. She has no concept of a fair and impartial judicial system or of a government's ability to protect someone, because those concepts do not exist in her country. You are the person she came closest to trusting, but she 'knows' that you cannot protect her."

"She has no money or contacts," Lee said. "She probably can't get out of Boston."

"That may be the case," Sister Margaret said. "Ann also told me that Ludmila is a woman who believes she has nothing left to live for. She did not go into specifics…"

"I had that conversation with her two days ago," Lee said. "I can't disagree with her. Ludmila faces a terrible fate if she goes back to Russia. But she's still a suspect in Valentina Zhukova's death. And so I need to keep looking for her."

Sister Margaret tapped an unadorned fingernail on her desk, as though pondering a next move.

"She left you a note," Sister Margaret said. "I planned to call you this morning." She opened the desk's center drawer and withdrew a letter-size envelope. "Ann suggested she write this."

"You've read it?" Lee asked.

"No, it's not my place."

Lee took the envelope and opened it. The message was hand-written in an almost child-like scrawl.

Lieutenant Lee:

I cannot go back to Russia and I cannot let the FSB find me here. I must go find a safe place.

I did not lie to you tonight but I did not say some things. The most important of these is that I may have said something that caused Valentina's death. When we were finished in the ballroom, I was in the elevator with the designers from Thailand and Germany.

I told them Valentina is the kind of person who does not like to lose competitions. She sometimes plays with other peoples' designs before judges see them. This is a true thing. Then I told them it was a joke. But I saw the angry look on their faces.

I only said that thing because Valentina was very cruel to me.

Ludmila K.

Lee re-read and then re-folded the note.

"Is that helpful?" Sister Margaret asked.

"Maybe," Lee said, placing the letter in her purse. "Because of it I need to check on a few things."

Back in her car, Lee was scrolling through her address book when her phone chimed with a snippet from a Mozart piano concerto.

My parents? She thought. She looked at the phone which showed that not only was it her parents calling, but that the time was 9:04. It was three hours earlier in Vancouver. Warily, she answered the call.

"Is there something you need to tell us?" It was her mother's voice. No prologue, no pleasantries. But the words were spoken not with anger or fear but, rather, with hope or anticipation.

"I… don't know what you mean," Lee replied. "Isn't it awfully early there? Are you home or traveling?"

"We're home," her mother said. "But it looks like we'll be flying out this afternoon. Are you sure you don't want to tell us now?" Her voice had that same lilt that brought with it an expectation of impending good news.

"Flying where?" Lee asked, genuinely not comprehending what her mother was talking about.

"San Francisco!" her mother said. "We just got the tickets from Matt. His email says he wants us to be there for his parents' anniversary and that he may have an announcement of his own. He's even booked us a suite."

Lee dropped her phone, then spent fifteen seconds retrieving it from underneath the driver's seat. Her hand shook as she spoke.

"Mother, don't do anything right now. I promise to call you later. Please, please don't you and Dad do anything right now. I beg you."

"But what…"

Lee tapped the 'end call' icon. She could not cope with this right now. She gripped the steering wheel, her knuckles white from the force.

I do not need this right now….

Five minutes passed before Lee regained her composure. Only when the anger passed did she drive toward the Convention Center Plaza and BCEC.

* * * * *

Liz Phillips did her best to pay attention to the lecture. Marie Levy's PowerPoint presentation contained more than a hundred photos of hanging designs. Though some were tabletop size and some were eight feet across, there was a numbing sameness to them after the first twenty. It was only Levy's lilting French accent that stopped Phillips from speaking up sooner.

Levy knew her elements of design. What she was failing to do was to tie those elements to a handful of examples. At the half-hour mark, Phillips said so in explicit terms.

"But these are all classics," Levy said, and there were murmurs of assent from the two other 'listeners'.

"Start me with one example and build from it," Phillips said. "I once went to a talk by Roy Diblik on the incorporation of environmental principles in landscape design. The first slide up was of a single daylily plant in a sea of mulch in a park. I expected the slide to be up for a few seconds as an example of 'don't do this' Instead, the lecturer used that forlorn daylily to build his entire case. By the time he went on to 'good' landscapes, we knew what we were looking for."

Levy looked baffled. The other two women began to make noises defending Levy's presentation.

Phillips looked down at her notes. "Go back to the fifth slide. It has everything you need."

"But my talk is at two o'clock," Levy protested. "I cannot change it now. It is too late."

"It will be a much better talk if you do," Phillips countered.

"I wish we had photos of the designs done in the ballroom," one of the women said. "I hear they were stunning."

"I have some," Philips said. "I was in the ballroom the next day. They're on my phone."

Five minutes later, four photos had been mailed, received, downloaded, formatted and transferred to the PowerPoint program.

Looking at the four photos, Phillips winced and wished she had taken more time to compose them. To the three women, it was a revelation.

"This is the 'oomph' factor," said one. "To the best of my knowledge, only half a dozen people at the conference have seen those designs. You can talk about just these and everyone's attention will be riveted. We don't need anything else. These are the presentation."

Phillips looked at her phone. It was 9:57.

"Why don't the three of you work on the words and we'll try another dry run at noon?" Phillips asked.

Everyone agreed that they would be ready at noon.

At ten o'clock, Phillips was at Lost and Found. Leilani was looking over a printout.

"I'm looking for an X-Acto knife," Phillips said.

"I have no idea what that is," Leilani said. "Let me get the knife box."

Phillips held her breath until the box was retrieved. Leilani placed it on the counter. In ten seconds, Phillips knew she was wrong. There was no X-Acto knife in the box, much less one with blood traces or one that could be traced back to Zara Jretnam.

I was so certain, she thought.

"Was it valuable?" Leilani asked.

Phillips shook her head. "Just the opposite. It's one of those utilitarian things floral designers use. But for a few hours, I was convinced I had the solution to who committed a murder."

"The Russian woman?"

Phillips nodded. "I inventoried a group of carts for the police.

One – actually, two – of the designers had carts that were missing that kind of a tool. I had this vision that the killer used it, then threw it into a trash can. I'd find it here, with the blood still on it. I guess I was daydreaming."

Phillips added, "But right now I have to be at the Convention Center to make certain there's a pitcher of water for a speaker. I do have some items to look for. I'll be back a little later."

Leilani smiled. "I'll be here."

* * * * *

Detective Alvarez had crossed-indexed Ryan Bratt's cell phone with every call made on it during the preceding week. Two innocuous, one-minute calls led him to a so-called 'pay as you go' phone that yielded a cornucopia of information. There were a dozen calls to a "0117812" number – an international call to a telephone registered in St. Petersburg, Russia.

For someone who claimed only to be attempting to book the granddaughter of a Russian hero for a local talk show, Bratt made a great many calls to a number that likely was the FSB-issued device Alvarez had found in Zhukova's room on Wednesday morning.

The phone information helped make a case that Bratt was involved in espionage, and Alvarez dutifully organized it to give to the FBI. But as a lead to tying Bratt to the killing of Zhukova it was a dead end. Bratt had called Zhukova's number about the time his call-in show ended, then again when he was in the hotel. Both calls were under twenty seconds: long enough for the caller to go to a voice mailbox, and to hang up without leaving a message.

His great fear from earlier in the morning was being realized: the Boston Police Department's official investigation would reach a dead end. The FBI would announce that they had caught the killer after a manhunt that led them to New York. And a Latino male whose mug shot showed a vicious scowl would be the official killer. All over Boston, mothers would see that photo and show it to their children: *stay away from people like this.*

His feeling of failure was so great that he nearly did not bother to check his database management system. For two days it had been producing little but repetitive Russian propaganda about the evils of America, all now firmly planted in the fresh, rich soil of the murder of a golden granddaughter of the closest thing Russia had to royalty.

He idly glanced at topics. There was a query: *"Did you mean OSOAVIAKHIM?"* He hit the tab. *"DBMS has found 3 relationships for 'Operation Ossavakim'. There are additional relationships for 'Operation Osoaviakhim'. Do you wish to view these relationships?"*

Alvarez could not remember 'Operation Osoaviakhim' but he hit 'yes'.

The results came tumbling out.

The first was an excerpt from Google Books. At some time in the last decade, a book had been scanned and uploaded into a server. Webcrawlers had digested key words from it, awaiting a summons that might never come to produce the full text. Alvarez read:

Zhukov's signing on May 1, 1946 of Order 140 set in motion the effort that would culminate five months later with the NKVD's Operation Osoaviakhim. Zhukov personally selected more than a hundred Soviet officers under his command for the project, looking for a combination of intelligence and ruthlessness.

Within days, requests were issued at targeted factories for organizations charts. Those charts defined the critical roles within the companies: those who had designed and built specialized machinery, those who operated it, and those who maintained it. Factory managers were asked to identify the specific people in those posts.

While most companies readily complied with the requests, other German industrial managers connected the demands with the wholesale dismantling of factories going on within the Soviet Occupation Zone. When the information sought came to include names and ages of spouses and children, there could be little doubt of the Soviets' intent.

Some factory owners – especially those with multi-generation family ownership – stopped cooperating entirely. The results were deadly. In Leipzig, Otto Romfh, the fifth-generation owner of the sprawling Romfh Kugellagerfabriken that produced precision ball bearings, was publicly hanged for 'anti-government activities' with Marshal Zhukov in attendance…

Alvarez stopped at the word 'hanged'. His fingers went over the screen, settling on the word.

Here was a clue.

Rapidly, he scrolled through other results until he found from the 1939 German Census:

Romfh, Otto b. 12 Dec. 1896
Romfh, Gretel b. 6 May 1898
Romfh, Carl b. 9 Aug. 1935
Romfh, Elise b. 4 Dec. 1938

He narrowed his search to Carl and Elise Romfh. The August 1950 East German census showed Gretel, Carl and Elise still living in Leipzig. The December 1964 East German census showed only Carl. The January 1971 census showed:

Romfh, Carl b. 9 Aug. 1935
Romfh, Petra b. 22 Nov. 1937
Romfh, Eva b. 8 Jan. 1960

Alvarez crossed his fingers and switched to marriage records, hoping that such records were searchable. He was rewarded with:

Kirk, Josef and Romfh, Eva; Leipzig 3 May 1985

Eva Kirk's grandfather had been hanged on the order of Valentina Zhukova's grandfather.

For the first time, there was motive.

Alvarez had paid little attention to Eva Kirk. She had said all the right things at the interview Wednesday morning. Then, she had come forward later in the day to provide the information that Ludmila Karachova was the real designer, something she knew because she learned to speak Russian as a child in East Germany. With that clue, he and Lieutenant Lee had shifted their interest to

Zhukova's background and Karachova's role.

But it was hardly proof. It was only the beginning of a trail. Alvarez reached for his phone and called Lieutenant Lee.

Chapter 19

Lieutenant Lee read Alvarez's iPad screen as he explained the trail he had found. Lee, in turn, showed Alvarez the note written by Karachova, saying she had warned Kirk and Wattanapanit that Zhukova was not above tampering with competitors' designs.

"Is this enough to bring her in for questioning?" Alvarez asked.

"Not until I've spoken with the Captain," Lee said. "And I don't go to see him until we have something more solid. You keep on your computer. See if there are any images we can use when we talk to her. Those can be very powerful. I'm going to call Lois Otting and see if she has anything left in her file or her memory that might help us with physical evidence."

Lee then glanced at the corner of Alvarez's iPad. It was exactly noon. Sometime in the next few hours, the FBI was going to announce that they had a confession from Zhukova's murderer. A Venezuelan contract killer named Ramon Fortunato.

* * * * *

Liz Phillips looked at the crush of people below her on the Convention Center floor. There were easily thousands of people down there. They milled around floral designs, they congregated at the large freestanding displays and they browsed the vendor booths. IFDA was an unqualified success.

She pushed politely through a crowd of people waiting to get on the down escalator and made her way to the exits where two charter buses disgorged passengers.

She was five minutes late getting to the suite and, as soon as she entered she was greeted warmly.

"We have ordered up lunch from room service," Marie Levy said. "I hope you like a small steak and salad. It should be here in five minutes."

The three women had indeed made progress and they spoke in animated tones about the use of the four ballroom exhibits. Phillips was given full credit for pointing Levy in a better direction.

"We have just one problem," said one of the women. "Whether it's the lighting or something else, we keep finding visual flaws in three of the designs. They aren't the kind of things that you notice on first glance; they just annoy you after a while."

"Show her," the woman said to Levy. Levy, in turn, tapped her computer to life and pulled up the first photo.

"We are fairly certain this is Tomás Suarez's design," Levy said. "Beautiful rhythm and ingenious proportion. It is as though a sphere wants to do the tango, if that's possible." She pulled her fingers apart on the screen to enlarge a detail of the image. "But look here: right in the middle of these wonderful swirls of red and gold roses, we get what look like red-orange tulips. There are just a few, but they upset the color scheme."

"I took these photos early Thursday morning," Phillips said. "Plus, they're taken with my phone. Granted, it's twelve megapixels, but it's still a phone, not a 'real' camera. Also, no one had watered the designs since they were completed. There were already spent flowers on the floor."

"Maybe," one of the women said. "But these look like tulips." Turning to Levy, she said, "Show her May Wattanapanit's design."

Levy advanced to the next photo. "Again, beautiful work. Orchids and plumeria. You could teach a master class using this design." She again spread her fingers apart. "But look here." She indicated a sea of white orchids. "Why on earth would May put cream carnations into the mix? It is the sort of thing that drives judges crazy."

"Liz, do you know if anyone took photos of the designs the evening they were completed?" one of the women asked.

Phillips thought for a moment. "Kathy Thomas was there. She was helping May Wattanapanit. She's never without a camera. Her cell phone number ought to be on Winnie Garrison's emergency contact list."

A quick look around the suite turned up a phone list. Thomas said she indeed had fifty or more shots taken at 3 a.m. when everyone agreed there was nothing more to be done on the designs. She could be up to the suite in fifteen minutes.

"It would be nice to straighten this out," Levy said.

There was a knock at the door. It was lunch. Four trays were set on the conference table. "We can talk and eat," Levy said. "I just cannot believe I am changing my talk two hours before I am supposed to give it."

Phillips looked at the steak and salad; it was not the kind of lunch she would have chosen for herself but she appreciated being included. The three women were acknowledged stars in the tight-knit floral design world. She was a rank amateur whose role was supposed to be to agree with what the others said.

At the Northeast Garden and Flower Show where she oversaw the work of two hundred judges evaluating fifty or more landscape exhibits, the usual way judging panels were filled was to appoint two well-known and respected horticulturalists, and then fill out the third spot in the panel with a 'pigeon'. The pigeon was someone identified by the donor development staff of the New England Botanical Society as a prospective large contributor, and the reality of being in the presence of a famous landscaper or horticulturalist for a morning often led to the writing of a large check to the Society immediately afterwards.

Was she the pigeon? Was someone going to take her aside and ask if she would write a large check to IFDA? Or did Winnie Garrison truly believe Phillips had good instincts?

Listening to the chatter around her, Phillips cut into her steak. Placing the bite in her mouth, she replaced the fork and steak knife on the plate. There seemed to be no place in the discussion where she could interject a useful opinion and so she picked up the knife and fork to cut another bite of the succulent steak.

As she did, her hands froze.

The steak knife.

She had seen this steak knife before, or one exactly like it. Eight inches long, a medium-brown wooden handle with two gold-colored rivets. A sharp point and a serrated blade. Not some ridiculously expensive…

She laid the knife on the table and slowly rotated it. The three women stopped talking and watched her.

"Is something wrong?" one of the women asked.

Oh, my God… Phillips thought.

"I have to leave," she said. "I'm sorry, but I just thought of something very important I have to do… Please, go on without me."

Grabbing her purse, Phillips raced to the door and to the elevator. She stabbed at the down button.

Let her be there…

Four minutes later, Phillips was at Lost and Found. Leilani greeted her with a smile. "Back so soon?" she said.

"May I look at the knives again?" Phillips said, trying not to show the anxiety she felt. "I hate to be a pest…"

"Most fun I've had all week," Leilani said. "In fact, it's the *only* fun I've had all week." She went into the storage room and returned a moment later with a plastic bin.

Two hours earlier, Phillips knew she was looking for an X-Acto knife. It had taken her just a few seconds to know there was no matching item in the bin. Now, she used a ballpoint pen to gingerly push knives apart.

"Would it help to spread them out on the counter?" Leilani asked.

There were perhaps thirty knives in all. Half were Swiss Army knives. There were several professional looking hunting knives and Phillips briefly wondered why someone would have such a knife in a convention hotel.

Then her eye fell on the black-handled knife. Three rivets, well-worn but also well cared for with a blade edge that, even to the unaided eye, had been kept exceedingly sharp. The blade read, *'Zwilling J.A. Henckels'* with a square logotype. It was a small kitchen knife with a four-inch-long blade. It was the same size as the steak knife she had handled a few minutes earlier.

And the steak knife was the same as the one in Eva Kirk's design cart. The knife in the Lost and Found bin was a smaller version of the Henckels knives that were in the foam cut-outs.

There was no visible blood, but Phillips knew from watching an endless procession of criminal investigation dramas on television that blood traces lurked in crevices.

Maybe this was nothing. But maybe Eva Kirk had thrown the knife into a hotel waste basket, never suspecting that the trash would be meticulously sorted for recycling.

Phillips took a deep breath. She asked, "Has anyone else been down here to look at these knives?"

Leilani said no one other than Phillips had expressed any interest in knives in more than a week.

Phillips took her phone from her purse and found Lieutenant Lee's business card. She dialed the number. The call was answered on the third ring.

"Lieutenant Lee, I think I have something you want to see. It's a knife that I think belongs to Eva Kirk. I'm in the hotel's Lost and Found office." Phillips provided directions.

"Ms. Leilani," Phillips said, "either I've just helped find a clue to a murder or else there's a memo that's going to go around to every police department in Massachusetts saying to never, ever take a phone call from me."

* * * * *

Lee stared at her phone, unable to accept what she had just heard.

Alvarez looked at her, puzzled. "Was that good news or bad?"

Lee placed the phone back in her purse. "Unless Liz Phillips is completely Looney Tunes, which she gives no evidence of being, she may just have found the murder weapon. And she says it belongs to Eva Kirk."

Five minutes later, Phillips was explaining that Kirk's design cart contained four knives, each in a foam cutout. Three of them were distinctive Henckels pieces, the fourth was a steak knife that fit the allotted cavity but was not part of the set.

"I noted it to the technicians," Phillips said. "And I saw that they typed it into their notes. But I didn't think anything about it until a few minutes ago when I held one of the hotel's steak knives in my hand. It was the same type of knife as I saw in Eva Kirk's design cart, right down to the two, gold-colored rivets…"

Phillips stopped and opened her purse. There was a look of chagrin on her face. "In fact, I apparently took the one I was using with me. Here it is."

Using his phone's camera, Alvarez had carefully photographed the array of knives on the counter. Then, using latex gloves to ensure no further contamination of the evidence, he gingerly removed all but the black-handled knife Phillips had pointed to. Now, he took the steak knife from Phillips and laid it alongside the Henckels one on the counter. He photographed the two together.

"What made you think the knife might be here?" Lee asked.

"One of my responsibilities has been to retrieve things from Lost and Found," Phillips said. "Leilani showed me how the contents of every waste receptacle gets sorted. I saw the bin full of knives and just thought… it was worth looking at."

Lee nodded. In her mind she wondered why she had not thought of doing the same, and quickly concluded it would have been too much of a long shot; a waste of valuable time.

"Does any of this make sense?" Phillips asked.

Lee hesitated before answering. "Let's say that it complements some other information we've gathered and we need to take this very seriously." She turned to Alvarez. "Get two really good techs down here with full analysis gear. Get statements and fingerprints from everyone in the hotel who is associated with trash recycling. We need to establish a chain of custody."

She stopped. "What happened to the carts? And the techs' notes?"

Alvarez said, "The FBI kept only the cart shared by Zhukova and Karachova. They also took the notes though I suspect the files are still on the techs' computers. I had the hotel return the carts to their owners."

"What about Lois's autopsy notes?"

"The FBI has all the physical evidence," Alvarez said. "But I think she's smart enough to have kept duplicates of her notes."

Lee listened and digested what she heard. If there were blood traces on the knife in Lost and Found, there was a foundation for an arrest. But the FBI had a very different agenda and their resolution of the case was built around geopolitical concerns.

She needed to talk to the Captain.

Lee's thoughts were interrupted by the chiming of a phone. Phillips looked at her phone, apparently not seeing a familiar number.

"I can take this in the corridor," Phillips said. "May I leave for a moment?"

Lee nodded consent.

Phillips tapped open the connection. The voice was the distinctive one of Kathy Thomas. "I heard you rushed out of here like you just saw a ghost," Thomas said.

"This isn't a good time…" Phillips said.

"You really want to get back up here," Thomas interjected. "We've got a real mystery on our hands. Maybe you have some ideas. If you're still in the hotel, please come back up. Marie goes on in a little over an hour and it would be nice to clear this up."

Phillips went back into the Lost and Found office.

"Do you need me right now?" she asked.

"I need to get a statement," Alvarez said.

"Can it wait for…" Phillips picked a plausible time frame. "…half an hour?"

Alvarez looked at Lee, who nodded imperceptibly. He took a card from his wallet. "Call me as soon as you're free."

* * * * *

Phillips rode the elevator to the eleventh floor. *"We've got a real mystery on our hands…"* She walked briskly to the end of the corridor and Winnie Garrison's suite. She opened the door. Four women were looking at images projected on a wall, everyone talking excitedly. Framed prints had been removed from the wall, the curtains were drawn and all lights turned off.

Thomas motioned Phillips to look closely at the image on the wall. It was two images in one frame. Both were of one of the four hanging designs from the ballroom ceiling. One, Phillips knew, she had taken. The second, shot from a slightly different angle, was by someone else, presumably Thomas.

Thomas wielded a laser pointer. "Look at this," she said to Phillips. "This is the photo I took, according to the jpeg stamp, on Wednesday morning at 2:55 a.m. This is Tomás Suarez's design." She then moved the laser pointer to the adjoining image. "This is your photo. The time stamp is Thursday at 7:18 a.m. Twenty-eight hours later."

Thomas circled a spot on her own photo. "Look here. Red and gold roses." She went to the same location on Phillips' photo. "Six reddish-orange tulips have been added." She turned off the pointer. "This is just one example, but you and I were standing in almost exactly the same spot when we took these two photos and the red and gold roses are dead center in both photos. Someone added those tulips after we left."

Thomas asked for the next slide. "This is your photo of May

Wattanapanit's design. I know every flower in it because I placed every single one of them." She turned on the laser pointer and circled an area. "I'll swear on a stack of bibles that not only did I not put any carnations in that design, May didn't have any in her flower tubs. And, if she *had* them and told me to add them to the design, I would have told her she needed to 're-think' the idea." Thomas asked for the next photo. "Here's the one I took Wednesday morning. No carnations."

Thomas walked over to a table lamp and turned it on. "If fact, none of us used carnations, and the only tulips were in Eva Kirk's design, and those tulips were a honey yellow." She walked to another lamp and turned it on. "Between three o'clock Wednesday morning and seven o'clock Thursday morning, three of the four designs got additional flowers. Not enough to scream at you. Just enough, as Marie said, to annoy you if you looked at them long enough."

"And the one that didn't have additional flowers was Eva Kirk's," Phillips said.

Thomas looked at her, shook her head and smiled. "Wrong. The one that wasn't monkeyed with was Valentina Zhukova's."

Phillips was speechless. She thought about the Grand Ballroom and the four hanging designs, one with a puddle of blood beneath it. While she was brought to the ballroom by Lee after Zhukova had been taken down and the wire removed, she assumed the sphere with the blood underneath it was Zhukova's design.

"Lieutenant Lee brought everyone in for questioning in the ballroom," Phillips said. "You saw the crime scene. By the time you got there a big circle of carpet had been cut out from underneath one of the designs. You didn't notice whose design that was?"

Thomas laughed. "Honey, we were working on three hours sleep. We were dragged into the ballroom and told Valentina had been murdered – hanged. I saw everything I wanted to see in about three seconds. Your Lieutenant Lee was kind enough to let us keep our backs to the crime scene while she asked us questions and that suited me just fine."

Phillips also remembered all the tables that had been pushed away from the crime scene by the time the designers were brought into the ballroom. They formed a visual barrier such that no one could see the floor from the vantage point of where the questioning had taken place. All anyone could see were the spheres.

"Lieutenant Lee never asked everyone to identify their designs," Phillips said, as much to herself as to the group. Then she said, "Marie, let's look at Valentina Zhukova's design."

Levy advanced the projector two images.

"Kathy, you're certain this was Valentina's?" Phillips asked.

"I remember every tantrum she threw," Thomas said. "Of course it was hers."

"And this is the one that no one tampered with." Phillips asked, wanting to be absolutely certain.

Thomas nodded.

Phillips drew a deep breath. "The blood was under Eva Kirk's design. Presumably, Zhukova was also hanged from that design."

"Oh, my God," said two of the women simultaneously.

"Then what happened?" Thomas asked.

A thought struck Phillips; a remembered snippet of a conversation. "Yesterday during judging. I was clerking for a group of women who were telling stories about Zhukova," she said. "Gossip, really. 'She was murdered by the Russian Mafia', things like that. But one of the women said Zhukova had a reputation for 'making little changes' to other designs after everyone was done but before the judges started their work."

"But Eva Kirk?" one of the women asked. "Why would she do something like that?"

More conversations swirled inside Phillips' head. "At the Judges' Dinner last night. The woman seated next to me was telling a story about being on a bus tour with Zhukova through the eastern part of Berlin. Zhukova was telling everyone about how her grandfather – the great Marshal Zhukov – saved the country from starving. The tour bus guide apparently offered some polite disagreement and Zhukova exploded. Eva Kirk told me she was born and raised in East Germany and hated being dominated by the Russians."

"You mean it was personal?" Levy asked.

Phillips shook her head. "I don't know…" She thought about mentioning the knife in Lost and Found but thought better of it. "I think we need to get the police here."

"I speak at two o'clock," Levy said. "I really can't stay."

"I'm reasonably sure the only people the police will need to speak with are Kathy and me," Phillips replied. "We took the photos. Kathy can say definitively which design belonged to whom."

Phillips stepped into the corridor as the women continued their discussion. She tapped a number into her phone.

"Detective Alvarez," she said. "I think I have another piece of the puzzle."

* * * * *

Thirty minutes later, Alvarez had reviewed the photos, uploaded them to his iPad and taken statements from Phillips and Thomas.

Only after they had left the conference room he had commandeered for the meeting did he allow his anger to rise to the surface.

The damned FBI.

They had hijacked the investigation within hours after he and Lieutenant Lee had begun it. They had seized the physical evidence and shared nothing except their ludicrous plan to use a murder to destabilize a country.

But in the process the FBI had made the Boston Police

Department – and him especially – look stupid and inept. The ballroom had been sealed within hours. There was no way to do follow-up interviews because there was nothing to follow up on; the evidence was now somewhere in an FBI room, and probably in Washington or New York.

He also marveled at how a civilian – Liz Phillips – had pieced together two critical pieces of evidence using nothing but perseverance and intuition. In a more orderly investigation he would have reviewed all of the physical evidence, or so he told himself. He would have noticed the out-of-place knife and kept asking questions until its significance was uncovered.

Most importantly, he would have learned within hours that Zhukova had been killed beneath and then hung from Eva Kirk's sphere. The investigation would have immediately focused on her. He would likely have already had a confession in hand.

Damn the FBI.

But he could also have done those things even without the handicap. Though the one man and five women in the ballroom were groggy from lack of sleep and uncomfortable from being at the scene of a fresh murder, it would have taken thirty additional seconds to have each woman identify the arrangement on which they had worked. He had not done so because it did not seem important at the time. Further, he sensed their discomfort at even looking at the crime scene and did not want them made even more uncomfortable.

Now, two and a half days later, he realized that oversight – that lapse in the investigation – had been the single most crucial error. It was a rookie mistake. And somehow, sometime in the future, he would be reminded of that mistake.

His phone showed that it was 1:30. He needed to call Lieutenant Lee before she spoke with the Captain.

* * * * *

Lee was sitting outside the Captain's office, waiting for him to finish a phone call, when her phone began playing the snippet from the *William Tell Overture*. She looked at the Caller ID and immediately pressed the 'connect call' icon.

Five minutes later, the Captain beckoned her to come into his office.

"That was the FBI. They're timing their announcement for the evening news cycle," the Captain said. "Four o'clock here and midnight in Moscow. They'll make the announcement from here, but it will be Washington people doing the talking. They want us on hand to share the credit. Are you good with that?"

"We have the murderer," Lee said. "The real one."

"You haven't been keeping me up to date," the Captain said.

"This all happened today," Lee said. "In fact, we're still processing what we believe is the murder weapon."

"Then tell me everything," he said.

"Eva Kirk," Lee said. "One of the designers who worked alongside Zhukova Tuesday night. It was personal on two levels. Zhukova's grandfather, Marshal Zhukov, headed the occupation army in the Soviet Zone for a year after World War II. Part of his job was to dismantle German factories and ship those factories back to Russia, sometimes with the key personnel. Kirk's grandfather owned a ball-bearing firm the Russians wanted. He dragged his heels. Zhukov ordered him hanged as a warning to other factory owners."

Lee took out the note left for her by Ludmila Karachova and showed it to the Captain. "Then, as Kirk was riding back up to her room, Zhukova's assistant let slip that her boss may have remained behind to tinker with everyone's designs – something she apparently had a habit of doing when she thought she could get away with it. Zhukova wasn't stabbed under her own flower arrangement; it was Kirk's."

The Captain nodded. "And you want permission to bring her in."

Lee nodded. "But it is your call. You understand the lay of the land."

The Captain leaned back in his chair and looked at Lee for perhaps a minute. Finally, he said, "Bring her here. Let's do this formally. I'll ask the FBI if they want to be present, and I think I know their answer." He added, "You do know where to find her?"

Lee hoped the answer was 'yes'.

* * * * *

Alvarez hovered over the two crime scene technicians who used Luminol in the now-darkened and black-lighted Lost and Found office to determine that there was both blood on the Henckels knife and that there had been an effort to wipe it clean. All of this was documented on video. The knife would now go to a forensics lab to analyze the blood – whether it was human or animal and, if human, what further information could be drawn from it.

There would also be an intense effort to recover fingerprints from the knife. Obtaining all that information, he knew, could take four to eight hours even with calls from those well up the chain of command.

Lee's most recent call gave him the timeline and resources: two detectives would complete the taking of statements from everyone associated with the knife's discovery. Alvarez needed to turn his notes from his conversation into a coherent narrative. A warrant was being prepared to bring Eva Kirk's design cart to the District C-6's headquarters.

Oh, and he also had the task of locating Kirk and getting her to West Broadway before 3 p.m.

At 2:12, he entered the large meeting room where six hundred designers watched in near darkness as a woman with a French accent spoke at the podium while discussing a photo spread across a fifty-foot-wide screen behind her.

Alvarez did a double take as he saw the photo: it was one of the designs from the ballroom. The woman was discussing it in animated tones, using a laser pointer to describe its merits.

Jesus Christ, he thought.

He had stationed policeman at each of the three entrances to the meeting room. They had an enlargement of Kirk's passport photo and the added information that Kirk now wore her blonde hair short.

He waited for his eyes to adjust. The reflected light from the screen was the only illumination in the room and the photo was not especially bright. While he had a flashlight, he was hesitant to use it. He did not want to call attention to himself.

After ten minutes Alvarez had scanned less than a quarter of the audience. The image changed. He glanced up and saw it was Eva Kirk's flower-filled sphere. The speaker began analyzing it, moving the laser pointer around the massive screen.

From the corner of his eye he saw a movement. A woman near the back of the room rose from her seat and began inching down the line of seated attendees, some of whom stood but most remained in their seats. The woman was the right height and he thought he caught a glimpse of blonde hair.

He walked quickly up the aisle. The woman reached the end of the seat row and turned toward the door, never glancing back into the room.

He was twenty feet away when she opened the door and went out. Alvarez raced toward the exit, reaching it a few seconds after it had closed.

Let the policeman see her, he thought. *Let him be doing his duty.*

When he pushed open the door, he immediately heard the altercation.

"….You have to wait for the Detective to clear you, ma'am."

"I do not have time to be 'cleared', I must leave now," the woman said angrily.

"I have no choice, ma'am…"

The woman turned to sidestep the policeman.

It was Eva Kirk.

"I'll take it from here, Officer," Alvarez said. Turning to Kirk, he said, "I've been asked to take you to my district headquarters for a formal interview." He spoke quietly but firmly.

"And if I refuse?"

"The Officer and I will see that you get to the interview." He was polite but he left no room for doubt as to the outcome.

Chapter 20

The Interview Room at District C-6's headquarters was a plain, beige rectangle containing a conference table and four hardback chairs; two on either side of the table. A mirror ran the length of one wall. Occupants of the room assumed it was one-way glass and that they were being observed from the other side. They were inevitably correct.

Three people were in the Interview Room. Lieutenant Lee and Detective Alvarez sat on one side of the table with their backs to the mirror. Eva Kirk sat on the other side. She stared at the mirror; not looking at her own reflection but at whomever was on the other side, unseen.

Lee began. "Ms. Kirk, we have asked you here to respond to certain information regarding the death of Valentina Zhukova that has come to our attention since our last interview. Detective Jason Alvarez and I have gone over specific details of the events of Tuesday evening and Wednesday morning. We ask for your cooperation in reconciling our recent discoveries with the account you gave us Wednesday morning and a voluntary statement you made Wednesday afternoon."

"Am I under arrest?" Kirk asked.

"You are not under arrest," Lee replied.

"Must I answer your questions?"

"You have the right to say nothing, but because this is an interview seeking facts, you could potentially face an obstruction of justice charge at a later date if we learned that you hindered our investigation."

"May I have an attorney?"

"I stress that this is an interview seeking facts," Lee said. "You are not under arrest."

"English is not my first language," Kirk said. "May we conduct this interview in German?"

"Only if you wish to remain in our custody overnight while we find a fluent German speaker."

"May I have someone from my embassy present?"

"Germany has only a consulate in Boston and the Consul's specialty is in trade issues," Lee replied. "It might take several days for the German Embassy to determine if they wanted to send someone and, in the end, they might refuse. You would be in our custody during that time."

Kirk paused. Finally, she said, "Ask your questions."

Lee placed a photo in front of Kirk. "This is a design you did for the International Floral Design Alliance here in Boston. Is that correct?"

Kirk looked at the photo for an unnecessarily long time before saying, "Yes, it is."

"That first photo was taken at approximately 3 a.m. by one of the assistants who helped the designers assemble their work." Lee placed a second photo in front of Kirk. "This photo was taken by a crime scene technician at 6:15 a.m., just over three hours later. Do you see any difference between the two photos?"

Kirk again studied the photo for almost a minute. "No, should I?"

Lee took out two more photos. "Here is a detail from the 3 a.m. photo and the same area at 6:15. Do you see the areas highlighted?"

Kirk studied the two photos at length. "There are additional flowers in the later photo."

"Do you know how they came to be there?"

"I know I did not place them there."

"Do you know who did place them in your design?"

"I cannot say with certainty, and I would not care to speculate on something for which I was not certain."

Lee nodded at Alvarez, who went to a corner of the room and took a cloth cover from an object. It was Kirk's floral design cart. He opened the top of the cart, revealing an array of tools, each in a foam cutout.

"Is this your design cart?" Lee asked.

"It appears to be mine. I could not say for certain without examining every item in it."

Alvarez removed the top layer of foam, revealing the layer with, among other objects, the knives.

"Then we'll make this easier," Lee said. "Are the objects you see here yours?"

Kirk peered at the objects. "I have ones very similar to these."

"I call your attention to the three black knives. Are those yours?"

"I have ones just like them. They could be mine."

"Let me stipulate that your fingerprints are on these knives," Lee added.

Kirk shrugged. "Then they must be mine."

"The fourth knife," Lee said. "The brown one. Is that yours as well?"

Kirk again shrugged. "It, too, must be mine."

Lee leaned across the table toward Kirk. "Would you be surprised to know that we found blood on this knife? We have very sophisticated tests we can run on objects to find blood on them, even if they have been washed."

For the first time, Kirk smiled. "I would be very surprised indeed. But I have no idea how it got there."

"It was animal blood," Lee said. "Cow blood to be specific. This knife was used to cut a steak. We're curious how it came to be in your design cart. You said it was yours."

The response took the smile off of Kirk's face. "I do not know how it came to be in my cart. Perhaps I placed it there accidentally."

"Would you like something to drink or eat?" Lee asked. "I was thinking about a cup of coffee."

"Let us continue," Kirk said, her voice cold. She thought she had won a point. Instead she had lost one.

"Then let us go back to Wednesday afternoon," Lee said. "You came to us with the information that Valentina Zhukova was not really a floral designer. You overheard her speaking, in Russian, to her assistant, Ludmila Karachova. Is that correct?"

Kirk paused, processing Lee's words. She sensed no hidden meaning. "Yes, that is correct."

Lee pushed two sheets of paper across the table. "This is the statement you gave us, is that correct?"

Kirk did not read the statement. Instead she waved dismissively. "If you say this is my statement I believe you."

"Had you ever met Ms. Zhukova or Ms. Karachova before?"

This time, Kirk thought for a very long time before answering. "We may have – no, we have been at the same conference on several occasions. I have been in the audience at least once when Zhukova spoke. But I have never formally met either person."

"So the first time you ever spoke to either woman was Tuesday evening?"

"We barely spoke except to exchange pleasantries."

"How soon before the IFDA conference did you become aware that you would be designing with Ms. Zhukova?"

Kirk seemed unprepared for the question and she was silent for perhaps thirty seconds. Finally, she said, "I was invited by the IFDA committee last spring. I believe the written confirmation included the names of the other designers. I cannot remember when that arrived."

"In your statement, you said you understood Russian because you grew up in what was then East Germany." Lee kept the question conversational.

"That is correct." Lee sensed wariness in the answer.

"You grew up in Leipzig," Lee made it a statement.

Kirk nodded and Lee now saw wariness on Kirk's face.

Lee reached into a file folder Alvarez had given to her minutes before the interview began. She withdrew a photograph and placed it on the table. "This is Otto Romfh, your grandfather." It was a black and white portrait of a businessman in his thirties or forties, wearing the kind of stiff, European suit men wore in the 1930s. It was a face that was at once serious and kindly.

Lee saw the look of astonishment on Kirk's face. She touched the photograph and ran her fingers over the face of the man.

"We found this in the online photography collection of the Leipzig History Museum – I won't try to pronounce the German name." Lee said the words softly.

"The Stadtgeschichtliches Museum," Kirk said, her fingers on the photograph.

Lee pulled an image of a postcard from the folder. "This was your family's factory. I think it was taken around 1935."

Lee took out a third photo. "You may also recognize this one." It showed the same man, but now seemingly older or more careworn. With him were a woman and two young children, a boy and a girl. Written across the bottom of the photo in white ink was a date 1943-7-23.

"I gave this photograph to the museum," Kirk said, nodding. There was now wetness around her eyes. "My grandfather and grandmother, my father and my aunt."

"And this." Lee removed a reproduction of an interior page of *Neues Deutschland* bearing the date of May 15, 1946. A grainy photo showed a square outside a factory building. Several dozen people populated the square, in the center of which was a man hanging from a makeshift gallows. The headline read, "*Leipzig Industrieller für Verrats hingerichtet*" – 'Leipzig Industrialist Executed for Treason'.

Kirk saw the photo and turned away. She was now crying.

"I have two more things I must show you," Lee said, continuing to speak softly. From a large envelope, she withdrew a coil of purple florist wire contained within a plastic bag marked 'Evidence'. The wire used in the hanging was in an FBI office; this was a length that Alvarez had purchased or begged from someone. She said nothing about the wire, but left it on the table.

The final item was a color photo of the Henckels knife showing the blue chemoluminescence of blood smears on the blade.

"This was dropped into a trash can in the hotel sometime Tuesday night," Lee said. "You probably expected that it would be somewhere in a landfill by now. That was my thought, too. But the hotel does a very meticulous job of recycling all of its waste. Anything that a guest might have inadvertently thrown away gets sorted out and taken to Lost and Found. That's where we found the knife this morning."

She continued. "The knife is at a laboratory in Boston. We are running tests on it to determine if the blood matches that of Valentina Zhukova, but I think we all know that it will. There were also recoverable fingerprints and I suspect they will be yours."

Lee touched Kirk on her arm. "We can keep questioning you, but it seems pointless. We know. We know Valentina Zhukova was not a nice person. In fact, she was a horrible person. A monster. She delighted in hurting people. She was also a cheat. After everyone left the ballroom Wednesday morning, she stayed behind and began compromising the other designs so that hers would be the only 'perfect' one. Except that the design wasn't really hers. The true artist was her assistant, Ludmila. And when you rode up the elevator at three o'clock in the morning, Ludmila told you that Valentina was likely up to her old tricks."

"And we know that Valentina traded continually on her grandfather's name, even as she was blind to the things he did. She believed the world saw him the same way the Russians do, and when someone disagreed – especially someone who knew what he did while he was commander of the Soviet Zone – she went on rampages…"

Lee paused. Kirk had begun picking up the photos one by one. The last one she handled was the 1943 photo of her family. Her mouth was open to speak. After a few moments, Kirk spoke in a low, soft voice.

"Zhukov ordered that my grandfather's family be present at his execution. His wife, his son and his daughter. It was an act of pointless cruelty. My father was only ten, my aunt just seven. They watched as Zhukov, his uniform gleaming with medals, raised one gloved hand; a signal for the execution to commence. Both my aunt and my father were scarred for life by the event. And, of course, two days later, the factory's machinery was dismantled, placed on trains, and sent to Russia. Twelve of my grandfather's best workers and their families were told that they would go with the equipment or face the same fate as my grandfather."

Kirk wiped a tear from her eye. "The Russians left an empty building. There were no jobs. Zhukov did not care if we starved. Russia had a ball-bearing factory and the people to run it, or at least to operate it until they trained Russians to do the job. Those Leipzig men and their families never came home. That, too, was part of my father's legacy: first, that he must watch that which he could not stop, and then he must know that ten more families likely perished as a result. Some, he said, had children who were his friends and playmates."

"He became an engineer and tried to emigrate to the West. But he was the son of an enemy of the state, and the Stasi forgot nothing. In time he married and I was born. The horror of that day in 1946, though, stayed with him all his life and he died a broken man when I was eighteen."

Kirk now looked directly into Lee's face. "It was not that I vowed some kind of vengeance. I hated the Russians, but then most of us did. When the DDR disintegrated, we were finally free of that past. It was only about six years ago that I heard about a Russian woman who claimed to be the granddaughter of the great Marshal Zhukov and that she was an internationally acclaimed floral designer. I had established my own reputation by that time and was beginning to travel regularly beyond Germany to compete. I sat in three lectures given by Zhukova, and I admitted to myself she was very good."

"It was pure…" Kirk searched for a word. "…*Spürsinn*. I have no translation. IFDA invited me to design in Boston and then told me that Zhukova would be one of the others. I did not come here to kill her. But from the moment she arrived in the ballroom, I could hear and see the woman that she was. She told her assistant – in Russian – that she had encountered 'the pitiful Jretnam woman' and had put 'the ignorant whore' in her place. Zhukova bragged that she 'left her in tears' and hoped for 'another go at her' before the conference was over. I had heard that Zara Jretnam had lost a sister to the airplane shot down over the Ukraine, and I could not understand why anyone would take such pleasure in tormenting someone who had endured such a loss."

"By the end of the night, I understood all too well. Zhukova was a sadist. She delighted in tormenting people because she also got pleasure out of tormenting her own assistant. She called her a 'stupid cow' and a 'peasant'. Yet as they conversed I also came to realize that it was Karachova who was the gifted designer. All Zhukova did was hand Karachova flowers when asked, and then criticize Karachova at every opportunity. She threw tantrums and disrupted our work."

"Also by the end of the night, I had come to hate Valentina Zhukova passionately. She was, in her own way, just like her grandfather. She inflicted needless suffering on those around her for her own pleasure. But even then I would not have physically harmed her, though I had made up my mind that I would 'expose' her as a fraud. It was only when Karachova told us in the elevator that we would come down tomorrow morning to find that our designs had been altered that I could no longer contain my anger."

"I waited perhaps fifteen minutes, then changed my clothes, took my short cutting knife and the remains of a spool of wire and went down to the ballroom…"

Lee held up a hand to stop Kirk. "We didn't see you on the elevator cameras."

Kirk nodded and gave a hint of a smile. "When you grow up in a police state, you learn to notice cameras. It becomes part of your habits." Seeing that Lee was satisfied, Kirk continued. "I went into the ballroom. It was just as Karachova had said. Zhukova was just finishing up Tomás Suarez's design, jabbing in flowers from a bucket she had apparently concealed somewhere. She moved a ladder to my design, took up a handful of stems and began doing the same."

"I remember she was humming an old Russian folk tune, and she had her back turned to me. I was able to walk right up to her. I stabbed her twice in the back. She screamed, turned around and fell off the ladder, landing face up. She was still screaming and I placed my hand over her mouth. I told her, in Russian, 'your grandfather, of whom you are so proud, destroyed my family. Their fate is now your fate.' Then I stabbed her through the heart."

"I did not know if I was strong enough to lift her, but I had not counted on the rush of… I think the word is the same in English… adrenaline. I tied the wire around her neck, leaned her against the ladder, and pulled her up so her feet were off the ground. I secured the wire and looked back at what I had done. I felt an odd sense of calm. My father, my aunt, my grandfather and my grandmother could now be at rest."

"I threw the knife into the first trash receptacle I passed and, yes, I thought it would never be seen again. But as I made my way back up the stairs, I worried about the empty spot in my cart and so I took a knife from a tray in the hallway. Then I went back to my room and fell into a deep sleep. Three hours later I was awakened by the news that we were all to be questioned in the ballroom. You know the rest."

Lee asked, "You thought you would not be caught?"

Kirk considered the question. "I did not know if I would. I avoided the hotel cameras, but until this morning there was a black sweatshirt with Zhukova's blood on it in a paper bag in my closet. I waited to be questioned further, and I concocted suitable answers, but the questions never came. This morning, I disposed of the sweatshirt in a trash can in the Convention Center so I guess I thought I was 'home free' as you say."

"But in the lecture hall this afternoon, Frau Levy discussed each of our designs in detail. When she got to mine, she seemed to be telling me, 'we know, we know'. I knew it was time to leave. I would have packed my bag and left for the airport. But now I am caught, and I assume you will place me under arrest. You have my confession."

Chapter 21

Lee excused herself, leaving Alvarez with Kirk. She went into the adjoining office where the Captain stood by the one-way mirror. Next to him was FBI Agent Grimes and a woman who had not been there when she started the interview.

"This is Linda Foster," the Captain said. "She's with the State Department."

"Excellent work," Foster said, shaking Lee's hand. "Impressive work."

"So what do we do?" Lee asked, looking at the Captain.

The Captain nodded at Foster.

"I want you to understand our problem," Foster said. "Let me give you a few statistics. This year, Germany will get thirty-eight percent of its natural gas from Russia and thirty-five percent of its oil. All of that flows through pipelines under the Baltic directly from Russia. In addition, Germany imports twenty-five percent of its coal from Russia, all of which comes in via rail. In all, Germany depends on Russia for a quarter of its energy and has no way to easily replace it."

"Which means what?" Lee asked.

Foster said, "Let's suppose that this afternoon the Boston Police announce the arrest of a German national for the murder of Valentina Zhukova, the famous granddaughter of the revered general who saved the Motherland and who is a close, personal friend of Vladimir Putin."

Foster continued. "There is no free press in Russia. One hundred newspapers and nine television networks will parrot whatever line the Kremlin wants. And what they will want is retribution. For starters, they'll call for shutting off that oil and gas. For Putin, it's a masterstroke. He can turn it off for a few days, watch the DAX drop twenty percent, and then offer to turn it back on… for a fifty percent hike in rates. The Germans would have no choice but to comply."

"All this because of a flower show and Valentina Zhukova?" Lee asked.

"You have to read or listen to the Russian press for the past few days," Foster replied. "Zhukova has been elevated to sainthood along with her grandpa. Right now, the anger is directed at the United States, but it is just proof that we are a crime-ridden cesspool that allows innocent Russians to be murdered on the street even as we plot to crush the Russian people through sanctions. Turn that anger toward Germany and all hell breaks loose."

Agent Grimes cut in. "Which is why our way is better. Ramon Fortunato is the silver bullet Putin won't see coming. Fortunato fingers Boris Gusinovich. Putin puts the FSB on the case and they find out that, yes, Gusinovich hired Fortunato for another hit and bragged about it and, yes, Gusinovich wants a piece of the cyber-warfare pie. Putin purges Gusinovich, who swears to God to his fellow oligarchs that he's being framed. Gusinovich's friends start feeling even more uneasy about Putin. Fearless Leader has already presided over the biggest percentage drop in oil and natural gas prices in history, and the price for everything else Russia sells on the world market is down."

Grimes continued. "Gusinovich's buddies are wondering which one of them is going to be next. Was it worth annexing Crimea? Invading Ukraine? Turning rebels loose to shoot down airliners? If this turns out right, Putin is gone in three to six months. And the world will be a little better off. Even if he isn't, the oligarchy's trust of Putin is in tatters, making it harder for Russia to make trouble around the world."

"And what happens to Eva Kirk?" Lee asked.

"We put her on a plane," said the Captain. "We thank her for her cooperation. We tell her we will review her case at some time in the future. When she gets home, she reads that some Venezuelan has confessed to the crime. She'll figure it out."

"And what if we did pursue a conviction?" the Captain added. "This is manslaughter, not even second-degree murder. Any lawyer worth his salt would plead diminished capacity and any judge would nod in agreement. She'd do a psych evaluation and court-mandated supervision. I'm not saying it's right, but we just saved the Commonwealth about three hundred thousand bucks."

"Have you forgotten about Ludmila Karachova?" Lee asked.

The response came from Agent Grimes. "We took her into protective custody this morning. There was a pair of FSB goons shadowing her, presumably waiting for orders to grab her and get her down to New York. When she left the shelter this morning, we introduced ourselves. She is in a safe house…" He started to say more, then stopped himself. "She's safe and will stay that way. She can go home when all of this plays itself out. She can also stay here. It's going to take her some time to comprehend those options."

"And what about Detective Alvarez and me?" Lee asked.

The Captain nodded and smiled. "The two of you are golden. I saw what young Alvarez was able to do with that museum's website photography collection in less than an hour while pulling together all of the other material you used in that interrogation. That confession wouldn't have happened without his work. Well, on Monday he starts trying to teach us old geezers how to do that stuff. He is far too valuable a talent to waste on the streets. If this was the course in Alvarez 101, I can't wait to see Alvarez 102."

The Captain shifted and looked at his watch. "As a courtesy to you and to see how your interview played out, the FBI's announcement got pushed to 4:30. I'm going to be there, Agent Grimes and a few special guests are going to be there. You're invited to join us. Whether you do or not, there's a formal commendation awaiting you. You have earned my respect. I still think getting out of town for a few days would be a good idea, though."

Lee listened and absorbed the information. When she realized a response was expected, she said, "I think you're right."

* * * * *

At five o'clock, Lee stood at the United Airlines' first class concierge desk at Logan Airport. Her tickets lay in front of the bookings agent.

"I'm ready to leave now, and two hours in San Francisco seems like such an unnecessarily long layover," Lee was saying. "I can get to Vancouver more quickly through Chicago or Denver. Or, should I just take these tickets to Alaska Air and ask if they'll honor them?"

The concierge glanced at the ticket total and assured Lee that United would make every accommodation to get a valued customer to Vancouver as quickly as possible. Five minutes later, Lee was being escorted through a priority security line en route to Seat 3A on United's 5:26 p.m. flight to Chicago with a short connection to Vancouver.

The flight was already boarding and Lee took her seat. She called her parents and told them she would take a cab to their home. She wouldn't arrive in Vancouver until midnight and so they shouldn't wait up.

"But what happened to San Francisco?" her mother asked. "What was the big announcement?"

"There was never an announcement," Lee said cheerfully. "It was all a mix-up. We'll have a fun weekend together, just the three of us. I'll explain everything."

Her second call was to Matt's cell phone. It went to voice mail, which could mean Matt was already in the air, or any number of other possibilities.

"Hi, Matt," she said. "I'm taking you up on the tickets. You're right; it's a nice gesture on your part. Sorry I'm going to miss your parents' anniversary party tomorrow. If they ask where I am, just tell them the truth. I'm the wrong girl for you. I'm too stubborn and not nearly pretty enough. I won't take orders and I can't be bought, much less rented for the weekend. But tell them you're looking hard for that right girl and, when you find her, you'll bring her out for their approval. Have a good life."

Lee closed the connection and powered down her phone. She leaned back contentedly in her seat and smiled.

* * * * *

In their Charlestown condominium, Jason and Terri Alvarez sat on a sofa, their daughter played with a stuffed animal at their feet. A bottle of wine was open on the coffee table, the television showed the six o'clock news. Terri Alvarez lay against her husband's chest.

An hour earlier he had recounted the events of the day including his meeting with the Captain. When the formal meeting with the FBI ended, the Captain had pulled Alvarez aside.

"You start a new career on Monday," the Captain said. "Get used to some big changes in your life, and I am going to make certain those changes are for the better. I understand your daughter's special needs. I have some pull around this place, and I think I can make some things happen that will solve your time problems. Please trust me."

Now, they watched the FBI's announcement that Ramon Fortunato had confessed to the murder of acclaimed international floral designer Valentina Zhukova in a Boston hotel ballroom three days earlier. Fortunato's arrest was the result of diligent work by both the FBI and Boston Police.

At the side of the FBI Deputy Superintendent – someone whose name had not previously been mentioned by anyone Alvarez had spoken with – was the Captain. At the words, "diligent work", Alvarez was certain he saw the hint of a smile on the Captain's face.

* * * * *

In Winnie Garrison's suite, five women gathered around the large, flat-screen television, trying to make sense of the six o'clock news.

On the screen was video of the joint FBI and Boston Police announcement about the solving of the murder of a Russian tourist in Boston earlier in the week at the still-ongoing International Floral Design Alliance convention and show. A Venezuelan national, a professional killer named Ramon Fortunato, had been apprehended by the FBI two days earlier in New York. Under questioning by the FBI and Boston detectives, Fortunato had admitted killing the Russian.

The story had taken several twists. The Russian in question, Valentina Zhukova, was the granddaughter of a revered Soviet military commander from World War II, and Zhukova was married to a high-level Russian army officer. The murder was described as 'a warning shot', ordered by one of Russia's powerful business interests intent upon getting lucrative contracts from the Army.

The FBI was prepared to turn over all evidence in the case to the Russian government, but said Fortunato would stand trial in the United States.

Kathy Thomas turned off the television. "I don't get it," she said to the others. "We saw that Zhukova had messed with everyone's designs. Wasn't that the reason she was killed? Where did this Venezuelan guy come from?"

"It means we were wrong," said Marie Levy. "We are civilized people. We do not kill people over floral designs. We may get mad, but we always find some other way to get back."

Liz Phillips said nothing. She listened as the others made their own conjectures but ultimately concluded that they had been wrong about Kirk. Phillips had a suspicion that she understood what had really happened and that a 'more acceptable' outcome had been devised at a higher level.

It wasn't for her to question the outcome. She was pleased to have played a part in solving a crime. She expected that, tomorrow, the Convention Center would be overflowing with people with a sudden, newfound interest in floral design. Winnie Garrison would need all the help she could get.

Acknowledgements

I am often asked where I get the ideas for my books. The genesis of *'Murder in Negative Space'* goes back four years when I had the pleasure to share a banquet table with Deen Day Sanders, an irresistible force in the flower show world. She was about to bring the World Association of Flower Arrangers, or WAFA, to Boston and she shared with me her enthusiasm for the pending event.

I was so intrigued by the notion of such an undertaking that, a month later, like Liz Phillips, I was pushing staging into place before the show's opening. Further, like Liz, my wife, Betty, was escorting groups of designers through the Boston Flower Market in the pre-dawn hours. I thought at the time that an international floral design show would make a great setting for a mystery, but other projects took precedence.

Then, last April, friend and reader Linda Jean Smith of Chelmsford, MA shared with me a vivid recollection about an obnoxious floral designer who noisily directed and berated an assistant working on a balcony above him; annoying everyone else in the room. Afterward, I could not get that image out of my head.

The final pieces of the story clicked into place with the reading of a biography of Marshal Georgy Zhukov, a pivotal figure in World War II who is largely unknown in America; and the unfolding of events in the Ukraine over the spring and summer of 2014. By June, Valentina Alexandrovna Zhukova had come to life in my imagination, and Lieutenant Victoria Lee, ably assisted by Detective Jason Alvarez and Liz Phillips, had been dispatched to find her killer.

I'm also asked why I sometimes mix fictional with real locations in my stories. Why, for example, would I invent the Harborfront Exposition Center for *'A Murder at the Flower Show'* yet use the real Boston Convention and Exposition Center for '*Negative Space*'? The answer is simple: if the location has some culpability in the story, I invent it. If not, I'm inclined to use familiar landmarks to anchor my story. So, BCEC is real while a vacant lot occupies the site of the Convention Center Plaza Hotel.

My characters, on the other hand, are wholly fictional and I take pains to ensure that I don't inadvertently sweep real people into my stories without their permission (though, for worthy causes, I sometimes auction off the right to make a cameo appearance in a book). '*Negative Space*' almost came to a screeching halt when I learned that a rising figure in the art world shares a surname with one of my characters. Diligent research uncovered no link to my plot line. I breathed a deep sigh of relief.

When I do use historical characters and events ('*The Accidental Spy*' is chock full of them), I make every effort to keep those portrayals accurate. In this book, much research went into ensuring that the fictional events in the Soviet Occupation Zone I created have historical precedents. In other words, yes, the Soviet Army did dismantle entire factories and ship them to Russia as 'reparations', sometimes with key managers and their families. And the effect on the German economy was devastating.

On the other hand, I throw myself at the mercy of the floral design community for whatever egregious errors I have made in enumerating design principles or describing their implementation.

It has been an extraordinary year for me. Thanks to a program called 'Gardening Is Murder' (and, starting this fall, a second program called 'Gardening Will Kill You'), I have had the opportunity to meet thousands of readers at garden clubs, women's clubs, senior groups, libraries and, in an ironic twist of fate, flower shows. Those invitations now stretch ahead more than a year and take me far beyond the Boston metro area. I cherish those opportunities more than words can express. But I also continue to enjoy the intimate settings of book clubs and book stores. All I can say is, please keep the invitations coming.

It takes a community to produce a book, and I am indebted to a group of readers who both castigate me for my inability to properly use commas and who subject my story line to tests of plausibility. That group includes Jan Martin, Faith Clunie, Marilyn Racette, Connie Stolow, and Linda Jean Smith.

At the head of the thank-you list is my wife, Betty, who is both my biggest fan and sternest critic. It wouldn't be possible without you.

Made in the USA
Middletown, DE
20 February 2015